GUSTAVE FLAUBERT, a doctor's son, was born in Rouen in 1821, and sent at eighteen to study law in Paris. While still a schoolboy, however, he professed himself 'disgusted with life', in romantic scorn of bourgeois society, and he showed no distress when a mysterious nervous disease broke off his professional studies. Flaubert retired to Croisset, near Rouen, on a private income, and devoted himself to his writing.

In his early works, particularly *The Temptation of St Antony* (begun in 1848), Flaubert tended to give free rein to his flamboyant imagination. However, he later disciplined his romantic exuberance in an attempt to achieve total objectivity and a harmonious prose style. This ambition cost him enormous toil and brought him little success in his lifetime. After the publication of *Madame Bovary* in the *Revue de Paris* (1856–7) he was tried for offending public morals; *Salammbô* (1862) was criticized for the meticulous historical detail surrounding the exotic story; *Sentimental Education* (1869) was misunderstood by the critics; and the political play *The Candidate* (1874) was a disastrous failure. Only *Three Tales* (1877) was an unqualified success with public and critics alike, but it appeared when Flaubert's spirits, health and finances were at their lowest ebb.

After his death in 1880 Flaubert's fame and reputation grew steadily, strengthened by the publication of his unfinished comic masterpiece, *Bouvard and Pécuchet* (1881) and his remarkable *Correspondence*.

KITTY MROSOVSKY went to French schools in Carthage, Rome and London before reading English at Somerville College, Oxford. Formly a lecturer at York University, she now lives in London and reviews drama for *Quarto*.

GUSTAVE FLAUBERT

THE TEMPTATION OF
SAINT ANTONY

*Translated with an Introduction and Notes
by Kitty Mrosovsky*

PENGUIN BOOKS

Penguin Books Ltd, Harmondsworth, Middlesex, England
Penguin Books, 625 Madison Avenue, New York, New York 10022, U.S.A.
Penguin Books Australia Ltd, Ringwood, Victoria, Australia
Penguin Books Canada Ltd, 2801 John Street, Markham, Ontario, Canada L3R 1B4
Penguin Books (N.Z.) Ltd, 182–190 Wairau Road, Auckland 10, New Zealand

Originally published in French under the title *La Tentation de Saint Antoine*
This translation first published by Martin Secker & Warburg Ltd 1980
Published in Penguin Books 1983

Printed and bound in Great Britain by
Cox & Wyman Ltd, Reading
Set in Fournier

CONTENTS

ACKNOWLEDGEMENTS

I am grateful to my mother for reading and commenting on my translation. And I have benefited from many helpful criticisms and suggestions offered by Antony Wood. My thanks go also to Ann Douglas for her early appreciation of the project, to Alison Samuel, my editor, for her kind diligence, and to both my sisters and all my friends for their interest and optimism (including Roger Sherman, who reminisced about the dramatisation of the sixties). The money which allowed me time in which to prepare this book was left to me by my father: for this, as well as for much else, I remember him with very great gratitude.

INTRODUCTION

INTRODUCTION

1. Flaubert and Saint Antony

Why Saint Antony? Was Flaubert casting himself as a saint? Or was he excavating a corner of hagiography? Or converting a bizarre painterly tradition into words? Each of these conjectures is plausible, given the familiar image of Flaubert as worshipper of Art, painstaking realist, magician of the *mot juste*. But I prefer another triple conjecture: he wrote *The Temptation of Saint Antony* because he knew about psychic disturbance, because he was interested in religions and religious feeling, and because the desert saint's demonic illuminations could figure the arid tedium of life and the dangerously empty power of words. *Saint Antony*[1] was a quarter of a century in the making. It was first written in 1848–9, rewritten in 1856, and again rewritten before it was published in 1874 – not an easy birth. But there was no text of his that Flaubert loved more.

His upbringing had not encouraged religious orthodoxy. Both his parents were apparently freethinking deists in the tradition of Voltaire and Rousseau, and Doctor Flaubert was possibly attracted to freemasonry.[2] But Flaubert later declared: 'I'm a mystic at bottom and I believe in nothing.'[3] More expansively he wrote in a letter of 1857:

> What attracts me above all is religion. I mean all religions, no more one than another. Each particular dogma is repugnant to me, but I regard the sentiment that invented them as the most natural and the most poetic of humanity. I have small liking for philosophers who have seen nothing but trickery and nonsense in it. I myself discover there humanity and instinct; indeed I respect the negro kissing his fetish as much as the Catholic at the foot of the Sacré-Coeur.[4]

3

It would seem to follow that Flaubert also respected St Antony.

The real St Antony was an Egyptian anchorite, celebrated indeed as the trail-blazer for that style of life, and his story was told by St Athanasius in what is regarded as the first classic of Christian biography. He was born in Middle Egypt in about the year 250. His parents, both Christians, died when he was eighteen or twenty. He soon gave away his inheritance and set out to practise the ascetic life in some neighbouring tombs. After fifteen years he moved to an abandoned fort on the East side of the Nile at Pispir, later known as his Outer Mountain. There he spent another twenty years struggling alone against besieging demons. But admirers gradually tracked him down. He retreated again, further into the desert of Upper Egypt, to Mount Colzim near the Red Sea, known as his Inner Mountain. His eremitic vocation could no longer entitle him to complete isolation. He visited Alexandria on three occasions, and made regular trips to see his disciples at Pispir. By the time he died in 356, not a few people had risked a journey to the Inner Mountain for the sake of advice and cures.

Athanasius's biography is chock-full of the suspense, the near-defeats, the hard-won victories of the spiritual life – enlivened by the villainous interventions of resourceful demons. There emerges a picture of a gentle, humble, infinitely patient and fairly unsophisticated saint, of compelling charm and serenity, never agitated or gloomy. But Flaubert's Antony is a far cry from his original: cantankerous, bitter, envious, greedy, sadomasochistic. Closely though Flaubert had studied his Athanasius, much though he relied on authentic details, his Antony is St Antony in name and circumstance, not in character. However, his portrait of the anchorite mentality is by no means a wholesale travesty of the truth. He had read quite enough to know that Athanasius's portrait of St Antony is striking precisely because the saint's gentle sensibility was a rare asset in the desert. Among his ascetic followers there were plenty who refined and prolonged their self-tortures in the grimmest and most unlovely spirit of competition.

But it was St Antony who represented the arch-anchorite, the very type of the solitary. His temptations make up a long and brilliant iconographical and popular tradition, a major stimulus to

Flaubert. With the revival of religious art in the mid-nineteenth century the subject again became highly fashionable (though it was often treated with dreadful vulgarity), and in the second half of the century there was renewed scholarly interest in the saint's life.[5] There was never any question of Flaubert fixing on a lesser figure. On the front of his first manuscript, which he insisted he must finish before setting off to Egypt with his friend Maxime Du Camp, he wrote:

> Messieurs les démons,
> Laissez-moi donc!
> Messieurs les démons,
> Laissez-moi donc!

This deferential pleading with tormenting familiars plainly echoes the saint's popular trials. Years after his childhood, Flaubert enjoyed bringing George Sand to see the marionette theatre run by Père Legrain at the fair of Saint-Romain at Rouen. A fifteen-minute *Saint Antoine* would end with the saint's legendary pig taking flight with its tail on fire.[6] The verve and ludicrous contrasts of this kind of entertainment may have coincided with Flaubert's taste for crude and cynical farce. The flavour seems strong in his first *Saint Antony* and still persists in the last version: for instance, I suspect, in the saint's stance of boggle-eyed rigidity in front of the Queen of Sheba's outrageously cheeky advances.

Flaubert had far to go before he put the last touch to the vertiginous, slippery but scrupulous structure of his final *Saint Antony*. To understand the bottomless appeal which the subject held for him, one must turn to his personal life. The outstanding fact of Flaubert's biography is best quoted from his own account:

Yesterday, we set off from Pont l'Evêque at half past eight in the evening, in such darkness that one couldn't see the horse's ears. The last time I went that way, it was with my brother, in January 44, when I fell, as if struck down with apoplexy, on the floor of the cab I was driving and for 10 minutes he thought I was dead. It was much the same sort of night. I recognised the house where he bled me, the trees opposite (and, a marvellous harmony of things and ideas) at that very moment, a wagon also went by on my right, like the time when ten years ago almost, at 9 o'clock in the evening, I suddenly felt myself carried away in a torrent of flames.[7]

The drama of the event may be exaggerated, but the diagnosis is euphemistic. It is now mostly accepted that the 'nervous illness' which periodically assailed Flaubert was epilepsy.[8] The first and most serious attack was apparently sparked off by the light of the oncoming wagon. Later attacks were accompanied by streams of images. Flaubert has left us very vivid descriptions of his feelings during these attacks. There was a sort of orgasmic anxiety followed by a huge eruption of the memory into images, or else a single image would gradually engulf like a great flame the whole of objective reality.[9] In a letter of 1853 he wrote:

Lunacy and lust are two things which I've so fathomed, through which I've so well navigated by my willpower, that I shall never be (I hope) either alienated or a de Sade. But I didn't get off lightly, take my word for it. My nervous illness was the foam from those little intellectual joy-rides. Each attack was a sort of haemorrhage of the nervous system. It was like seminal losses of the pictorial faculty of the brain, a hundred thousand images at once, exploding into fireworks. There was a wrenching of soul from body, atrocious (I'm convinced of having been dead several times). But what constitutes the personality, reason's being, went on to the end; without that the suffering would have been nothing, because I would have been purely passive and I was always *conscious*, even when I could no longer speak. The soul then was wholly withdrawn into itself, like a hedgehog hurting itself with its own prickles.[10]

But the attacks gradually began to space out. By 1847 Flaubert was writing that he believed he could wear down his disease, and by 1857 that he had cured himself through force of will and a determined clinging to reason.[11] Indeed, the impression of intimacy between Flaubert and his illness, the note of manipulation, may lead one to suspect that the attacks were in some way intentionally engineered (such is Sartre's opinion). After all, the most immediate result of the crisis was that Flaubert was justified in leaving off his despised law studies in Paris. He himself claimed that his illness was the 'logical' outcome of the period of his youth, and added:

'To have had what I had, something must, have happened, before-hand, in a fairly tragic way inside my brain-box.'[12] No superficial explanation of this 'something' is likely to stick. Interestingly, it's possible to deduce that Flaubert's appreciable period of sexual abstinence (he claimed two to two and a half years) must have begun well before his first attack – to be broken, presumably, when he began his spasmodic liaison with Louise Colet in July 1846.[13] Be that as it may, after his illness he was perforce debilitated, ensconced in family life, in bed under the medical care of his eminent father and his elder brother Achille, and complaining – as he did all his life – of the boredom of it.

The first year of his new mental leisure went towards completing *L'Education sentimentale*, the early novel drawn from his curtailed experiences in Paris (not to be confused with the mature novel of the same title). But in mid-1845 a new idea began to form. The whole family was accompanying Flaubert's fragile sister Caroline on her honeymoon. When they visited the Balbi palace at Genoa Flaubert was struck by the painting *The Temptation of Saint Antony*, then attributed to Pieter Brueghel the Younger or 'Hell' Brueghel, and at once, so he wrote to his friend Alfred Le Poittevin, thought of dramatising the legend – only to toss aside the idea. His first allusion to 'my *Saint Antony*' occurs two years later. But already by mid-1846 the orientation of his reading is clear.[14]

By that time his life had set into its definitive pattern. His father died in January 1846 and his much loved sister only two months later, leaving a two-months-old daughter, Caroline Hamard. On the grounds that the baby's father was unbalanced, her grand-mother and uncle bore her off to the country house at Croisset. It was against Flaubert's rock-hard commitment, on the one hand to this odd version of the nuclear family, and on the other to his colossal intellectual programme, that Louise Colet was to pit herself with such scant success.

2. Friends and influences

In 1847 Flaubert travelled through Brittany and Normandy with his friend from student days, Maxime Du Camp, with whom two years later he was to set out for the East. They jointly described the trip in *Par les champs et par les grèves*. One discovers here how Flaubert is impressed by two human foetuses, a pair of siamese piglets in a jar of spirits, and the exquisite ferocity of two savages' heads, in the natural history museum at Nantes; how the blood-thirsty sights and sounds of the abattoir at Quimper prompt him to a cannibalistic fantasy; and how pleased he is by the naïve piety of the peasants at Quimperlé. An eye for physical grace, anger at human encroachment on nature, and a pantheistic élan are characteristic of Flaubert's part of the travelogue. His feelings on the beach at Belle-Isle were ecstatic:

> We regretted that our eyes might not reach to the heart of the rocks, to the bottom of the seas, to the ends of the sky, so as to see how the stones grow, how the waters are made, how the stars light up, that our ears might not hear the gravitation in the earth of granites forming, the push of sap through plants, the rolling of corals in the solitude of the ocean. And in sympathy with this contemplative effusion, we could have wished that our soul, irradiating every-where, might go and live among all this life so as to assume all its forms, to last like them, and varying for ever, for ever to push forth under the sun of eternity its metamorphoses![15]

Such emotional, abandoned pantheism is typical of Flaubert's early writing. In letters of 1846 he refers baldly to his 'pan-theistic faculty' and his 'pantheistic belief'.[16] Much of his reading at the time fitted in with these tendencies, for instance the rather more austerely pantheistic *Bhagavad Gita*. Antony's *cri de coeur*, the wish to 'be matter', grows out of Flaubert's sensuous responses.

More important than Maxime Du Camp was Flaubert's long-standing friend Alfred Le Poittevin. From the vantage of his five years of seniority he made a deep impression. Flaubert later wrote that he had never known a more transcendental spirit.[17] For us, Le Poittevin survives in his few short works and his letters as a rather wretched type of intellectual, tormented by metaphysical doubts and obscene fantasies. It's obvious that the two friends shared a sense of disillusion, an ironic disgust at the platitudes of bourgeois life, a cynical distaste for involvement, and a determination to remain proudly impassive. Sartre associates Le Poittevin with the Devil of *Saint Antony*, arguing that his sophisticated 'strategy of inertia' found its natural conclusion in unmoving void.[18] Certainly Le Poittevin's intellectual attitudes must have affected the younger Flaubert. Like many of his contemporaries he admired Byron. But in addition to its suitably satanic irony about human behaviour, his short work *Bélial* illustrates a belief in a Hegelian dialectic of matter and spirit, and a blend of metempsychosis and pantheism, all baked into vaguely progressivist mould. On his death-bed he was reading Spinoza.

Alfred Le Poittevin's death in 1848 was for Flaubert yet another shock. He watched by the corpse for two days and nights, reading Creuzer's huge work on comparative religion. The letter he wrote to Maxime Du Camp at the time gives some insight into his intensities of response to life, to literature, and to loss:

> I lifted him, turned him over, wrapped him round. I was left with the impression of his limbs, cold and stiff, all day at the end of my fingers. He was horribly putrefied, the sheets were wet through. We put him in two shrouds. When he was arranged like that he looked like an Egyptian mummy tight in its linens and I experienced I can't say how enormous a feeling of joy and liberty for him. The mist was white, the woods were beginning to stand out from it. The two tapers were shining in this dawning whiteness, two or three birds sang and I repeated to myself this phrase from his *Bélial:* 'He will go, joyful bird, to greet among the pines the rising sun . . .', or rather I could hear his voice saying it to me and all day I was deliciously obsessed by it. . . .
>
> So that . . . is what I've lived through since Tuesday evening. I've had incredible apperceptions and untranslatable light-bursts of ideas. Heaps of things came back to me with choruses of music and gusts of scent.
>
> Until the time when it had become impossible for him to do anything, he would read Spinoza till 1 o'clock in the morning, every evening in bed.[19]

It was in the following month, as we see from the title-page of the manuscript, that Flaubert began to write *Saint Antony*. His pantheism, his epilepsy, Alfred's death, and also literary and philosophical influences, all contributed to persuade him to adopt shifting tableaux and a passive protagonist to dramatise insistent questions about good and evil, illusion and reality, spirit and matter. One giant predecessor was Goethe, whose *Faust* was familiar to Flaubert's generation largely through Gérard de Nerval's translation. And the influence of Hugo, with his Romantic mixture of grotesque and sublime, was inescapable.[20] Flaubert was also quick to become acquainted with Michelet's writing. But more like the original *Saint Antony* than anything else in its vaulting lyricism and void-obsessed questioning is *Ahasvérus*, the story of the Wandering Jew as retold by the great comparative religionist Edgar Quinet. This is no amateur exercise in nomadic Romanticism. Anyone who reads how Ahasvérus echoes to the melancholy of each place he passes, or how the death-figure Mob sees the poet plunging into the transparent sea of things and retrieving a dozen words, glistening wet, in a world which is nothing but one great zero or void, will understand that Flaubert was haunted by the rhythm and scope of Quinet's work.

At the point when he undertook to write *Saint Antony*, Flaubert had just completed his early *Education sentimentale* in which he writes not only of a realist aesthetics that must demonstrate the strict concatenation of cause and effect but also of how art imitates the great concert of nature. The line of causality linking Flaubert's works was never to be simple to follow. One can appreciate that *Saint Antony* was first produced by a Flaubert far removed from gregarious and seedy student life and that, as Thibaudet wrote, the book is one of 'solitude and desire'.[21] But it's important to know that some of its themes are clearly anticipated in stories written before Flaubert's crisis or his discovery of the supposed Brueghel. His juvenilia are at their worst a farrago of Romantic melodrama and cloying subjectivism, at their best a powerful and disturbing evocation of adolescent sensibilities, and at all events a very rich source of psychological speculation about their author, as Sartre has brilliantly shown. Suffice it here to say that in *Rêve d'enfer*

(1837) an azure-haired superman proves indifferent to all temptations, that in *La Danse des morts* (1838) the hallucinatory spree is well under way, and most importantly that *Smarh* (1839) describes how a hermit's faith is undermined by Satan's revelation of the vacuity of the cosmos and the paltry nullity of human life. So when Flaubert later referred to *Saint Antony* as a 'metaphysical howl'[22] he was referring to a genre which he had early cultivated, in defiance of the wasting leprosy of *ennui*, the emptiness of reality and the deliquescence of the ideal.

There are intricate connections between Byron's *Cain*, Le Poittevin's *Bélial*, Spinoza, and Flaubert's own work. The second act of *Cain* is entitled 'The Abyss of Space' and describes how Lucifer flies through space with Cain, who is 'intoxicated with eternity' but dismayed by the prospect of extinction. Such an extra-terrestrial flight had, of course, been anticipated in *Faust*. But it was *Cain* that provided the idea of the space-trip as philosophical platform used by Flaubert as early as 1839 in *Smarh*. In the first *Saint Antony* the episode becomes a dizzy blend of Spinozism and Romantic pantheism. But in the last version Antony's experience is less happy.

The notion of air-borne speculation was later to become tinged for Flaubert with nostalgia. Of Le Poittevin he wrote: 'What voyages he made me make into the blue!'[23] And indeed in *Bélial* the diminishing effect of scientific argument on humanity's status is compared to the belittled look of the world when seen from a balloon, from heights at which the 'cold of the atmosphere' and the 'infinite space' result in a trembling vertigo. It was in very similar terms that Flaubert eventually described the effect of Spinozism on Bouvard and Pécuchet: 'They felt they were in a balloon, at night, in icy cold, being swept away on a never-ending course, towards a bottomless abyss, and with nothing around them but the ungraspable, the motionless, the eternal. It was too much. They gave up.'[24]

Flaubert's own admiration for Spinoza was long-lasting. He had read the *Ethics* before first writing *Saint Antony*, and he reread them and discovered the *Tractatus Theologico-politicus* before completing the last version. What Flaubert saw in Spinoza was both confirmation of his own unitarian pantheism, his notion of an endless diffusion of forms through a radiant infinity of space, and something more. Jean Bruneau has pointed out that his nature-ecstasies can be traced back at least as far as his Corsican travels of 1840, and that it was afterwards easy for him, as it was for his contemporaries, to conflate Spinoza's rational intuition with the mystical naturalism of the German idealists as well as with Oriental pantheism.[25] But Spinoza also deeply impressed Flaubert by his revelation of a deterministic universe in which good and evil are regarded as limited human concepts, a universe of cosmic harmony in which each thing must fulfil the potential of its own nature. Bruneau argues, however, that the 'hypothesis of the void', the 'problem of existence', haunted Flaubert despite his respect for Spinoza. In fact I think it might be more accurate to deduce that Flaubert eventually recognised the gulf between his own sensuous response to nature and the philosopher's abstract system: haunted by the last moments of his friend's life, he came to associate Spinoza himself with ideas of chill, numbness and void.

When Flaubert drafted a plan for a novel based on his illness, a plan which has been variously ascribed to 1853 and 1860–61, the title he gave to it was *The Spiral*.[26] He had already used the metaphor to describe Le Poittevin's *Bélial*, in which the 'overall idea' struck him as that of a whirling, infinite spiral.[27] It seems an apt metaphor for pure form or in structuralist terms for a whirl of signifiers without signifieds. *Saint Antony*, coloured as it is by Flaubert's brilliant hallucinations, can be seen both as an esoteric personal record and as an experiment, teased out over a quarter of a century, to perfect an 'infinite spiral' of images.

3. The three versions

Antony's urge to become sheer matter is in Flaubert's final text the last shot in the nocturnal fusillade of temptations. The distance between this urge and his own juvenile ecstasies is hard to map, involving as it does the whole development of his writing life. He finished the first *Saint Antony* in 1849, aged twenty-seven. Then came his travels in Egypt, then *Madame Bovary*. He was soon back at work on a second version, shortened and reshaped; a few sections of this were published in 1856–7 in *L'Artiste* but Flaubert was reluctant to risk publication of the whole book, perhaps because he wasn't satisfied with it or perhaps because the prosecution for obscenity of *Madame Bovary* in 1857 made him wary. After *Salammbô* and *L'Education sentimentale* he returned in 1869 to *Saint Antony* and set to work on a radically remoulded version. In the 1850s he had referred to his obsession with the subject and noted that he himself had been the Antony of the first *Saint Antony* – hence its self-oriented and personal passion, which he deplored as a fault. But in 1872, as he was completing the last version, he could claim it as 'l'oeuvre de toute ma vie', his life's work.[28]

Spasmodic rewriting was only the tip of the iceberg. Flaubert's long exploration of the classics, his early attempts to learn Greek, his interest in religions, dogmas and heresies, in freaks and monsters, science and insanity were also part of the obsession. There are twenty-five years of reading and experience between the first *Saint Antony* and the last version published in 1874, to be followed by the publication of *Trois contes* in 1877 and *Bouvard et Pécuchet* in 1880 (seven months after Flaubert's death). But the first version is by far the longest. It took Flaubert four days, reading out loud from midday to four p.m. and again from eight p.m. to midnight, to reveal it to his friends Maxime Du Camp and Louis Bouilhet.[29] He anticipated yells of enthusiasm. But as the words undulated onwards, as Antony was tossed from heretical pillar to hallucinatory post with never the beginnings of dramatic action, the two listeners secretly flagged in everything but their determination to be frank. The verdict was delivered by Bouilhet after the last midnight lap: the work should be incinerated and not again mentioned. The author was horrified.

Why such severity? Flaubert's prose, magnificently lyrical, swirls around its suite of subjects, flickers with cynicism, clings tight with obscene intentions, or offers itself as sheer linguistic palpitation – this last being one of his favourite words. Eroticism is never far, lust is free to linger: 'At all the crossroads of the soul, your song is to be met, and you pass at the end of ideas as the courtesan passes at the end of the street.'[30] Can such allures cloy? The vortex of pictures and ideas was at any rate too bewildering for Flaubert's friends. And matters were perhaps not much helped by the farcical interjections of the pig, that companion who insinuated himself into the saint's iconographical entourage in the Middle Ages, apparently because some monks of the Order were allowed to keep pigs which scavenged the streets. All the same, one can't help noticing how suggestive this character is of Flaubert's gargantuan proclivities, especially when recounting a piggy dream about a great pond of greasy dish-water:

> A whole world's rotting filth was spread around me to satisfy my appetite, I caught sight of clots of blood through the fumes, blue intestines and every kind of animal excrement, and the vomit of orgies, and like slicks of oil the greenish pus that runs from wounds; it all thickened about me, so that I was walking with my four trotters almost sinking into this sticky slime, and on my back there fell a continuous drizzle of hot rain, sweet and sickly. . . . All this gurgled inside my body, all this lapped against my ears, I was gasping, I was howling, I was eating and swallowing it all. Ugh! ugh! . . .[31]

Flaubert admired the quality of *grotesque triste* that he saw in Jacques Callot's engraving *The Temptation of Saint Antony*, which he hung on his wall in 1846. But his blend of porcine and lyrical fantasy, of raillerie, flamboyant melancholy, near-slapstick, voluptuousness and argumentative harangue doesn't quite manage to achieve consistent piquancy.

The 1856 version is the only one to include one of the most disturbing of Flaubert's visions. A thin trickle of sand falls noiselessly down into the interior of a tower, at the bottom of which are strange grey masses; as 'a sort of palpitation quivers across them', they can be identified as men, fierce and desperate, yellow-eyed and black-nostrilled, their hair and beards white with dust, each holding a knife; a rat passes, they fall upon it and bloodily tear up its carcase; then with rolling eyes they repeat: 'Our fathers have eaten sour grapes and our teeth are all on edge'; the sand rises to their

lips, to their eyes, to their foreheads, to the top of their heads –
until there is nothing left to be seen or heard.[32]

Interesting as the 1856 version is, it is mainly a thoroughly
slimmed reincarnation of the 1849 one. The evolution of Flaubert's
text can be essentially sketched by comparing the first and last
versions. The ousting of the pig is only one obvious change. One
may wonder once or twice whether Flaubert has deleted things
that might shock, notably the Montanists' sacrificial bleeding of a
child and the hermaphrodite who appears among the monsters.
But the first version is above all stiff with personified abstractions.
The Seven Deadly Sins as well as an eighth, Logic, and the Three
Theological Virtues play a taxingly traditional part in Antony's
trials. Much though Flaubert warms to some of their allures, the
parts seem rather stale. He rightly banished them from his final
text, though their influence persists: Antony's opening mono-
logue runs through the whole gamut of evil inclinations.

But the most important changes are structural and thematic. The
final version is divided into seven chapters. The first version is three
times as long but falls into only three parts. Part one introduces the
seven deadly sins and the heresies. Part two consists of a long-
drawn-out contest between sins and virtues, with Science joining
in the fray until Antony is conquered by Pride; then come assorted
appearances including the Queen of Sheba, the Sphinx and the
Chimera and the monsters; when Antony declares that he longs to
become matter so as to 'know what it thinks', the Devil arrives and
bears him aloft. In part three he is dazzled by space and wants to
diffuse himself into it, to be one with nature which he sees as the
manifestation of an all-pervasive god: here is the Spinozism of the
young Flaubert, coated with Romantic pantheism and with a soft
centre of belief in 'the hidden breath that lies at the heart of things'.
Admittedly, Antony's rhapsody is undermined by the Devil's
suggestion that the whole show may be one big illusion. And once
back on earth he is treated to a competitive dialogue between
Death and Lechery, then to a line-up of obsolescent gods heading
for the abyss. The work ends in irony and doubt. The Devil,
confident that lusts of the spirit cannot be eradicated, promises to

be back and his laughter sounds in the distance as Antony turns to his prayers.

Flaubert did not burn his manuscript. But he did take the criticism of his friends to heart. He later wrote to Louise that he would never recover the stylistic abandon of the early days of *Saint Antony*, but added: 'How lovingly I chiselled the beads of my necklace! I left out only one thing, and that's the string.' Better planning was needed. Flaubert reflected that the strict sequence of ideas was not paralleled by a concatenation of events, that drama was wanting. But in spite of these misgivings he went on hankering for the heady panorama of *Saint Antony* even while he pored over the moulds and mildews, as he put it, of the nineteenth-century soul for the writing of *Madame Bovary*. He insisted that what came naturally to him was 'the non-natural for others, the extraordinary, the fantastic, the metaphysical and mythological howl'. Since he looked back to the first composition of *Saint Antony* as 'the most profoundly voluptuous' time of his life, it's perhaps not surprising that in 1856 he remained under the influence of his earlier mood at least to the extent of not tampering with the basic shape of the book, though he pruned it thoroughly. In 1869 he was looking again for the 'logical link' between Antony's hallucinations. But this time he was more fearless. He threw himself into the work, partly to escape from his problems. As a 'dramatical exposition of the Alexandrine world of the IVth century', *Saint Antony* allowed him to forget the evils of his own times, to work simply for the sake of Art. When the Prussians invaded he abandoned Croisset; returning on 31 March 1871 he found his carefully concealed material on *Saint Antony* still intact.[33]

Alongside Flaubert's infinite capacity for taking historiographical pains, the old threads persist. He more than once refers to the subtitle of the book as 'le comble de l'insanité', the acme of insanity. But the work is so restructured, the emphases so redistributed, and such new touches added, that an excitingly altered book emerges, stylistically sparer than its predecessors and sharper in its contrasts. There are now seven chapters. Antony's opening speech provides both the historical context and a piquant hors-d'oeuvre of the sins which assail him in his desert retreat. In chapter two the Devil appears, and these temptations take on glowing form in the hallucinations that lead up to the Queen of Sheba's exotic arrival. The short third chapter introduces Hilarion, Antony's one-time disciple, an apparition who adopts the intellectually subversive role filled by Logic and Science in the first version. Having sown some theological doubts in Antony's mind, Hilarion acts as ironic companion and commentator throughout the heretical hubbub of chapter four and the procession of gods in chapter five. Once the gods, including the Lord of Hosts himself, have fallen silent, the Devil carries Antony off on his trip through the heavens.

But now there is none of the euphoria that Antony felt in the first version. The whole passage is much shorter, and the atmosphere much bleaker. A Spinozistic universe no longer offers the promise of blissful pantheism. The refusal to make man the measure of all things and the belief in a Creator immanent in Creation doubtless still have their grandeur. But the Devil's lucid exposé of the infinity of space, his intellectual extrapolation from orbit to orbit, lead inexorably to an acute sense of the illusoriness of human experience: it may all 'have rushed away towards a lie . . . into space . . . uselessly – like the cry of a bird.' As in the first version, Antony homes back to earth and to Lechery, Death, Sphinx, Chimera and monsters. But now – and this is the really crucial change – these freakish creatures lead him into fascinated scrutiny of nature, of the smallest imaginable particles of living matter. The euphoria of self-diffusion is with us again. But whereas it was provoked in Flaubert's youthful work by the grand sweep of space, it is now transferred to give a climax to the whole book and is elicited from a combination of fantasy and science, monsters and molecules, that ushers Antony to the brink of quasi-amoebic bliss.

In July 1872 Flaubert wrote that *Saint Antony* was finished. But in May 1873 he made a final all-important alteration. He replaced a last appearance of the Three Theological Virtues by Christ's face appearing in the sun. Manuscript fragments show that he had earlier considered introducing at the end of the episode on the gods a very old and reviled Christ, repeating his passion obscurely in the modern world.[34] One doesn't know at what point this idea was dropped, but it would certainly have impaired the simplicity and impact of the chosen final image. The increasing importance of the rising sun can be traced throughout the three versions.[35] In the first Flaubert simply indicates a few pages before the end that the sun rises; for the second he dug into his Grecian travel notes for a dazzling and dramatic description of sun and clouds; but only the last version concludes with Christ's face shining out of the sun. It seems likely that this image was chosen as a suitably cross-mythological one, combining the ubiquitous belief in the sun's divinity, the idea of Christianity in its most human and least dogmatic form, and a sense of the sun as the vivifying force which it certainly is. Meanwhile it may be recalled that the image of the rising sun was associated for Flaubert with the death of Alfred Le Poittevin, to whom he dedicated the final published version of *Saint Antony*.

4. 'The real riddles of life'

Flaubert had a way with idiots and animals. They seemed to love him, he seemed to understand them. He also claimed that during his illness he had felt and seen all that Saint Teresa, Hoffmann and Edgar Allen Poe describe.[36] It was the greatest of Poe's admirers, Baudelaire, who had some of the most perceptive things to say about *Saint Antony* when extracts from it were published in 1856–7 (these included the feast of Nebuchadnezzar, the arrival of the Queen of Sheba and the account of Apollonius of Tyana). After drawing attention to the 'suffering, subterranean and mutinous power which runs through the whole work, the dark vein which illumines – what the English call the *subcurrent* – and which serves as a guide throughout this pandemoniac junk-shop of solitude', Baudelaire concludes that Flaubert 'deliberately veiled in *Madame Bovary* the highly lyrical and ironic powers manifested without reserve in the *Temptation*' and that 'this last work, his spirit's secret chamber, clearly remains the most interesting for poets and philosophers.'[37]

Baudelaire could recognise that Antony's saintly megalomania is an icy surface covering a bewildering torrent of images or a black chill of disintegration. If one looks at Saint Teresa's autobiography or at Esquirol's impressively eloquent volume, *Des Maladies mentales* – both listed in Flaubert's long bibliography of his reading during 1870–72 for *Saint Antony* – it's obvious that these books were more than pathological reference-books for him. Teresa's 'saintly folly', her passionate solitude, her physical feelings of being transported outside herself, and her sense at such times that everyday life was a tedious irrelevance, can be readily compared to Flaubert's account of his hallucinations. Notably, Teresa describes the paradoxical conjunction of outer inanition with an explosively intense inner flux of images. And Esquirol describes how monomania may take the form of a 'fugaceous delirium' in which a versatile abundance of ideas and images can reach almost sublime heights, or may take the form of exclusive fixed attention on a single object.[38] I suppose that Flaubert's Sphinx and Chimera (erroneously pigeon-holed as Reason and Imagination) may owe something to his own experience of such moods, either in alternation or coexisting in painful tension.

What have others since Baudelaire made of Flaubert's 'secret chamber'? The official reception in 1874 was poor, indeed hostile. *Saint Antony* was criticised as inexact, immodest, chaotic, in bad taste, boring, a sure artistic suicide. In a more specialised vein, Taine praised Flaubert for combining the hallucinations of a fourth-century ascetic, incoherent as these must be, with a 'tableau of the grand metaphysical and mystical orgy, of the pell-mell of systems' which marked the period; and Renan, with a touch of condescension, praised the work as a brilliant and painterly fantasy, of nightmarish charm.[39] But there were also more poetic responses to the book's peculiar flavour, which detected in its opulence and anxiety something other than learned fantasy, a mesmeric quality which spoke from mind to mind. If Hugo's phrase 'full as a forest' is a little too pat, Huysman's seductive commentary in *A Rebours* (1884) shows what a powerful stimulant the book could be for such a decadent refiner of the cerebral and the sensuous, tingling to the Chimera's feverish incantation.[40] Of course various *fin de siècle* works which exploit similar exotic or heretical territory, by such writers as Louis Ménard, Anatole France, André de Guerne and Rémy de Gourmont, can be loosely affiliated to Flaubert's work.[41] It has also been argued, on slight but not negligible evidence, that echoes from the 1874 *Saint Antony* contribute to some of Rimbaud's writing.[42] But the greatest admirers of the book were painters.[43] It inspired pictures by Cézanne, James Ensor, Fernand Khnopff, and above all Odilon Redon, whose lithographs were in turn recycled into more of Huysman's inexhaustibly filamentous prose. These three series of lithographs are extraordinary. Flaubert, we know, was adamantly against the illustration of his books. But even Jean Seznec, whose beautifully meticulous research on *Saint Antony* is unrivalled and whose respect for the text is unimpeachable, is convinced that there was a 'kinship of genius' between the two artists that made Redon the 'ideal interpreter' of Flaubert's vision.[44] Redon's shadowy surrealism is grotesque without vulgarity, mysteriously sad with a melting minimum of outline, or shocking in its detail as in his flagrant floating eyeball. Perhaps he so got under the skin of the book because, as Jean Seznec points out, like Flaubert he was fascinated by the monstrous and the minuscule and was interested in physiological research.

Several theatre productions have been inspired by Flaubert's work.[45] In 1887 at the *Chat Noir* café Henri Rivière produced a colourful shadow-play of characters drawn partly from the book and partly from contemporary life. In 1930 Raoul Brunel treated the subject in a more down-to-earth vein, adapting the ending to show Antony joining a group of workers and setting out to till the Thebaid. In 1967 Jean-Louis Barrault starred at the Théâtre de France in Maurice Béjart's adaptation, an ambitious attempt to give expression to the wide sweep of Antony's vision, presented with the help of convulsive mime and dance, fantastic costumes, and the more rigorous support of a gradually mounting steel spiral.

It was the sensuous microscopy of Flaubert's descriptions that Jules Laforgue responded to, in his own florid style. In *Salomé* (largely a parody of Flaubert's *Hérodias*) he tours a palatial

Aquarium and revels ironically in 'a whole foetal and claustral and vibratile flora, agitated with the eternal dream of one day managing to exchange whispers of mutual congratulation on this state of affairs'. Another great obsession of Flaubert's time, the Void, also gets short shrift. Three clowns chant the refrain:

> Néant, la Mecque
> des bibliothèques![46]

Reductive in another fashion is the study published in 1912 by Theodor Reik, a Freudian analysis of what *Saint Antony* may betray about Flaubert.[47] The gratuitous presence of Antony's mother (more insistent from version to version) is of course good grist to the Freudian mill. Antony's guilt at having left her, his fantasies about her lonely death, do suggest that here an emotional charge has travelled straight from life into literature. Anyone who looks up Flaubert's letters from Egypt will find Madame Flaubert figuring not only as a conventionally worried parent but as the very incarnation of maternal grief. Reik is confident that the artist's garish neuroses – sadism, erotic writing-drive, hankering for married women and prostitutes, curiosity about Nature – can safely be explained in terms of the child's incestuous desire for his mother, prostituted to his hated father. All, of course, is sublimated in the 'Sanatorium of Art'.

Freud himself had been far too impressed by *Saint Antony* to quarry it so condescendingly. In a letter of 1883 he describes it as

> this book which in the most condensed fashion and with unsurpassable vividness throws at one's head all the dross of the world: for it calls up not only the great problem of knowledge [*Erkenntnis*], but the real riddles of life, all the conflicts of feelings and impulses; and it confirms the awareness of our perplexity in the mysteriousness that reigns everywhere.[48]

What Flaubert's mother, who lived until 6 April 1872, really meant to him as alibi, incentive or emotional absolute, I don't propose to gauge. That he was devoted to her and appalled by the notion of ever having children himself is certain. But however great his individual neuroses, his development was obviously in some ways typical of his class and time and expressed through common attitudes and themes. 'The prostitute is a vanished myth,' he wrote to Louise Colet in 1846, adding: 'I've stopped frequenting her, in despair of ever finding her.'[49] But how potent this myth remained for him is shown not only by the latter account of his voluptuously poignant night with Kuchuk-Hanem on the Nile,[50] but by *Saint Antony*, *Salammbô* and *Hérodias*. I must confess that the strands of nineteenth-century erotica as unpicked by literary critics sometimes seem to me monotonously predictable. Flaubert was not alone in imagining, beyond the squalor and disease of the brothels which he used, as did many of his class, for the satisfaction of his staple sexual needs, an exotic woman who would combine the frank availability of the whore with a kind of sensuous transcendence. He was not likely to find in the respectable or even the less respectable women of his own class, however attractive and intelligent and friendly, either what he was used to or the inarticulate intensification he dreamed of. The Oriental Woman fascinated him as an unknown, and his night with Kuchuk-Hanem was memorable because it was a climax to the wordless communication of dance. The evidence is that Flaubert, again like so many others, eventually contracted syphilis – possibly before going to Egypt and certainly by the time he got back.[51] But already in 1846, at the very beginning of his liaison with Louise Colet, he was writing to her that people who love each other should be able to spend ten years comfortably apart.[52]

Nineteenth-century decadence, masochistic and morbid, is the context in which Mario Praz placed *Saint Antony*, suggesting that it influenced D'Annunzio and Swinburne and that Oscar Wilde skimmed from it some rare rhyme-words for *The Sphinx* (perhaps 'catafalque', 'mandragores', 'oreichalc'?). Praz is clearly right to be sceptical of Flaubert's protest against Sainte-Beuve's accusations about sadism in *Salammbô*. Flaubert admired Sade, though he was capable of pointing out that his were among the few vicious characters who made him laugh, since 'crime here attains to the ridiculous, for nature is so exalted, so pushed to extremes that it becomes impossible and disappears, one has nothing but a *notion* of fantastic beings supposedly human and in contradiction with humanity.'[53] For all the exaggeration, a Sadian protagonist such as Madame Delbène can argue very tenaciously that thought is by no means distinct from matter – which is after all a real concern in *Saint Antony*. And anyone glancing at the women in Flaubert's book – the writhing Ammonaria, Ennoia with her bitten face and bruised arms, the Queen of Sheba with her needle-sharp nails harking back to the hooks (*angles*) on Antony's whip – cannot but realise that here the voluptuous is also the sadomasochistic.

That Antony's obsessions were also Flaubert's is shown by his letters. In the 1850s he was writing to Louise:

> There comes a time when *one needs to make oneself suffer*, to hate one's flesh, to throw mud in its face, so hideous does it seem. If it weren't for my love of form, I might perhaps have been a great mystic.[54]

In another letter he expands nostalgically on his love of prostitution, the sheer idea of it, remembering how the lusts of his student days in Paris seemed all involved with the cadences of biblical fornication, and comparing the beating of his heart at the sight of the gas-lit flesh of passing girls to the tickling of some profoundly ascetic corner of his soul at the sight of a monk's knotted girdle. He sees in the idea of prostitution 'so complex a point of intersection – lust, bitterness, nullity of human relations, muscular frenzy and ringing of gold – that looking to the bottom of it makes one dizzy, and what a lot one learns there!' (Perhaps this encomium is 'the page in Flaubert on prostitution' noted in his diary by Kafka, who read *Saint Antony* in 1908–9, but reserved his greatest admiration for *L'Education sentimentale*.)[55]

The Oriental exoticism so rife in the nineteenth century provided an easy literary highway towards all kinds of dubious fantasies. However, Praz's thesis that 'sadism and Catholicism ... become the two poles between which the souls of neurotic and sensual writers oscillate' and his description of *Saint Antony* as 'from beginning to end an orgy *à la* Sade'[56] amount to a sadly simplistic view of the work, a reduction of it to the lowest common denominator of the morbid aesthetics which he maps. Death and sex are deep companions in the human mind, and their nagging, overlapping solicitations in *Saint Antony* may represent something more than a decadent period piece or a purely personal trauma. Nevertheless the period flavour is strong. The best recent discussion of Flaubert in relation to the 'Oriental Renaissance' of his time is by Jean Bruneau, who suggests that his lifelong dream of sunlight is something of a key to his aesthetics, that his two outstanding Orientalist predilections were for India and for the desert, and that he evolved a complex and original sense of the Orient which acted as a vital source for his meditations about the world and indeed about nineteenth-century France.[57]

Taking into account the post-Romantic atmosphere in which many artists felt alienated from their bourgeois surroundings, one may also relate Flaubert's idea of art as a type of martyrdom to Baudelaire's idea of it as a type of prostitution. Baudelaire, perhaps influenced by Joseph de Maistre, saw himself as a sacred prostitute whose self-imposed degradation was for a high anti-materialist cause.[58] Both martyrdom and sacred prostitution involve an idea of reciprocity, however brutal, in that there is a level of complicity between victim and executioner, sacrificer and sacrificed, created by recognition of the possibility of absolute allegiance. But the artist acting out his excessive, violent and violating procedure in the name of his allegiance must victimise himself. It's entirely appropriate that Flaubert should have created a kind of *alter ego* out of St Antony, who was not a martyr at all, and whose sufferings were self-inflicted.[59] The desert anchorites tried to equal in their masochistic practices the sufferings of the martyrs, and Flaubert throughout his life pursued a similar course: the literary vigil rivalled the religious, and the strokes of the pen bit as deep as the lashes of the whip – which is not to say that he made himself a martyr for words, but that he tried to martyr himself by means of words for the sake of something else. Antony's whipped-up frenzy in Chapter II, and also the moment of reward and relief when the sun finally rises, are well paralleled in Flaubert's description of the artist's calling in a letter of about 1853:

> Art, like the God of the Jews, thrives on holocausts. Go on! Rend yourself, whip yourself, roll yourself in ashes, make matter vile, spit on your body, tear out your heart! You'll be alone, your feet will bleed, an infernal feeling of disgust will accompany you the whole

way, none of what makes other people's joy will go to make yours, what are pinpricks to them will be laceration to you, and you'll flounder on, lost in the storm, with this little light on the horizon. But it will get bigger, it will get bigger like the sun, its golden beams will cover your face, they'll pass into you, you'll be lit up from inside, you'll feel airy and all spirit, and after each letting of blood the flesh will weigh less.[60]

The ascetic ideal penetrated deep into Flaubert's artistic conscience. Indeed, his career could be interestingly considered in the context of Nietzsche's analyses of European asceticism and nihilism, not least because Nietzsche raised the question of the corrupting effect of the ascetic ideal on artistic creativity – though his references to Flaubert are few, and he appears to have associated him somewhat superficially with the realist school, whom he viewed as Parisian decadents with petty and impoverished aims. Flaubert belongs neither with the realists nor with an art-for-art's-saker like Gautier. While he refused, in common with such contemporaries, to subject art to utilitarian morals, he could sport neither an epicurean belief in pleasure nor a naïve faith in naturalistic method. Excess, licence, a gigantic indulgence in every possibility, are in fact, as Jean-Pierre Richard[61] has demonstrated with some subtlety, quite as fundamentally Flaubertian as any ascetic impulse towards lean and attenuated truth. 'Excess is proof of ideality: to go beyond need', wrote Flaubert in his notebook. And such excess can lead past Blake's palace of wisdom to a savage sensuality. He further noted that 'cruelty through sensuality provokes less revulsion than cruelty which is ignorant of itself, the cruelty of ideas, of principles. Is it because the first is a necessity for man in the plenitude of his faculties and the second is a vice of the intellect? Art can turn the one to account, it steers clear of the second.'[62]

Flaubert was aware of the imaginative drive in outrageous cruelty. And the power of illusion is a crux of his aesthetics. In early days, writing to Louise of his hallucinations, his travel fantasies, his bookish habits, he announced: 'I believe in the eternity of one thing only, of *illusion* that is, which is the real truth (*la vraie vérité*). All the others are only relative.'[63] Jean Bruneau argues that

Flaubert could have owed a direct debt to Hegel and quotes a key-phrase of the *Aesthetics*: 'Indeed, far from mere appearances being purely illusory, the forms of art comprise more reality and truth than the phenomenal existences of the real world. The world of art is truer than that of nature and history.'[64] However, one must be cautious about interpreting the final *Saint Antony* in the light of these quotations. The Devil's most disturbing proposition persists in Chapter VI: 'Unless – the world being a perpetual flux of things – appearance on the contrary were to be all that is truest, and illusion the one reality.' But it comes in the form of a taunting question, rather than a ringing belief, and Antony circumvents it with a gesture of hope.

The notion of illusion does go some way towards explaining the force of Flaubertian temptation. The classic sensuous and psychological temptations, that's to say the Seven Deadly Sins, are for Antony perhaps only facets of the fundamental temptation of illusion itself. His hallucinations are temptations irrespective of what they contain. Form and content are one, he is tempted by endless desire. An early and well-known passage from Flaubert's letters is again relevant:

> Now I, so long as no one will have separated out, in a given phrase, form from content, shall maintain that here are two words empty of meaning. There are no beautiful thoughts without beautiful forms, and vice versa. Beauty transudes from form in the world of Art, as in our own world the outcome is temptation, love.[65]

For all the surface clarity, there is some ambivalence here. Beauty is lined up with temptation and love. But the concepts are too big to explain each other. In *Saint Antony* in particular, the question persists: what kind of beauty, what kind of temptation, what kind of love?

5. Modern critiques

Valéry had a weakness for what he called Flaubert's 'intimate antidote' to the boredom of building monuments to bourgeois provincialism; but he also (as a man used to getting up at four to pursue pure notions running through his head) felt that *Saint Antony* left him at the mercy of a 'dizzily unleashed library' of vociferous tomes.[66] Writing two decades later, in the sixties, Michel Foucault [67] has had a lot more to say about the text's 'erudite onirism' which he views as an exciting form of imaginative life, not meant to deny or compensate for reality, but appearing in the 'interstices' between signs, books and commentaries. Existing by virtue of this network of the ready-written, *Saint Antony* is 'the book of books', the fantastic figuration of all imaginable books 'taken up, fragmented, displaced, combined, distanced by dreamy thought, but also drawn closer by it for the imaginary and scintillating satisfaction of desire'. It opens the way towards Mallarmé, Joyce, Roussel, Kafka, Pound, Borges: 'the library', says Foucault, 'is ablaze.'

The open Bible which Antony pores over (a feature of the last version) is of key importance, the very locus of temptation. It engenders the whole visionary sweep and shows that 'evil is not incarnate in characters, but incorporated in words'. Foucault goes on to distinguish five different orders of language, and a relay of figures who prolong the imaginative dimension of the work. There is the actual reader, then the implicit spectator who describes the décor, then Antony, then Hilarion, and within the vision conjured up by this satanic disciple there are then figures who evoke their rites and histories – and whose discourse in turn gives rise to still more shadowy figures. The five orders are defined as 'book, theatre, sacred text, visions and visions of visions'. They do not produce a vanishing perspective but a kind of 'retrograde envelopment', so that the most far-fetched fictions are in a way the most vivid and immediate, seeming materially to overwhelm Antony and Hilarion. As the successive points of vantage tend to merge into a single sense of dazzlement, one is drawn to identify with the remotest figures and to see through their insubstantial eyes: such is the temptation of vision.

Having analysed the dramatic strata of *Saint Antony*, Foucault detects an ordering in the sequence of visions. First comes a cosmological pattern: we start with the hermit's heart, then move on to Alexandria, the Christian East, the Mediterranean, Asia, then to the dilating universe of space, then to the minuscule cell; this is a circular return to the point of departure, since Antony is gently contemplating 'the larva of desire'. There is also a historical pattern: Antony reaches back through his past life, the recent history of the Church, the other countless beliefs of men, and so to the primal universe, the stars, matter without memory, the origin of all things. The third pattern is prophetic. Hilarion speaks for Western science, guiding Antony through theology and comparative religion and providing a rationalistic view of the universe. Foucault suggests that 'like a nocturnal sun, *The Temptation* goes from East to West, from desire to learning, from imagination to truth, from the oldest nostalgias to the formulations of modern science.' Antony's Egypt is at a 'zero point', in a 'fold of time', in the 'hollow of history'. And his 'temptation' is that of 'a Christianity doubly fascinated by the sumptuous fantasmagoria of its past and the limitless acquisitions of its future'. These glittering images do not mask reality but reveal it because, so Foucault argues, Christianity was indeed created when the last 'reflections' of the ancient world played upon the beginnings of the new. Finally he detects a theological pattern: Faith, Hope and Charity, the Virtues of the first version, implicitly persist since the heresies compromise Faith, the doomed gods undermine Hope, and the vision of a deterministic universe makes nonsense of Charity; in the end Antony can only transform Charity into 'dazzled curiosity', Hope into an 'unmitigated desire to merge into the violence of the world', and Faith into identification with 'the mutism of nature, the dull and gentle stupidity of things'.

Michel Butor, writing in 1970, picks instead on the Seven Deadly Sins.[68] He suggests a set of better qualities to match the negative ones, so that each sin is two-faced. We are offered sloth/detachment, greed/refinement, avarice/curiosity, anger/indignation, envy/emulation, pride/science, and lust/realisation. This hierarchy is supposed to mirror the stages of literary activity, from solitude to ultimate publication. Butor believes that one of the sins is dominant in each chapter: sloth in the first, greed in the second, the avarice of logic in the third, anger among the heretics, envy among the gods, pride when the devil rides into space, and in the seventh chapter lust.

In my opinion this sort of scheme is not well founded in the text. In particular, greed and anger are not outstanding in the third and fifth chapters respectively. Flaubert dissolved the Seven Deadly Sins into Antony's opening monologue and re-crystallised them in his selected Bible verses, but they don't provide the fundamental structure of the work. All the same, temptation is presumably something to be withstood, and if Antony is doing more than putting up a traditional resistance to traditional vices then one may well wonder what sort of ethical wear and tear he suffers and what the upshot of his night of tribulations is.

Foucault believes that Antony's impulse towards matter is innocent; he wants to let thought lie and to rejoin 'the stupid sanctity of things'. A similar interpretation was offered some years ago by Louis Bertrand, who saw Antony's passivity and inertia as indications of his spiritual condition as *la chose de Dieu*. A passage about this type of saintly stupidity, with specific mention of St Antony, was copied by Flaubert from a novel of 1863 by George Sand and found among his notes. Bertrand suggested that Flaubert found in it confirmation of his own insights, since there is another manuscript note apparently belonging with the first *Saint Antony* that can be translated as: '*General tone of debasement, idiotism and fatigue* on Saint Antony's part, set off by his sharp anger, at the end, when he chases Logic away.' He assessed the overall mood of the book as that of 'moral nihilism', and its ambiguous conclusion as a result of Flaubert's principle that the artist has no more business to conclude a work than God to put a full stop to creation.[69] But for Foucault there is a victory over temptation, over desire. He elaborates the point by noting a contrast with *Bouvard et Pécuchet*: whereas Antony achieves a state of 'brute sanctity' by abandoning the attempt to be what he sees and turning to the activity of prayer (the French speak of 'doing' rather than 'saying' their prayers), Bouvard and Pécuchet reach a similar state of freedom from desire by abandoning their attempts at active manipulation and returning to their copying, content simply to be 'the fold of discourse on itself'.

Butor, on the other hand, discerns no dramatic break. He

describes the sun as a hieroglyph of the idea of divine incarnation
that has haunted Antony in so many unexpected shapes. This
analysis has the advantage of showing how the longing to be
matter is linked to the obsession with illusion: a god, a creator, can
materialise his illusions. Having detected a subtly engineered
'genealogy of desire', Butor defines the creatures of the last chapter
as the offspring of 'the grand lust that invention is'. His account of
this chapter is itself very persuasive. The sensuous surface of the
text deserves recognition, and I notice that it can be related to much
of what Lust has to say in the first *Saint Antony*, for instance: 'If
only, for feeling, I had hands all over my body! If only, for kissing,
I had lips at the ends of my fingers!'[70] In Butor's dynamic inter-
pretation there is no breaking free from the spiral of illusion and
desire, from the proliferation of forms. Day and night are alternate
faces of one same eclosion of energy. Temptation is a splendi-
ferously seductive art, and the rising sun provides no escape; on
the contrary, the divine face is possibly equivalent to the nocturnal
devil just as, at the end of *Saint Julien l'Hospitalier*, the hideous
leper masks the Saviour.

This last suggestion seems to me perverse. The Devil in *Saint
Antony* is still the doubter, the metaphysical underminer, that he
was in Flaubert's early writings. And I think that the leper's
metamorphosis from disease-ridden flesh to luminosity, if it does
parallel the switch at the end of *Saint Antony* from twitching
globules to solar image, shows that Flaubert is in his element when
so far insisting on the physical and organic (to adapt his comment
on Sade) that it disappears in favour of a bare notion of being. In
the last stretch of *Salammbô*, the bleeding Mâtho is 'completely
red'; only his eyes retain any human appearance, and from their
orbits come 'two flames which seemed to reach up to his hair'; his
heart is torn out and exposed to the arrowy rays of the setting sun,
which sinks into the sea just as the heart-beats cease: 'at the last
palpitation, it vanished.'[71] In *Saint Julien* Flaubert was again
attempting the impossible rather than the impossibly clever: 'And
his eyes all at once took on the brightness of stars, his hair spread
out like the rays of the sun . . . . The roof flew off, the firmament
was unfolding – and Julian rose towards spaces of blue, face to face

with Our Lord Jesus, who was bearing him up into the sky!'[72]

Does Antony transcend the *idiotisme* Flaubert noted, the *abêtissement* recognised by Taine, the *bêtise* Foucault writes of? Critics disagree. Certainly Flaubert was fascinated by dumb-beastedness, animal lethargy, obtuseness, heavy-lidded physicality – witness the monstrous Catoblepas, whose stupidity 'attracts' Antony. The obsession was connected with intense religious nostalgia. In early days he wrote to the mystified and antagonistic Louise:

> I don't indulge, as you fancy, in intellectual orgies. I've worked very simply, very regularly, and even fairly foolishly [*bêtement*]. I don't write any longer, what's the point of writing? All that's beautiful has been said and well said. Instead of creating a work, it's perhaps wiser to discover new ones beneath the old. It seems to me that the less I produce, the more pleasure I take in contemplating the masters. And since, above all, what I ask is to pass my time agreeably, I'll hold this. You call me 'the Brahman'. It's too great an honour, but I do wish I were. I have aspirations enough towards the life to drive me wild. I wish I could live in their woods, turn like them in mystical dances and exist in that immeasurable absorption. They're beautiful with their long hair, their faces running with sacred butter and their great cries which answer those of elephants and bulls. Once upon a time I wanted to be a Camaldolite, then a renegade, a Turk. Now it's a Brahman or nothing, which is simpler.[73]

It's the implications of the 'simple' that are so hard to interpret. Foucault's admiration for *Saint Antony* is of a piece with his love of works which suggest disjunction and silence. One knows from his *Histoire de la folie* that he admires writers such as Nerval and Artaud whom he cites with eloquent approval as having abandoned the habits of the Western world to achieve an absolute rupture, a 'profile against the void'.[74] And it's worth referring to this work for Foucault's account of the changing view of the relation between folly and animality. He argues that whereas the animality of the insane was earlier seen as a totally negative quality, once an evolutionary perspective had been established it could be seen as part of a natural mechanism.[75] In Foucault's eyes, Antony's insanity acquires a thoroughly salutary status.

31

Turning from Foucault to Sartre, the contrast is colossal. I can't, of course, undertake a full discussion of Sartre's voluminous work on Flaubert in its bearing on *Saint Antony*. But I must draw attention to one double kernel of his argument. He believes that Flaubert's concentration on style and form represents a compulsive reification which turns words into objects; and he believes that Flaubert is out to 'derealise' the world, to create nothing but nothingness. For Sartre, Flaubert is the great technician of irrealisation whose sense of his own void or nothingness is looking for assuagement in the metaphysically virulent void he creates. A bourgeois artist alienated from his milieu, product and accomplice of it nonetheless, he irrealises himself and becomes the 'gigantic depository of the Spinozistic substance',[76] identifying this Spinozistic All with a negative Nothing. Sartre is indeed very interesting when he discusses the relation between Flaubert's sense of the void and his sense of pulverulent and pullulating matter. He argues that a 'first or *idealist* negation of the real engenders, disappointed, negation through a ludicrous ultramaterialism'; subsequently 'the silent, icy, infinite laughter of Nothingness' cuts across the huge *fou rire* of matter.[77]

It's certain that for Flaubert matter and void are intrinsically linked, since death means the scattering of organisms into dust. But even Sartre seems to admit that by his pantheism Flaubert runs counter to his tendency to irrealise and dehumanise and that he can make of his pantheistic effusion something 'neither miserable nor ridiculous' – at least when, in *Madame Bovary*, Emma's *baisade* in the woods becomes 'a privileged moment when language is dead' and when 'the mute awareness of dazzlement and the dazzling sunset are one and the same thing. Emma, on her back, her body rifled by a man's organ, her eyes burnt by the fire of a star, is very near to realising the wish of the last *Saint Antony*, "to be matter".'[78] However, Sartre's left-wing psychoanalytical approach is most likely to shed light on the first *Saint Antony*, where the sexuality is more unremitting, the void more insistently canvassed, and the artistry less. When it comes to the last version, the complex product of a quarter of a century's development, something other is needed than the Sartrean projection on paper of Flaubert's psyche, like an immensely magnified and capillary hypothesis, which tends to lead back again and again to the same main artery of criticism. Sartre's claim that 'the Artist, for Flaubert, is he who adopts with respect to Being the point of view of Nothingness, with respect to life the point of view of death,' is the kind of challenging, simplistic generalisation that belongs with Nietzsche's note on 'that typical transformation of which G. Flaubert offers the clearest example among the French . . . , in which the romantic faith in love and the future is transformed into the desire for the nothing.'[79]

From the point of view of Sartre's hostility to the literary, a work such as *Saint Antony* becomes purely an illusory solution to Flaubert's neuroses, a pouring of absence and irreality into words. His discussion is often absorbingly interesting. But his central claim is that the imaginary, which he equates with 'dream', is autistic, passive and empty:

> Rational thought is forged in action or rather it's action itself producing its own lights. If then there exists a thought proper to inaction, to impotence, it can only be dream. In autism, that extreme form of passivity, desire failing to carry over into reality falls back on itself as self-image, that's to say as imaginary assuagement or, if one prefers, as transcendence retracted into immanence. . . . Gustave, we have seen, has long since been a child of the imaginary; dream in his case is the site, empty and gaping, of impossible *praxis*.[80]

Estimates of *Saint Antony* depend on attitudes to dream, to the imaginary. Jonathan Culler's book on Flaubert is partly indebted to Sartre's work, and especially in his account of 'reverie' the affiliation is clear – although he moves beyond Sartre's study to a more 'positive' appreciation of Flaubert's writings. He defines the goal of 'open and exploratory reverie' as stupidity or *bêtise*, and suggests that *Saint Antony* is a 'synthesis of Flaubert's attitudes towards stupidity'. This 'mode of perception', he argues, 'produces a correspondence between mind and its objects so that both come to partake of the same quality. The world is ordered but, seen *sub specie inanitatis*, that order is without point.' The quality is found to be pervasive: in the ridiculous wrangling of the heretics, the 'boring self-satisfaction' of Apollonius, the laughable suite of primitive gods, the 'solidified language' of the Buddha, and at last in the limp-headed Catoblepas.[81]

Having situated Flaubert in the deserts of 'ironic negation', Culler looks for evidence that he can reach 'beyond irony to a point where one can find the positive in the negative',[82] and he finds it in 'the notion of a sacred order'.[83] He explains that 'the purity and inviolacy of the sacred' may be defined as 'arbitrary meanings guaranteed not by man but by god'.[84] Such meanings are to be found in the sacred veil or Zaïmph of *Salammbô*, the parrot of *Un Coeur simple* – and perhaps Culler might have included, though he does not, the rising sun of *Saint Antony*. But the point is that since, for him, 'meaning' is an 'aspiration towards a secure and fully self-conscious understanding',[85] he obviously cannot reconcile it with reverie. His emphasis on Flaubert's irreverence for the codes of human intercourse is very Sartrean: 'What I should want to maintain . . . is that a desire not to understand, not to grasp the purposes that language, behaviour, and objects serve in ordinary practical life, is one of the determining features of Flaubert's writing.'[86]

Perhaps so. But states of fascination, of mental and physical attraction or repulsion, may be of value not only to Flaubert as a pathological writer but to his readers – and to the extent that he has suggested such states, they have been communicated and they do in any case enter the realm of meaning. Culler's determination to link 'meaning' with 'self-conscious understanding' results in a very one-sided treatment of the element of 'mystique' in Flaubert's writings. Hot on the tracks of the imposition of sacred order, he sadly neglects the seering sensuality of Flaubert's performance. For instance, it needs saying that the presence of the sacred veil in *Salammbô* leads, not to a self-conscious state of order, but to a barbaric event – the torture-gauntlet run by Mâtho – described in sadistic voyeuristic style. I am aware that there is much self-conscious ordering in Sadian scenes: my point is that Mâtho's well mapped death-agony is not 'strictly fabulous' (as Roland Barthes has described Sade's novels)[87] but in part naturalistic and emotive. Cruelty, sensuality, mesmerism, Flaubertian qualities *par excellence*, are not given adequate attention by Culler. Indeed, his lack of response to the rhythm and tempo of *Saint Antony*, to those atmospheric qualities which elicited Redon's remarkable lithographs, and his incuriosity about the semiological complexities of the text, make me suspect that he is here guilty of just that 'premature foreclosure' that he would have us all guard against.

Let it be recognised that Flaubert has failed to satisfy at least two of the greatest French writers of this century. Valéry found the hero of *Saint Antony* so 'mortally passive' that he longed, like the Queen of Sheba, to pinch him; and in the beautifully characteristic conclusion to his article 'The Temptation of (Saint) Flaubert', he wondered why the inner appetency, the whole physiology of temptation, was not more fearlessly realised. Proust, equally characteristically, protested long ago that in the whole of Flaubert's works there is not to be found one single fine metaphor. But in the very teeth of his frustration at the apparent clumsinesses and lack of distinction of the writing, the 'heavy materials which Flaubert's phrase lifts up and lets fall with the intermittent sound of an excavator', the homogeneous monotony of the 'great moving escalator' of which the pages consist, he reflected on the linguistic originality, the revolutionary handling of bare verbal tenses, which was Flaubert's achievement, and he could not but admire 'the narrow, hermetic continuity of style'.[88]

6. Text and context

Flaubert sensed the closeness of people and things. He knew what it is to lose oneself gazing at a burning log, a stone, an animal, a drop of water, a shell, or just a hair.[89] In *Un Coeur simple* the old servant Félicité shares her life with an idolised stuffed parrot. While the parrot is credited with meaning, Félicité enjoys feeling: 'Sometimes, the sunlight coming in through the attic window would strike its glass eye so that there leapt from it a great luminous ray which put her into ecstasy.'[90] This passage is clearly a reimaging of one from the first *Saint Antony*, which did not survive into the 1874 text, in which Antony's watch by a girl's corpse is described.

A voice reminds him: 'The gold ring on her finger, struck by one of the torches, threw out a great ray which came straight to your eye.' And Antony responds: 'It was a night like this, the air was close, I felt weak in the chest . . .'[91] At the end of *Un Coeur simple*, Félicité dies of pneumonia, breathing up azure vapours of incense with 'mystic sensuality'.

Perhaps Félicité's experience harks back to Flaubert's watch beside the corpse of his dead sister. This is pure speculation. But I suppose that currents of feeling and association resurface in Flaubert's works just as they do in those of writers less addicted to irony and impersonality. We ourselves, of course, have only the texts to go by. For us, 'Flaubert' is the impression left in our minds by the collection of texts by and about him. Hence the interest of *Saint Antony*. It isn't a polysynthetic left-over from Flaubert's youth, but the work among all others which most interconnects with his whole writing life. On its own merits the text is striking and sticky – beautiful to some, rebarbative to others. It challenges one to reflect on what counts as 'meaning', on how far one will go in search of it.

In *Bouvard et Pécuchet* Flaubert shows the futility of trying to come to grips with the world. Neither books nor transparently good intentions are of any help to the two ex-copyists. Reality – whether cultural, natural or metaphysical – eludes their control. At the point when Flaubert had just finished *Saint Antony*, he mentioned in his letters that he would like to see it published simultaneously with the 'quite different' book he was planning: 'I'm working on one at the moment which could form a pendant to it. Conclusion: the wise thing is to stay still.'[92] The links between the two books are in fact many. In particular, chapters III, VIII and IX of *Bouvard et Pécuchet* provide a sample of ideas similar to those in *Saint Antony*. The two friends ponder over the purpose of the universe, over stars and monsters, over the origins of life, and especially over the thorny problem of how spirit and matter are connected. Bouvard plays the corpulent materialist and the Spinozistic devil, Pécuchet the defensive Cartesian and the self-flagellating idealist. Disgusted with the inconsistencies of their respective positions they clamber onto suicide-chairs, but change their minds and go to midnight mass – only to be driven back into scepticism, nay Buddhism, by the priestly aplomb with which the local *curé* soon ignores their objections about martyrs and miracles (much the same ones that Hilarion dismays Antony with). Returning home in fine argumentative fettle, they discover the hair-lipped idiot Marcel kneeling beneath the madonna on the stairs like an ecstatic fakir. While the two protagonists' zoological craze, like all the others, has been short, the final return to copying that Flaubert planned for them is certainly comparable to Antony's return to his prayers. And underpinning the two books is the same immensely erudite honeycomb.

Flaubert's indefatigable, apiarian reading programme should not be dismissed either as some sort of elaborate obsession or as a mere preliminary gathering of ingredients for a realist syrup. That he kept an eye open for historic local colour is of course true. And he certainly deleted some anachronisms from *Saint Antony*, for instance the picture of the Virgin Mary which originally provoked Antony's erotic fantasies. But he was in any case working away from the luxuriance and the hearty cynicism of his first version. And even in the last version he takes plenty of historical liberties, some of which I indicate in the notes. While he was clearly avoiding what Henry James has called the 'affront to verisimilitude' in his broad historic canvass, he was no stickler for rigid authenticity. Jean Seznec has done invaluable research on the sources of *Saint Antony;* he brings to light the range of Flaubert's knowledge, his punctiliousness, his ability to make subtle combinations of his sources and to extrapolate imaginatively from what seems like unpromisingly arid material. Such work is an inspiring model of scholarly and aesthetic decoding combined with keen insight.[93] Yet at this point, we need to be reminded once more that these sources are more than curiosities, more than mere antique-markets of signs and images from which Flaubert concocted the lacquered visions of his Egyptian anchorite.

It is a familiar fact that Flaubert can mercilessly blow the fuse between words and things. Bouvard and Pécuchet's attempt to classify the clouds as nimbus or cirrus, stratus or cumulus, is cautionary: 'the shapes altered before they had found the names.'[94]

But the words Flaubert read can still help us to understand the words on his pages. 'Intertextuality' is a term sometimes used to point to a text as a part of a cultural nexus rather than the expression of an artist's subjectivity. But some of the grossest strands in the network of texts to which a single work is linked will be, in the traditional critical formulation, the sources. Perhaps one may wish to put aside certain connotations of the word, those of purity and of some sort of organic, ineluctable growth, and to think in terms of parallels and contrasts, overlappings and disjunctions. But a work is not a complete synchronic system (though it may be a synchronic sample of the author's creative language) and its elements can't be purely defined by their simultaneous relationships to each other. The work is of course part of the larger synchronic system of the language of the time. But moreover, just as in linguistics it becomes very difficult to separate synchronic from diachronic facts where semantics or meanings are concerned, so in the case of a work of literature a study of its relatedness to an array of other texts may help one to understand and appreciate the equilibrium of the end-creation. Meanings persist, provided they are perceived.

In terms of their dates of composition, the source-texts are in a superficially definable diachronic relation to the author's work. But the diachronic perspective peculiar to the work is that formed by the author's reading of his source-texts; and given that the notion of synchronism implies a state of relative interdependence of meanings rather than any rigorously simultaneous production, a source-text may alternatively be regarded as being brought at the period of composition into synchronic relation to the author's work. Either way, the fact remains that an awareness of the semantic potential of a work is sharpened by knowledge of the sources, the context. It is thought that by the disunities of their work creative writers show the edge between the ideology of their time and more progressive consciousness, but one can also argue that the tension of a work, what prevents it from being a limp bundle of language, depends as much on the pull of the past as on that of the future. The work must be a taut trampoline of signifiers on which meanings can bounce. And indeed, once one begins to locate the textual hooks and eyes of *Saint Antony* – its sources and its affiliations to more modern texts – the meanings start to sparkle, swing, coagulate or drop free.

Take Mani, the first of Flaubert's heretics. Impressively pale, surrounded by emblems of his skills as painter and cosmologist, he speaks both as a serene pantheist and as an acrid opponent of soul-weakening sensualism. His attitude is deeply troubled. Now among Flaubert's sources was a notorious article by the philosopher Pierre Bayle, who made Mani a hero of dualist thought.[95] Bayle was above all intent on the question, how could a good God be responsible for evil? He wrote with fervent conviction of this incompatibility in creation – before abjuring the unorthodox line of thought and flaunting an arbitrary volte-face under the banner of faith. The unchronological pride of place which Flaubert gives to Mani owes something to this tradition.

Mani's heroic dualism leaves the way free towards pantheism (in another article Bayle himself had concluded that a God responsible for the whole of creation could only be envisaged in Spinozistic terms).[96] Of course, the dominant nineteenth-century trend was to see nature-worship and pantheism in all primitive religions. And Flaubert had only to go to Jacques Matter's elegant work on Gnosticism to find the religion of Mani and the Gnostic movement treated as a variety of pantheism, modified by Asia's ancient dualism.[97] Via the notion of emanation, both Matter and Creuzer firmly linked Gnosticism and pantheism. So to Flaubert the Gnostics were not simply a babble of bizarre voices appropriate to Antony's time and culture, but troubling reminders of permanent anxieties. Moreover, whereas Matter had little difficulty in harmonising the tortured sexual abstinence of some of his sects with the abstract pantheism he attributed to them – he simply took it for granted that the most ascetic were the best – for Flaubert the problem bit deeper. 'From the heart of a rigorous system there issues a doctrine of laxity,'[98] wrote Matter; hardly any one sect can be labelled ascetic or orgiastic, since followers differed from founders and accusations flew freely. What strikes one, scanning Flaubert's heretics, is the alternate glorification and condemnation of the flesh. The wild oscillation between abandon and rigid control fascinates him. And this is where he chooses to put his emphasis. He is very willing to echo the charges of fornication and obscene practices made against the Manicheans.[99] Although theological clashes are outlined, sensuous counterpoint prevails in Chapter IV.

When Antony wonders 'What then is the Word? ... What was Jesus?' he receives an avalanche of brief rattling replies. Discriminations are slid over. Flaubert was too far from belief in Christianity to be strictly interested in Christology or in the doctrine of the Trinity. He probably agreed with Albert Réville who dismissed the Trinity as a pseudo-Gnostic formulation, saying that the doctrine is in effect polytheistic and that the early church only triumphed over Gnosticism thanks to its own opposing brand of gnosis.[100] What did interest Flaubert was the idea of immanent divinity. The Gnostics' attitude towards the world was anguished and contradictory. They believed that divine elements were trapped inside matter. They believed in the utter incompatibility of spirit and matter. Their anxieties run parallel to Flaubert's, who inherited the Descartian assumptions of his culture about the dualism of mind and matter, but fought to interfuse the two by impersonating a creative Logos in his books, and by appealing to advanced intellectual and scientific notions. A letter of 1859 in which he mentions the 'psychomedical' studies undertaken for *Saint Antony* is highly relevant, since it shows the habits of mind which Flaubert can hardly shake off in the very act of arguing for a different philosophy:

I'm convinced that the most furious material appetites are formulated *unknowingly* by impulses of idealism, just as the basest fleshly extravagances spring from pure desire for the impossible, ethereal aspiration after sovereign joy. And besides I don't know (nor does anyone know) what is meant by these two words: soul and body, where the one ends, where the other begins. We feel *forces* and that's all. Materialism and spiritualism still weigh too heavily on the science of man for all these phenomena to be studied impartially. The anatomy of the human heart is not yet perfected. ... The *historic sense* is quite new in the world. Ideas are going to be studied like facts, and beliefs dissected like organisms.[101]

If the anxieties of the Gnostics appealed to Flaubert, so did their meticulous cosmology (here his flair for the futile is also at work) and the atmosphere of search, the addiction to the difficult. Both Matter and Réville saw in Valentine's system a complicated solemnity, a moving quality of aspiration. Réville described it as 'this quasi-pagan religion in which the whole world had as its cause and as its mainspring passionate love, the draw of the unknown'.[102] Flaubert too conveys this admiration, especially when Valentine, Mani and Apollonius speak.

But these moments of lyrical respect occur in what is often a stinging exposé of the ludicrous and illogical postures of the heretics. Indeed, Taine accused Flaubert of keeping too close to the calumnies of Epiphanius, to the Christian side of the polemics.[103] One must remember in any case that Gnostic studies are by now vastly better informed and more sophisticated. For instance, Flaubert does not anticipate the account of Basilides's nihilistic views given by R. M. Grant, who argues that they amounted to an 'extreme statement of the illusory nature of the universe', looking forward to 'a state of cosmic oblivion'.[104] Beausobre, who wrote two and a half centuries ago and whose huge work on Manicheism Flaubert naturally pored over, concentrated more specifically on the question of the illusoriness of Christ's suffering on the cross.[105] And it's this heresy that Flaubert picks out: for him, Basilides is a Gnostic much like another, brandishing his obscure amulets and wanting to escape from other men's systems. However, when R. M. Grant writes of the 'passionate subjectivity' of the Gnostics and their 'self-centred' character,[106] one feels that Flaubert had already conveyed something of this quality in the opinionated palaver of all his heretical voices clashing under the great dome. I wonder also whether he was struck by reading in Matter that one Gnostic maxim was: 'You shall know all others, yet you yourself no one shall know.'[107] This rigid demarcation between the self and surrounding people must have had its appeal to the arrogantly solo Flaubert. To sum up, one need not exaggerate the extent to which he was attracted by the intellectual construction of the Gnostics. Although modern scholars find much to admire in their complexities, a study of the way Flaubert selects his details and lays his emphases suggests that it was above all the quality of their un-ease about the world and their existence in it that he found com-pelling, and their pantheism that he found congenial.

Flaubert's own concerns show clearly again in the chapter on the gods, especially in his descriptions of three gods new to the final version: the Buddha, the unnamed Babylonian goddess, and Isis. The Babylonian goddess who enjoyed a cult of virgin prostitution is the famous Mylitta described by Herodotus. From his reading of Creuzer Flaubert also gleaned the suggestion that she was probably symbolised by a conical figure and by a yoni, per-haps together with a phallus.[108] This conjecture he inserted into his book as a solid 'block of stone representing a woman's sex-organ', nostalgic for the primitive equivalence of cunt and stone, the naïve congelation of human and mineral – and never mind the barbarity of the rituals.

Uncivilised and brutish behaviour never disqualified anyone from Flaubert's admiration (except in the case of the invading Prussians, whose depredations he regarded as a sickening be-trayal of their evolved intellectual status). It's at once plain that the Brahman's dung-steeped absorption appealed to him far more than the sophisticated and articulate reflections of the Buddha. While the cruder sallies of the first version have often been discarded and the portraiture of the gods owes much to the enlightened per-spective of the comparative religionists, the Buddha still has little chance of retaining his dignity when in the grip of Flaubert's mature undermining irony. Pompous and peculiar, he sandwiches together his indeterminate virtues, faculties, forces and substances, boasts of his temptations and stickles over the size of a single grain of rice in the good old days. This is a thoroughly deflating por-trait. But it isn't an arbitrary chunk of irony. Consultation of the pages of Eugène Burnouf, Flaubert's main authority on Budd-hism, suggests exactly why the Buddha must be debunked.[109] Burnouf contrasted the moral, practical and egalitarian system of Buddhism to the ontological, metaphysical and speculative emphases of the earlier Brahmanist religion; he noted the relative mediocrity of Buddhist literature; and he pointed out that whereas the Buddhist cult centred on the image and relics of

Buddha, the Brahmans sacrificed to a crowd of minor divinities scattered throughout nature. The élitist, masochistic, pantheistic, individualistic nuances of Brahmanism form a much more attractive nexus for Flaubert than the ethical, altruistic teaching of the Buddha. Cow-dung spoke louder to him than charity.

But Flaubert's later additions are not all of an ironic detached quality. The Isis episode is an instance of near-passionate involvement. In the first *Saint Antony*, Egypt was represented by the bull Apis who made an ingloriously bellowing exit. In the last version we have the veiled Isis holding her child Horus like the Virgin Mary (as Flaubert indicates in a manuscript note)[110] as well as a very beautiful evocation of the country. To some extent Flaubert echoes Creuzer, who describes with eloquence the majestically systematic religion in which every animal, every natural object, played its part in the national cult and contributed to the sacred order of the Universe.[111] But to this is added Flaubert's own feeling for what he imagines as the superior intensity, the luminosity of past ages. His passionate longing for the past had not lessened since he wrote in 1847:

> Spelling out antiquity, an immeasurable sadness overwhelms me as I think of that age of magnificent and charming beauty passed beyond recall, of that world quite vibrant, quite radiant, so coloured and so pure, so simple and so varied. . . . As if we hadn't enough of our past we chew over that of all humanity and we luxuriate in this voluptuous bitterness. After all, what does it matter! If it's only there that one can live! If that's all that one can think of without scorn and without pity![112]

The words of Isis have something of this poignant glitter. Noting in Creuzer how the goddess 'uttered cries so piercing that one of the king's sons died of fright',[113] Flaubert gives to Antony this empathetic role, writing that Isis lets out 'so piercing, desolate and harrowing a cry that Antony responds with another cry, opening his arms to hold her up'. Here one glimpses just how close Flaubert felt to being engulfed by past myths; his temptation was not that of scholarly scrutiny alone, but of absolute emotional identification. Is such intense reverie an instance of futile escapism? Or is there an impressiveness to this melting into myth, although

Antony is 'crushed with shame' when he finds that Isis isn't there to be supported?

Well might Flaubert have problems establishing a linear logic of events. In *Saint Antony* reason opens onto *rien*, nothing, as the Devil's arguments show. What Flaubert wanted was inner coherence, not some sort of domino game of temptations. When he wrote to Louise in 1852 of his stringless necklace, this was no chance metaphor. In Creuzer's Introduction one finds the phrase: 'this visible world is hung upon me, as the pearls of a necklace on the string which holds them' – a quotation from the *Bhagavad Gita*, with which Flaubert was in any case familiar.[114] So that even when he was trying to meet the conventional criticisms of his friends, he was also trying to be true to his basic pantheist ideal, implicitly comparing his work to a universe in which mind and matter are inextricable. As Antony says, 'There must be, somewhere, primordial figures whose bodies are nothing but their image. If one could see them one would discover the link between matter and thought, what Being consists of!' The same letter to Louise, in which Flaubert remembers the joys of first writing *Saint Antony*, also contains one of the most famous and curious formulations of his artistic ambitions:

> What strikes me as beautiful, what I would like to do, is a book about nothing, a book with no external tie, which would support itself by its internal force of style, a book which would have hardly any subject or at least where the subject would be almost invisible, if that can be so. The most beautiful works are those where there is least matter; the nearer expression draws to thought, the more each word sticks to it and disappears, the greater the beauty. I believe the future of Art lies in that direction. I can see it, as it grows, etherealising itself as best it may, from Egyptian pylons to Gothic lancets, from the Indians' poems of twenty thousand verses to Byron's spurts. Form, increasingly skilled, becomes attenuated; it gives up all liturgy, all rule, all measure; it abandons the epic for the novel, verse for prose; it no longer acknowledges any orthodoxy and is as free as the will that produces it. This enfranchisement from materiality is to be found in everything and governments have followed suit, from oriental despotisms to the socialisms of the future.

> That's why it is that there are neither beautiful nor ugly subjects

and that one could almost establish it as an axiom, adopting the point of view of pure Art, that there are none at all, style on its own being an absolute way of seeing things.[115]

Saint Antony is by no means the very book Flaubert here outlines. But it is interesting that the first, the ultra-lyrical, the disorganised *Saint Antony* seems to give rise to these ideas, and that even while Flaubert talks of freeing himself from 'materiality' his most vivid expression for the desired identicalness of work and thought is somewhat glutinous. What the last *Saint Antony* offers is at most a further facet of the envisaged emancipation of art from subject-matter. That's perhaps why Antony, the central subject, and the little vibrating globules, subject-*matter*, are indeed almost invisible by the end of the book. And the rising sun is not the least self-supporting of images with which to conclude.

But beneath the aesthetic sunshine there are still plenty of subjects to worry at. The nadir of traditional temptation comes in the dialogue between Death and Lust. In a manuscript note Flaubert suggests that the plastic contrast between them only underlines their essential agreement: death and orgasm, nothingness and life, illusion and reality, are much of a muchness.[116] They first vie for Antony's allegiance, then merge in a macabre embrace which gives rise to the image of a skull with a worm's body, crowned with roses. The disturbed eroticism that has run through the book bursts into this incarnation of the death-wish. In a sense, this is also the point at which the vein of lyrical, subjective despair, as it were the breath of *Ahasvérus* still blowing an occasional film over Flaubert's prose, disappears from the text. With the appearance of the Sphinx and the Chimera out of the mist – their dialogue is a *tour de force* reintegrated from the first version – Antony is gradually impelled towards unselfconscious astonishment and away from the self-conscious attractions of Death and Lust.

What did Flaubert mean by these creatures? The Sphinx-Chimera dialogue had already been drafted when he wrote from Egypt that he found the impression made by the great Sphinx at Gizeh 'indescribable'; he was reduced to saying it was frankly *chouette*, though not before he had noted the ancient monster's fearful stillness.[117] His juxtaposition of the two monsters is in itself curious. In Greek mythology the Sphinx propounds the eternal riddle and the Chimera is the fire-snorting monster, part lion, part goat and part dragon, killed by Bellerophon. Hesiod calls both creatures the progeny of the serpentine nymph Echidna. But as Almut Pohle has pointed out, not only the Nile setting but also the masculinity of Flaubert's Sphinx make it Egyptian, while his Chimera has little to do with the Greek monster and appears to depend on the evolved concept of chimeras as any wild and illusory notions.[118] There are one or two interesting indications in Flaubert's notes: 'After the Chimera, vague monstrous forms: her children, the products of her mind. . . . The Sphinx and the Chimera outline, contain every order of Nature. . . . The Chimera is the appearance [*l'aspect*], the Sphinx, the substance [*le fond*].'[119] Alfred Lombard suggested that Flaubert's dragon-tailed monster probably owed something to Callot's engraving.[120] Flaubert, in any case, had always been very keen on monsters. He felt in them a real power reaching back to the mystery of origins. Here again is the belief in the truth of illusion. And nowhere is the idea more seductively sketched than in an early passage from *Par les champs et par les grèves*:

> Who has not found the Chimera charming, grown fond of her lion's nostrils, her eagle's wings that rush by and her rump with the green glints? . . . Neither were such dreams, any more than those of nature, created by one man, nor were they given birth to in a day; like metals, like rocks, like rivers, like gold-mines and like pearls, they seeped up slowly, drop by drop, forming in successive layers, taking shape on their own, drawing themselves out from nothingness by their internal force. We contemplate them likewise with a worried and retrospective amazement, inquiring perhaps beyond memory whether, before our life, we have not also like them existed, whether our thoughts have not cohabited in a common country with those thoughts now become forms, whether the first principle of our own form was not once hatched in the womb of the universal chrysalis, with the seed of oak trees and the springs that made the sea.[121]

The purely personal necessity of illusion was also one of Flaubert's convictions. He later wrote: 'Life is tolerable only with a hobby, work of some sort. As soon as one abandons one's chimera, one dies of sadness. One must cling tight to it and hope it will carry one off.'[122]

While the Chimera has quite rightly been interpreted as a facet of Flaubertian imagination, the conflict between the two monsters has led some critics wrongly to assume that the Sphinx must represent a ready opposite to imagination, notably reason. This is a case where Flaubert's sources offer little help. Pohle believes that Flaubert was influenced by the description in Creuzer, in which the Sphinx is associated with 'the idea of strength united to wisdom', or said to express 'divine intelligence reposing in itself and sufficing unto itself'.[123] But precisely what Flaubert's Sphinx is not is self-sufficient. On the contrary, it longs to exchange its melancholy boredom for the wings of fantasy. And to the Chimera the Sphinx is an *Inconnu*, an Unknown. The most important contrast between the two is also the most obvious, the contrast between rapid movement and absorbed immobility. The Sphinx is rigid, not with reasonable thoughts but through some sort of self-hypnotic condition as it traces out alphabets and fixes its gaze on the inaccessible horizon, until it admits that it has thought so hard that there's nothing left to say. There is something tormenting about such fodderless concentration, which should be compared to the ruinous state of the troglodyte, also tracing signs on the sand, in Borges's story 'The Immortal'. But it isn't unimaginative – far from it. The Sphinx and the Chimera, two monsters, both reflect Flaubert's conviction that monsters are more real, more surely significant, than normal creatures. And the interplay between them is the interplay between rival powers of the imagination, the power of concentration and the power of perpetual motion. Each creature has its cruel, aggressive and self-destructive streak. Each suffers, the Sphinx from the aridity of its stillness, the Chimera from the emptiness of its innovations. Their copulation manqué is a ponderously apt metaphor for every creative débâcle.

Words don't copulate any more than monsters. But in Flaubert's hands they can have a gross physicality, a weight of existence. One senses his regret that touch can never be incorporated into literature. Bookish though his medley of monsters is, he was quite as interested in natural monsters as in those between hard covers.

And although tiny-minded half animate creatures like the Scia-
podes expose the cautious bliss of the despised bourgeoisie –
signifying 'obscurantism itself', as Flaubert noted[124] – his sequence
as a whole points in a grander direction, on whose scientific and
philosophical colouring Jean Seznec has commented interestingly.
He points out that Flaubert in his early reading came across the
idea that natural history might one day confirm the existence of
such creatures as the pygmies, the unicorn, or the Queen of Sheba's
weird bird, and also that his reading of Spinoza is again relevant
because of the philosopher's belief in an infinite variety of forms.
Flaubert was anyway the son of a learned doctor, and his biologist
friend Georges Pouchet kept him alive to progress in the sciences.
His letters indicate that he read, for instance, in 1871 some of the
books of physiology-cum-psychology by Pierre Cabanis, who
tried to relate the intellectual processes to the nervous system. And
a reference of 1874 suggests familiarity with Darwin's writings.[125]

But the last thing that Flaubert was likely ever to succumb to
was a facile evolutionary fervour such as one finds in his friend
Louis Bouilhet's poem *Les Fossiles*, which progresses via primeval
lizards and pelicans to a grand convulsion from which must spring
a new masterful being yet more brilliant than man; or such as one
finds on the last page of Quinet's *La Création*, where he happily
envisages a time when man's triumphant successor will view the
Parthenon as a bank of polyparies, and the Iliad as a pretty bird-
song. Neither, on the other hand, does *Saint Antony* reflect a more
sober interest in the Darwinian struggle for survival. Nor can
Flaubert's trend be called Lamarckian, since he cannot think in
terms of a neatly planned universe or a scale of perfection culmin-
ating in the complex organisation of man. He has more in common
with the anti-systematic bias of Buffon[126] and the speculative spirit
of Diderot (both of whom were interested in the malformed and
the hybrid). While Diderot pushed the dominant eighteenth-
century notion of the great Chain of Being so far as to claim that
sensibility was a property of all matter, minerals included, he did
not interpret the notion with Deistic rigour, and he insisted on the
disorder and unpredictability of the universe: the meanest worm
wriggling in the mud might be proceeding towards colossal

animal stature, the largest animal might be gradually slipping back to worminess, might be a quite fleeting product of the planet; and everything might be tending towards 'a great inert and motionless sediment'. Meanwhile he saw the greatest prodigy as the transition from inert matter to sensibility.[127]

Interest in supposedly spontaneous generation was given new impetus by John Needham's ill-corked experiments on infusions in the 1740s. Among others, Buffon, Diderot and Lamarck gave credence to the theory, which is implied in Antony's delighted claim that he has seen 'the birth of life'. One of the books listed in Flaubert's manuscript reading-list for 1870–72 is a treatise on the subject by Félix-Archimède Pouchet (his friend's father) who had engaged in a celebrated polemic with Pasteur over this very question. How far Flaubert was convinced by conclusions which now look embarassingly hasty isn't known, nor is it altogether relevant. The point to bear in mind is that the state of scientific and philosophic play was such that there was no clear demarcation between organic and inorganic matter. One current hypothesis was that of primitive 'protoplasmic' forms of life which might arise from non-organic matter. Another was that of a primary organic substance from which all species had evolved. The conflicting hypotheses about the origins of life and the nature of matter were very much bound up with philosophically vexed questions: people were anxious to find solutions that would amount neither to downright materialism nor to blinkered idealism. For instance, the German biologist and Darwinian propagandist Ernst Heinrich Haeckel (whose *Creation* Flaubert seemingly didn't read until just after *Saint Antony* was published)[128] believed in an enigmatic universal substance, advocated a monistic religion, and admired Spinoza and Goethe.

Pouchet's book is of interest especially because of the way that he tries to integrate his views with past beliefs, and he too endorses a Spinozistic pantheism. Wrong though he was about the provenance of a 'worm' in a horse's eye, his views provide a valuable comment on Antony's quandary.[129] Pouchet's position, in brief, is that while spontaneous generation can take place provided organic matter is present, the appearance of the phenomena of life cannot be attributed 'to the caprice of blind matter' but must depend on a supreme principle 'identical to the substance of the world'. His arguments aim to restore to matter 'its true dignity' by showing its intimate links with spirit. To read his book is to get a vivid idea of how, through such a metaphysical bias, ancient beliefs in fallen and trapped sparks of divinity might be mixed up with the discoveries and experiments of modern science:

> In almost all cosmogonies it seems to be indicated that the divine spirit is in some sort infiltrated into each fragment of creation. . . . This indefinite penetration of particles of Divinity into all the molecules of matter, this pantheism, in a word, which animates with divine breath all atoms, conceived at the heart of antiquity and resuscitated by modern German philosophy, does it not come to lend its support to heterogenesis?[130]

It's interesting that Edmond de Goncourt noted in his diary for 18 October 1871 that Flaubert confided to him 'that the saint's final defeat is due to the *cell*, the scientific cell'[131] – interesting, but not all that enlightening, because this 'scientific cell' was itself the subject of so much debate. It seems plain that Antony's longing to become matter is other than a naïvely materialistic impulse. Flaubert's manuscript notes indicate the tension between the more narrowly Christian sense of giving in to an ungodly urge and the broader idea of pure discovery and admiration. One of these notes runs: 'But Nature seems filled with spirit and Antony feels quite close to it, wishes to be within it, wishes to be the grain of matter, and he is definitively going to succumb.' Another is more aspiring in tone: 'Arrive little by little, through a series of monstrosities (symbolic), to the living cell, to Being, to Matter. Thus Saint Antony has climbed back up the ladder. He reaches what primitively, eternally *is*.' What perhaps is the most interesting note underlines the bewilderment of the experience: 'Towards the end. He is too far, in an abstract land, having looked at everything, having no longer any consciousness of himself, and being just a looking-machine, a living contemplation.'[132]

Ezra Pound thought that in *Saint Antony* Flaubert was bogged down in nineteenth-century issues 'now dead as mutton'.[133] But scientists and philosophers are still arguing about the origins of life and the body-mind relationship, and no one seems very sure whether our potential for humane altruism lies within or without our genes. A hundred years later, Antony would doubtless find himself marvelling at the double helix of the DNA molecule – and Flaubert, maybe, would be ordering his own poppet-bead gene kit.

7. A twentieth-century bird's-eye view

Gods, heresies, hallucinations, symbols, myths, messages, molecules. There is no shortage of books on these topics, our own society turns them out in shoals, it hardly seems possible that the rich seas of system and meaning shall ever be overfished. The point at issue with *Saint Antony* is whether the book is more than a superb curio on the one hand, or a gift to analysts and theorists on the other.

Flaubert belonged, who could deny it, to his time. Jean Seznec stresses the fact when he argues that the author of *Saint Antony* saw antiquity in basically the same colours as his contemporaries Taine and Renan, that's to say as a baroque chaos of ideas bathed in an atmosphere of feverish hallucination, as a quickening religious vertigo which spun through every profanity, to be mesmerised at last by empty space.[134] He rightly draws attention to lines Flaubert wrote shortly before his death:

> God knows to what point I push my scruples on the score of documents, books, inquiries, journeys, etc . . . Well, I regard all that as very secondary and inferior. The material truth (or what is termed so) should be no more than a spring-board from which to rise higher. Do you reckon I'm such a simpleton as to be convinced that in *Salammbô* I've made a true reproduction of Carthage, and in *Saint Antony* an exact portrayal of Alexandrianism? Ah, no! But I'm sure of having expressed the *ideal* entertained today.[135]

But is Flaubert's account really left high and acrobatically perspiring in the nineteenth century? Parallels with some quite contemporary lines of thought suggest that *Saint Antony* is more durably provocative.

In 1963 E. R. Dodds produced a bold picture of the world of the third century. We were shown people who typically felt that human life was a dream or a nightmare, were obsessed with hatred of their bodies, expressed their death-wish in voluntary martyrdom, projected their guilt-feelings and forbidden thoughts into the image of the Devil and their sense of their own Unconscious into the image of the Valentinian Bythos or primordial Deep, and reacted to the 'progressive withdrawal of divinity from the material world'[136] with complex mysticisms. Dodds illustrated the 'extrovertive' type of mysticism by a quotation from the Hermetic Tract:

> Outleap all body and expand yourself to the unmeasured greatness; ... Embrace in yourself all sensations of all created things, of fire and water, dry and wet; be simultaneously everywhere, on sea and land and in the sky; be at once unborn and in the womb, young and old, dead and beyond death; and if you can hold all these things together in your thought, times and places and substances, qualities and quantities, then you can apprehend God.[137]

The sentiments are not unlike Antony's. And Flaubert, one feels, would be fascinated by the whole of E. R. Dodds's book, though not at all disconcerted. It seems that certain cruxes are well lodged into what has to be our imaginary anatomy of third century man.

Would he have made anything of Peter Brown's ideas on 'the crisis of freedom' in late antiquity, the rise of intolerance and the role of the Holy Man as an alienated and therefore objective 'stranger'who could arbitrate in disputes?[138] Not much, perhaps. A world without tyranny was about as unimaginable to Flaubert as a world emptied of the spiders and snails that suffer the fate of being squashed underfoot. He admired Nero as an instinctive sensualist, the barbaric culmination of antiquity.[139] And he could not anticipate the meticulous historiographical researches of our own century. Antony as a social outcast is very much a nineteenth-century individualist.

Flaubert's non-participation in the public life of his time is notable. But before passing judgement on this abstention, it is worth looking at the last section of Claude Lévi-Strauss's *Tristes tropiques*, which suggests, eighty years after the publication of *Saint Antony*, possible grounds for the incompatibility between commitment to causes and the type of cultural exploration that Flaubert carried out. Lévi-Strauss argues that the anthropologist's eclecticism, his ideal impartiality and scrupulous detachment, mean that he forfeits the right to repudiate the injustices and cruelties practised in particular societies. Must he then refrain from censorious comments on his own? The impasse is somewhat sidestepped by an appeal to the immanent notion of a model human society outside time and space. This can never be realised in any single civilisation, each of which will always contain a 'certain dose of injustice, insensibility, cruelty'. His own civilisation, and Flaubert's own, Lévi-Strauss nevertheless holds up as an example of an 'ogre' civilisation, boundlessly obsessed with blood and torture.[140]

The sweep of Flaubert's concerns, his curiosity about all religions and cultures, must be allowed to have something in common with the ventures of ethnographical research, even if he falls short of ideal impartiality. Lévi-Strauss later argues in *La Pensée sauvage* that historian and anthropologist are complementary. There is no real opposition between the diachronic study of history and the synchronic, cross-continental study of contemporary cultures.[141] Edmund Leach further explains that 'for the thinking human being all recollected experience is contemporaneous; as in myth, all events are part of a single synchronous totality.'[142]

It may be objected that Flaubert was not a historian but a novelist. Again, this type of opposition is too simplistic. It's only by recognising the open-ended, limitless quality of Flaubert's curiosity and the kind of far-reaching perspective it provided him with that the absorbingly dispassionate quality of his fictional recreations of his own and past worlds can be grasped. A passage from the last chapter of *La Pensée sauvage* is very much to the point:

The historian's relative choice, with respect to each domain of history he gives up, is always confined to the choice between history which teaches us more and explains less, and history which explains more and teaches less. The only way he can avoid the dilemma is by getting outside history: either by the bottom, if the pursuit of information leads him from the consideration of groups to that of individuals and then to their motivations which depend on their personal history and temperament, that is to say to an infra-historical domain in the realms of psychology and physiology; or by the top, if the need to understand incites him to put history back into prehistory and the latter into the general evolution of organised being, which is itself explicable only in terms of biology, geology, and finally cosmology.[143]

Flaubert's novels, in their different ways, can be seen as just such attempts to get 'outside history'. He could not have written *Madame Bovary* had he been encased in his own civilisation. No merely realist eye for the concrete details of the present could have given him adequate insight. Not forgetting the way in which the scream of Isis echoes in *Saint Antony*, one may note a passage from his letters which seems to outline some kind of attempt to reach beyond his own ogrish century to a supracultural awareness:

> Yes, I feel a deep disgust for the papers, that's to say for the ephemeral, for the fleeting, for what is important today and for what will not be so tomorrow. There's no insensibility in this. I simply sympathise quite as well, perhaps better, with the vanished and now unheeded miseries of dead peoples, with all the cries they uttered that are no longer heard. I pity the lot of the actual working classes no more than I do the ancient slaves who turned the grindstone, no more or quite as much. I'm no more modern than ancient, no more French than Chinese, and the idea of a native land, that's to say the obligation one is under to live in one corner of the world marked red or blue on the map and to hate the other corners marked green and black, has always struck me as narrow, hide-bound, and rabidly stupid. I am the brother in God of all that lives, of the giraffe and the crocodile as of man, and the fellow-citizen of all that inhabits the great furnished hotel of the universe.[144]

Flaubert's aspiration towards cosmic tolerance does not spring from political liberalism but from a sense of physical compatibility. When in *Saint Julien l'Hospitalier* the leper is kissed by Julien, physical prejudice is annihilated. At a time when it has been suggested that perfect tolerance is only possible in genetically identical colonies, perhaps we shouldn't underestimate Flaubert's sensuous egalitarianism.

The question of tolerance is linked to that of progress. The 'zealots of progress', as Lévi-Strauss says, misprise the 'accumulated riches of humanity'.[145] Once one assumes that the future precludes the vitality of the past, its first efforts, one has already adopted a conditional tolerance, which is no tolerance. In his refusal to go along with any assumptions about human progress, Flaubert diverges clearly from one trend of his times. Authorities such as Jacques Matter and Albert Réville shared a typical faith in humanity's ascensional impetus, and Etienne Vacherot was confident in the powers of reason, but Flaubert used their works without being at all swayed by such one-way optimism. That he was much influenced by the Oriental Renaissance of the nineteenth century has already been noted. Significantly, Matter observed that the Asiatics were superior to the Greeks in that they linked man's salvation to that of the universe he lived in, rather than making him the arbitrarily created receptacle for God's good grace.[146] Flaubert's Orientalism is fed both by his distrust of rationalist dogmas and by his refusal to regard human life as the most important fact in the universe. This traditional antithesis between East and West, subject to facile abuse though it is, remains conceptually powerful. Lévi-Strauss distrusts the 'juridical and formalist rationalism' of the West and admires Buddhism because it allows the very distinction between the meaningful and the meaningless to be abolished, so that knowing need not encroach on being.[147] The Flaubert of *Saint Antony* is very close to the Lévi-Strauss of *Tristes tropiques* who longs for moments of respite:

> ... the brief intervals when our species can afford to interrupt its hive-like labour, to capture the essence of what it once was and continues to be, this side of thought and that side of society: in the contemplation of a mineral lovelier than all our works; in the scent, wiser than our books, inhaled from the hollow of a lily; or in the wink laden with patience, serenity and reciprocal pardon, that an involuntary entente occasionally allows one to exchange with a cat.[148]

I don't, to conclude, want to leave Flaubert perched on some pinnacle for cat-loving contemplatives. His travel notes show well enough that his curiosity was often more cruel than compassionate. But I think that the sense of the world articulated in *Saint Antony* can give one pause. A very perceptive early Flaubertian critic, Albert Thibaudet, wrote that the book was about a reality that was coming undone.[149] The cosmos splits into ever smaller fractions. The single molecule is felt to be not so much the seed of infinite forms as the last refuge of a mysterious life, reduced within ever more infinitesimal bounds. Here again Lévi-Strauss (among others) provides a parallel line of thought, since he warns of how humanity is gaily precipitating a state of material disintegration which will one day result in definitive inertia.[150] The world of non-human things cannot remain intact but it can remain incorruptibly other, in the last resort beyond control. And Flaubert, who was prepared to level his irony at every human attempt to appropriate and make sense of things, might well hesitate when it came to the wordless signature of the sun.

THE TEMPTATION OF
SAINT ANTONY

TO THE MEMORY
OF
MY FRIEND

ALFRED LE POITTEVIN

WHO DIED
AT LA NEUVILLE-CHANT-D'OISEL
on 3 April 1848

I

The setting is the Thebaid, high on a mountain, where a platform curves to a half-moon, shut in by large boulders.

The hermit's cabin occupies the rear. It consists of mud and reeds, with a flat roof and no door. Inside it are visible a pitcher and a loaf of black bread; in the middle, on a wooden slab, a fat book; scattered on the ground some fibres of esparto, two or three mats, a basket, a knife.

Ten steps away from the cabin stands a long cross planted in the soil; and at the platform's other end a twisted old palm tree leans over the abyss, for the mountain falls sheer, and the Nile spreads like a lake at the foot of the cliff.

The enclosure of rocks cuts off the view to right and left. But out in the desert, as if more and more beaches were unfolding, immense parallel ash-blond undulations stretch on behind each other, gradually rising – while beyond the sands, in the far distance, the wall formed by the Libyan range is the colour of chalk, lightly blurred by a violet haze. Opposite, the sun sinks. In the north the sky is a shade of pearl-grey, while at its highest point crimson clouds, positioned like the tufts of a gigantic mane, comb out across the blue vault. These bars of flame become embrowned, the azure areas grow pale and nacreous; bushes, pebbles, the earth, all now seem hard as bronze; and in the air floats a golden dust, so fine as to be indistinguishable from the vibration of the light.

SAINT ANTONY

who has a long beard, long hair, and wears a goatskin tunic, is sitting cross-legged, making mats. As soon as the sun disappears he heaves a great sigh, gazing at the horizon:

One more day! one more day gone!

Surely I used to be less miserable! Before night was over, I began my orisons; then I went down to the river for water,

61

coming back up the rough track with the bottle on my shoulder, singing hymns. After that, I enjoyed tidying everything in my cabin. I took up my tools; I tried to make sure that the mats were even and the baskets light; because at that time my smallest gestures were duties which seemed painless to perform.

At specific hours I stopped work; and as I prayed with outstretched arms I felt as if a fountain of mercy were pouring into my heart from the height of heaven. It has now dried up. Why?...

He slowly walks about within the rocky enclosure.

They all blamed me when I left home. My mother collapsed, dying; from far off my sister signalled me to come back; and the other child was crying, Ammonaria, the one I used to meet every evening by the pool when she drove her oxen there. She ran after me. The rings on her feet shone in the dust and her tunic was open at the hips, blowing in the wind. The old ascetic who was taking me away shouted insults at her. Both our camels kept galloping; and I never saw anybody again.

First I chose to live in a Pharaoh's tomb. But a witchery winds through those underground palaces, where the aromatic smoke of long ago seems to thicken the shade. From the depths of sarcophagi I heard a doleful voice rising and calling me; or I saw, all of a sudden, the abominable things painted on the walls start into life; and I fled to a ruined citadel on the edge of the Red Sea. There my company consisted of scorpions slithering between the stones, and above my head perpetually eagles wheeling against the blue sky. At night I was clawed apart, pecked to pieces, grazed by limp wings; and appalling devils, screaming in my ears, knocked me to the ground. At one point indeed, some people from a caravan making for Alexandria came to my rescue and so took me away with them.

I then decided to study under good old Didymus. Blind though he was, no one could match his knowledge of the Scriptures. When the lesson was over he would request my arm to lean on. I would walk him to where, from the Panium, one can see the Pharos and the high sea. We would come back by way of the harbour, elbowing men of every race, from Cimmerians wrapped in bearskins to Gymnosophists of the Ganges rubbed over with cow-dung. But there was always a fight going on in the streets, on account of Jews refusing to pay tax, or of seditious parties who wanted to expel the Romans. The town is in fact full of heretics, the followers of Mani, of Valentine, of Basilides, of Arius – all of them accosting you to argue and convince.

Their talk now and again crosses my mind. Try as one will to pay no attention, it's unnerving.

I took refuge at Colzim; and my penance reached such heights that I no longer feared God. There were several who gathered round me to become anchorites. I imposed a system of practical rules on them, scorning the extravagances of Gnosticism and the dictums of the philosophers. Messages were sent to me from everywhere. People came from very far away to see me.

Meanwhile the populace were torturing confessors, and a thirst for martyrdom attracted me to Alexandria. The persecution had finished three days earlier.

As I was turning back, a flood of people stopped me in front of the temple of Serapis. The governor, so I heard, was making one last example. In the centre of the portico, in the hot sunlight, a naked woman was tied to a pillar, while two soldiers flogged her with whips; at each stroke her whole body writhed. She turned round, open-mouthed – and across the crowd, under the long hair which was covering her face, I thought I recognised Ammonaria...

Although ... she looked taller ... and beautiful ... quite fantastically!

He passes his hands over his forehead.

No! no! I don't want to think about it!

On another occasion, Athanasius called me to support him against the Arians. It was all confined to invective and ridicule. But since then he's been slandered, ousted from his see, put to flight. Where is he now? I have no idea! No one bothers to bring me news. My disciples have all left me, Hilarion with the rest!

He was perhaps fifteen when he came; and he had such a lively mind that he was constantly asking me questions. He would then listen thoughtfully – and whenever I needed anything he fetched it without a murmur, nippy as a goat and cheerful enough to make a patriarch merry. He was like a son to me!

The sky is red, the earth wholly black. Sweepings of sand rise up like great shrouds in the gusty wind, and fall back. Through a rift, suddenly a battalion of birds is seen passing in triangular formation, like a slice of metal quivering at the edges only.

Antony watches them.

Ah! how I wish I could follow them!

How often also I've gazed with envy at the long boats whose sails look like wings, especially when they carried away people whom I'd made welcome! Such good times we spent! so much at ease! No one could be more compelling than Ammon, telling me about his journey to Rome, the Catacombs, the Coliseum, the piety of eminent women, and a thousand things besides! ... And I wouldn't leave with him! Where do I get my obstinate commitment to a life such as this? I might as well have stayed with the monks of Nitria since they begged me to. They live in cells apart, but still communicate with each other. On Sunday a trumpet calls them to church, where there are three whips hung up for punishing delinquents, thieves and intruders, as their discipline is strict.

They're not short of certain luxuries, none the less. Devotees bring them eggs, fruit, and even gadgets designed to take the thorns from their feet. Around Pispir there are vineyards, and at Pabena they have a raft for fetching provisions.

But I would have served my brothers better by simply becoming a priest. One helps the poor, one administers the sacraments, one has authority over family life.

Laymen are anyway not all damned, and it was up to me to become ... say ... a grammarian, or a philosopher. I might have had a globe of rushes in my room, tablets ready to hand, young men around me, and a wreath of laurels hanging as a sign at my door.

But there's too much pride to these triumphs. Better have been a soldier. I was quite hardy and tough enough to stretch the engine cables, cross the dark forests, come helmeted into the smoking towns! ... Neither was there anything to stop me from putting down money for a post as toll-gatherer at some bridge; and travellers would have told me stories, pulling out all sorts of curious objects from their baggage ...

On feast-days the merchants of Alexandria sail down the Canopic river, drinking wine from lotus chalices, while along the banks the taverns tremble to the sound of tambourines! Beyond them are trees cut into cones, shielding quiet farms from the south wind. The roof of each tall house rests on spindly columns, set like sticks in a lattice; and through the gaps the master, lying on a long couch, can see his land all around him, the huntsmen in the wheat-fields, the vintage being pressed, the oxen threshing corn. His children play on the ground, his wife bends over to kiss him.

Here and there in the whitish obscurity of night appear pointed snouts, with cocked ears and brilliant eyes. Antony walks towards them. Pebbles are dislodged, the animals run off. It was a pack of jackals.

One of them remains, standing on two paws, with its body arched and its head on one side, in a posture of defiance.

What a pretty fellow! I'd like to stroke him on the back, gently.

Antony whistles to make it come. The jackal disappears.

Ah, he's off to join the others! What loneliness! What boredom!

He laughs bitterly:

A fine style of life this is, twisting pieces of palm tree into crooks over the fire, making baskets, stitching mats, and exchanging it all with the Nomads for bread that breaks your teeth! Ah, misery! will it never end? Better be dead! I can't bear any more! Enough! enough!

He stamps his foot, goes swerving about between the rocks, then stops out of breath, bursts into tears, and lies down on the ground on his side.

The night is calm; countless stars pulsate; the only sound is the tick of tarantulas.

The two arms of the cross cast a shadow on the sand; Antony, who is crying, notices it.

Good God, how feeble I am! Courage now, up we get!

He goes into his cabin, finds a buried ember, lights a torch and stands it on the wooden slab so as to illuminate the fat book.

Shall I take ... the Acts of the Apostles? ... yes! ... starting anywhere!

'*He saw the heaven opened, and something descending, like a great sheet, let down by four corners upon the earth. In it were all kinds of animals and reptiles and birds of the air. And there came a voice to him: Rise, Peter; kill and eat.*'

So the Lord wanted his apostle to eat some of everything?
... while I ...

Antony's chin sinks onto his chest. The rustle of the pages blowing
in the wind makes him look up, and he reads:

'*So the Jews smote all their enemies with the sword, slaughter-
ing and destroying them, and did as they pleased to those whom
they hated.*'

Then the count of how many they killed: seventy-five
thousand. They had suffered so much! Besides, their enemies
were the enemies of the true God. And how they must have
relished their revenge, as they massacred the idolaters! No
doubt the town was choked with dead! At garden gates, on
staircases, piled up so high inside rooms that the doors stuck
on their hinges ... ! – But now I'm plunging into thoughts of
blood and murder!

He opens the book at another place.

'*Nebuchadnezzar fell upon his face, and did homage to
Daniel.*'

Ah! that's good! The Almighty exalts his prophets above
kings; though this one was forever feasting, permanently
drunk on pleasure and pride. But to punish him, God turned
him into a beast. He had to walk on all fours!

Antony starts laughing; and as he spreads his arms he ruffles the
book's pages with the edge of his hand. His eyes light on this passage:

'*Hezekiah welcomed them, and he showed them his perfumes,
his silver and his gold, his spices, his scented oils, his precious
vases, all that was found in his treasure house.*'

I can just imagine ... the sight of the precious stones heaped
almost to the ceiling, the diamonds, the darics ... Whoever
owns such grand accumulations is a man apart. As he handles

them he thinks of how the result of unquantified effort, what amounts to the very life of nations drained dry, is his to scatter at will. It's a useful precaution for kings. The wisest of them all didn't fail to adopt it. His fleets provided him with ivory, with apes... Where is it all now?

He thumbs eagerly through the pages.

Ah! here!

'Now when the queen of Sheba heard of the fame of Solomon, she came to tempt him with hard questions.'

How did she hope to tempt him? The Devil did his best to tempt Jesus! But Jesus triumphed because he was God, and Solomon perhaps thanks to his magical science – that sublime science! For the world – as a philosopher once explained to me – forms one whole whose parts all influence each other, like the organs of a single body. It's a matter of knowing the natural affinities and repulsions of things, then setting them in action... So one might modify what seems an immutable order?

Leaping forward from behind him, the two shadows formed by the arms of the cross become huge and horn-like. Antony shouts out:

God help me!

The shadow has withdrawn into place.

Ah!... It was just an illusion! nothing else! – There's no point in worrying myself! There's nothing for me to do!... absolutely nothing to do!

He sits down and folds his arms.

All the same... I thought I could feel the approach... But why should *he* come? Surely I'm well enough versed in his wiles? I repulsed the monstrous anchorite who laughed as he offered me small hot rolls, and the centaur who tried to take me on his back – and that black child who materialised in the middle of the sands, very beautiful, calling himself the spirit of fornication.

Antony walks to right and left, excitedly.

It was by my order that those scores of holy retreats were built, full of monks wearing haircloth under their goatskins – enough of them to form an army! I cured the sick from a distance; I chased out devils; I crossed the river among all the crocodiles; the Emperor Constantine wrote me three letters; Balacius, who spat on mine, got torn to pieces by his horses; the people of Alexandria fought to see me on my return, and Athanasius saw me off. And what feats besides! To groan away more than thirty years in the desert! with my back bowed, like Eusebius, under eighty pounds of bronze, with my body exposed to the stinging of insects like Macarius, and with never an eye shut for fifty-three nights, like Pachomius; it may well be that the beheaded, the burnt, the pincered have less virtue, since my life is one long martyrdom!

Antony slows his pace.

Indeed, there's nobody in deeper distress! Kind hearts grow fewer. Nothing is ever given me. My coat's worn out. I've no sandals, no bowl even – because I gave everything I had to the poor and to my family, down to the last obol. I must – if only for the essential tools of my trade – have a little money. Oh, not much! a small sum! . . . I'd be sparing.

The Nicene Fathers, in robes of scarlet, sat like mages on thrones all along the wall; and they were treated to a banquet and loaded with honours, Paphnutius especially, because he was lamed and lost an eye in the persecution of Diocletian! The Emperor several times kissed his punctured eye. How idiotic! And the members of the Council were such a disgrace! A Scythian bishop, Theophilus; another from Persia,

John; and a cattle-man, Spiridion! Alexander was too old. Athanasius should have been easier on the Arians, for the sake of concessions!

Not that they would have made any! They wouldn't listen to me! The one who was speaking against me – a tall young man with a curly beard – coolly showered me with specious objections; and while I was searching for words, they watched with evil expressions, yapping like hyenas. Ah! if I could only get them all exiled by the Emperor, or better still, beat them, crush them, see them suffer! I suffer enough myself!

He leans unsteadily against his cabin.

It's the fasting! I'm losing my strength. If I could eat, just for once . . . a bit of meat.

He half shuts his eyes with faintness.

Ah! red meat . . . a bunch of grapes to bite into! . . . curds shivering on a plate!

But what's the matter with me now? . . . What is it? . . . I can feel my heart heaving like the sea, when it swells before a storm. I'm overcome with utter weakness, and the warm air seems to blow me a hint of scented hair. Surely no woman has arrived? . . .

He turns toward the narrow path between the rocks.

That's the way they come, swinging in their litters on the black arms of eunuchs. They alight, and clasping their hands loaded with rings they kneel down. They tell me their troubles. Tortured for want of a superhuman touch they long to die, in their dreams gods have appeared, calling to them – and the fringes of their dresses brush my feet. I push them back. 'Oh no, they say, not yet! What am I to do!' No penance would be too great. They demand the very harshest, to share my own, to live with me.

It's a long time now since I saw any! Maybe some will come? why not? What if I suddenly . . . hear mule bells tinkling up the mountain. I almost think . . .

Antony climbs onto a rock at the near end of the path; he leans over, trying to pierce the gloom.

Yes! a moving mass, down there, right at the bottom, like people looking for their way. It's over here! They're going wrong.

He calls:

This way! Come! come!

The echo repeats: Come! come!
He drops his arms, dumbfounded.

How shameful! Ah, poor Antony!

At once, he hears a whispered 'Poor Antony!'

Who's there? Answer me!

The wind that blows through cracks between the boulders is freely modulating; and in these confused sonorities he makes out VOICES, as if the air were talking. They are soft, insinuating, hissing.

FIRST VOICE

Is it women you want?

SECOND VOICE

Money bags, rather!

THIRD VOICE

A shining sword?

OTHER VOICES

– All the people admire you!

– Go to sleep!

– You'll cut their throats, you will, you'll cut their throats!

Objects are meanwhile transformed. At the edge of the cliff the old palm tree with its tuft of yellow leaves becomes the torso of a woman, leaning over the abyss, her long hair floating.

ANTONY

turns toward his cabin; and the stand supporting the fat book with its pages loaded with black letters comes to seem like a bush crammed with swallows.

It's the torch, of course, a trick of the light ... Out with it!

He puts out the torch, and is plunged in darkness.

And all at once, in mid air, first a puddle of water passes by, then a prostitute, a temple corner, the figure of a soldier, a chariot drawn by two white horses, rearing.

These images occur swiftly, percussively, showing up against the night like scarlet painted on ebony.

They gather speed. They wheel past at a dizzy pace. At other times, they halt and gradually fade, or merge; or else they fly away, and others instantly appear.

Antony closes his eyes.

They multiply, surround and besiege him. Indescribable terror sweeps over him; all he feels is a burning contraction in the pit of the stomach. Despite the uproar in his head, he is aware of a huge silence which cuts him off from the world. He tries to speak: impossible! The overall bond of his being seems to dissolve; and no longer resisting, Antony falls onto the mat.

II

And now a great shadow, subtler than any natural shadow, festooned along its borders with further shadows, etches itself on the ground.

This is the Devil, propped against the roof of the cabin, and folding under his wings – not unlike a gigantic bat suckling its young – the Seven Deadly Sins, whose grimacing heads can be dimly discerned.

Antony, still with closed eyes, enjoys his inaction; and he spreads his limbs across the mat.

It feels soft, more and more so – till it puffs out, it lifts, it becomes a bed, the bottom of a skiff; water laps against the sides.

To right and left rise two tongues of black earth topped by farmed fields, with a sycamore here and there. A ringing of bells, a drumming and a singing, echo in the distance: people are setting off for Canopus, to dream in their sleep by the temple of Serapis. Antony knows this – as he glides, driven by the wind, between the banks of the canal. Papyrus leaves and red nymphaea flowers, man-sized or more, hover above him. He lies at the bottom of the boat, one oar trailing in the water behind. Every so often a warm gust blows, and the thin rushes rub together. Little waves make a softer and softer murmur. A drowsiness overcomes him. He fancies himself an Egyptian solitary.

And he suddenly starts up.

Was I dreaming? . . . I can't have been, it was so vivid. My tongue's burning! I'm thirsty!

He goes into his cabin and gropes around, haphazardly.

The ground feels wet! . . . Has it rained? Why! broken pieces! my pitcher! . . . but the bottle?

He finds it.

Empty! quite empty!

To go down to the river would take three hours at least,

73

and on such a dark night I wouldn't see my way. My insides are churning. Where's the bread?

After searching for a long time, he picks up a crust rather smaller than an egg.

What? The jackals have run off with it? Ah, curse them!

In sheer fury, he flings the bread to the ground.

No sooner has he done so than a table stands there, spread with everything good to eat.

The byssus tablecloth, striated like a sphinx's fillet, produces its own undulating luminosity. On it are placed enormous hunks of red meat, huge fish, birds in their feathers, quadrupeds in their furs, and fruit of almost human coloration; while pieces of white ice and violet crystal flagons mirror each other's brilliance. Antony notices in the middle of the table a boar steaming from every pore, its legs under its belly, its eyes half shut – and the thought of eating this formidable beast gives him acute pleasure. Then come things he has never seen, minces quite black, jellies golden in colour, stews in which mushrooms float like water-lilies on a pond, and mousses like clouds in their airiness.

The aroma of it all brings him the salty smell of the ocean, the freshness of fountains, the strong scent of woods. He dilates his nostrils as much as possible. He drools. He tells himself that this will last him for a year, ten years, a lifetime!

As he lets his astonished eyes wander over the dishes, others accumulate, forming a pyramid whose corners crumble. The wines start to flow and the fishes to palpitate, blood bubbles in the platters, fleshy fruits come forward like amorous lips; and the table rises to his chest, to his chin – bearing one single plate and one single loaf, exactly opposite him.

He reaches for the loaf. Other loaves present themselves.

For me! ... all of them! but ...

Antony draws back.

There was only one – and now look at all these! ... It must be a miracle, like the one our Lord performed! ...

What for? Hey! None of the rest makes any sense either! Ah! demon! out! out!

He aims a kick at the table. It disappears.

Nothing more? no!

He draws a deep breath.

Ah! That was a strong temptation. But I escaped it!

He looks up, and trips against a ringing object.

What on earth!

Antony stoops down.

Well! a goblet! Someone must have lost it on his travels. Nothing unusual...

He wets a finger, and rubs.

Shiny, and metal! All the same, I can't make out...

He lights his torch and inspects the goblet.

This is silver, with an ovular decoration round the rim, and a medallion at the bottom.

He prises up the medallion with his finger-nail.

Here's a piece of money worth... seven or eight drachmas. Not more. Never mind! With that, I might well buy myself a sheepskin.

The torchlight flickers on the goblet.

Impossible! gold! yes!... solid gold!

Another larger coin lies at the bottom. Underneath it, he discovers several more.

But this is a sum big enough ... for three oxen ... for a small field!

The goblet is now quite full of gold coins.

Come now! a hundred slaves, soldiers, a mob, enough to buy...

The granulations along the rim become detached, forming a necklace of pearls.

With a jewel like this, even the Emperor's wife might be won!

With a shake Antony slides the necklace over his wrist. He holds the goblet in his left hand, and with his other he lifts the torch to light it more clearly. Brimming over like water from a fountain, pouring out in a continuous stream so as to form a little mound on the sand, come diamonds, carbuncles and sapphires, together with large gold coins bearing the effigies of kings.

Whatever next? Staters, cycles, darics, aryandics! Alexander, Demetrius, the Ptolemies, Caesar! But not one of them owned so much! There's nothing I couldn't do! No more suffering! How this brilliance dazzles me! Ah! I could cry for joy! This is good! Yes! . . . yes! . . . more! never enough! However much I might throw into the sea, I'll have more left. Why lose any at all? I'll keep the lot, without telling anybody; I'll have a chamber dug out of the rock, plated inside with bronze – and I'll go there to feel the piles of gold shifting under my heels; I'll plunge my arms into them as if they were sacks of grain. I want to rub my face in it all, sleep on top of it!

He lets go of the torch in order to hug the heap, and falls face down on the ground.
He gets up. The place is completely empty.

What have I done?
If I'd died meanwhile, I'd be in hell! Irrevocable hell!

He trembles all over.

So I'm damned? Oh no! It's my own fault! I fall into every trap! Who could be more stupid or more sordid? I'd like to hit myself, or rather to wrench myself out of my body! I've been holding back for too long! I need to take my revenge, to hack and to kill! I feel I've a pack of wild beasts inside me. I want an axe, and chopping through a whole crowd ... Ah! a dagger! ...

Noticing his knife, he rushes for it. The knife slips from his hand, and Antony remains propped against the wall of his cabin, his mouth wide open, unmoving – cataleptic.

The entire entourage has disappeared.

He thinks he is in Alexandria on the Panium, an artificial mountain coiled round by a staircase, rising in the centre of the town.

In front of him stretches Lake Mareotis, to the right the sea, to the left open country – and just beneath his eyes a confusion of flat roofs, cut through from north to south and from east to west by two intersecting roads which display down their entire length a series of porticoes rich in corinthian capitals. The houses overhanging this double colonnade have coloured glass in their windows. A few of them are fitted externally with enormous cages of wood where the outside air rushes in.

Monuments quite various in their architecture crowd close together. Egyptian pylons loom above Greek temples. Obelisks emerge like lances between red brick battlements. In the middle of squares appear the pointed ears of a Hermes or a dog-headed Anubis. Antony can see mosaics in the courtyards, and carpets hanging from beams in the ceilings.

With a single glance he takes in the two ports (the Great Harbour and the Eunostus), as round as two circuses, and separated by a mole which links Alexandria to the craggy island from which rises the tower of Pharos, quadrangular, five hundred cubits high and in nine storeys – with its mass of black charcoal smoking at the summit.

Little interior harbours are cut into the principal ports. The mole finishes, at either end, in a bridge which rests on marble columns planted in the sea. Sails pass underneath; and heavy lighters brimming with merchandise, state barges encrusted with ivory, gondolas covered with awnings, triremes and biremes, craft of every kind, manoeuvre or moor against the quays.

Around the Great Harbour runs an uninterrupted sequence of royal constructions: the palace of the Ptolemies, the Museum, the Posidium, the Caesareum, the Timonium where Mark Antony took refuge, the Soma which contains the tomb of Alexander; while at the other end of the town – in a suburb beyond the Eunostus – may be descried factories making glass, perfumes and papyrus.

Ambulant vendors, porters, donkey-drivers, are running and jostling. Also in sight: a priest of Osiris with a panther's hide on his shoulders, a bronze-helmeted Roman soldier, quite a few negroes. At shop entrances women stop, while artisans work; and the creaking of carts makes birds fly up from the ground where they are eating butchers' offal and scraps of fish.

Across the white uniformity of the houses the pattern of streets falls like a black net. Markets full of greenery form vivid clusters, dyers' drying-houses add patches of colour, and gold ornaments on temple pediments are luminous points – all contained within the oval span of the greyish walls, under the sky's blue vault, by the motionless sea.

But the crowd stops and looks westward, whence enormous clouds of dust are advancing.

Here come the monks of the Thebaid, clothed in goatskins, armed with clubs, and yelling their canticle of war and religion to the refrain: 'Where are they? where are they?'

Antony realises that they are coming to kill the Arians.

Suddenly the streets empty out – there is nothing to be seen but scampering feet.

Now the Solitaries are in the town. Their formidable truncheons, studded with nails, whirl like steely suns. Things are broken with audible crashes within the houses. There are intervals of silence. Then loud screams start up.

From end to end, the streets are a continuous eddy of frightened people.

A few of them have pikes. Occasionally two groups meet, merge into one; and this mass slips on the flagstones, falls apart, drops down. But the long-haired men always reappear.

Thin threads of smoke escape from the corners of buildings. Doors burst their panels. Sections of wall collapse. Architraves tumble.

One after another, Antony comes upon all his old enemies. He recognises some whom he had forgotten; he commits atrocities on these before he kills them – disembowelling, slitting throats, beating out brains, dragging old men by the beard, crushing children, hacking the wounded. And revenge is wreaked on luxury; those who cannot read tear up books; others break or damage statues, paintings, furniture, caskets, a thousand fragilities of whose function they are ignorant, and which, for that reason, exasperate them. From time to time they stop, quite out of breath, and then begin again.

The inhabitants shelter in courtyards, moaning. Women lift up their tear-filled eyes and naked arms to heaven. To make the Solitaries relent, they clasp them round the knees; they are knocked down; and blood spurts up to the ceilings, spills back down the walls, wells up from the decapitated trunks of corpses, fills the aqueducts, collects on the ground in large red puddles.

Antony is up to his thighs in it. He wades in it, he inhales the droplets on his lips, and he shivers with joy as he feels it against his body, under the hair tunic which is drenched with it.

Night falls. The immense uproar dies down.

The Solitaries have disappeared.

Suddenly, on the exterior galleries that rim the nine storeys of the Pharos, Antony notices thick black lines such as might be made by perching ravens. He runs up to it, and he finds himself at the top.

A great copper mirror, turned towards the open sea, reflects the ships out on the main.

Antony enjoys watching them; and the more he watches, the more there are.

They are crowded into a crescent-shaped gulf. Behind it, on a promontory, is displayed the Roman architecture of a new town, with stone cupolas, conical roofs, pink and blue marble, and a profusion of bronze applied to the volutes of capitals, the crests of houses, and the angles of cornices. A cypress wood rises beyond. The colour of the sea is greener, the air is colder. On the mountainous horizon there is snow.

Antony is looking for his way when a man accosts him, saying: 'Come! you are expected!'

He crosses a forum, enters a courtyard, stoops under a door, and arrives in front of the palace façade, ornamented with a waxen group representing the emperor Constantine felling a dragon. In the middle of a porphyry basin lies a golden conch full of pistachios. His guide tells him he may take some. He does so.

Then he becomes quite lost in suites of rooms.

Displayed along the mosaic walls are generals, offering conquered towns to the Emperor on the flat of their hands. All around are columns of basalt, grilles of silver filigree, ivory chairs and pearl-embroidered tapestries. Light falls from the vaults, Antony walks on. There are warm exhalations hovering; and he hears, occasionally, the discreet clack of a sandal. Posted in the antechambers are attendants – looking like automata – who hold vermeil batons on their shoulders.

At last he finds himself at the back of a hall, hung at the other end with hyacinth-coloured curtains. These draw apart to reveal the

Emperor sitting enthroned in a violet tunic, his feet in red buskins striped with black.

A diadem of pearls encircles the symmetric ringlets clustered on his head. He has drooping eyelids, a straight nose, a sly and heavy physiognomy. At the corners of the dais stretched over his head are set four golden doves, and at the foot of his throne crouch two enamel lions. The doves start to sing and the lions to roar, the Emperor rolls his eyes, Antony advances; and at once, without preamble, they tell each other of events. In the towns of Antioch, Ephesus and Alexandria, the temples have been sacked and the statues of the gods turned into pots and pans; the Emperor is thoroughly amused. Antony reproaches him for his tolerance of the Novatians. But the Emperor gets carried away – Novatians, Arians, Meletians, they are all a nuisance. However, he admires the episcopate, since the bishops appointed by the Christians depend on five or six persons, so that one need only win these over in order to make sure of all the others. Indeed he has not failed to furnish them with considerable sums. But he loathes the Fathers of the Council of Nicaea. – 'Come and visit them!' Antony follows him.

And they step straight onto a terrace.

It overlooks a hippodrome full of people and surmounted by porticoes where the remainder of the crowd walks about. In the centre of the racecourse stretches a narrow platform, and laid along it are a small temple of Mercury, a statue of Constantine, three bronze serpents intertwined, some large wooden eggs at one end, and at the other end seven dolphins with their tails in the air.

Behind the imperial pavilion are the Prefects of the Chambers, the Counts of the household and the Patricians, ranged in tiers as far as the first storey of the church, whose windows are all lined with women. To the right stands the tribune belonging to the blue faction, to the left that of the green, and beneath them a picket of soldiers, while on the level of the arena is a row of corinthian arches forming the entrance to the stalls.

The races are about to begin, the horses line up. Tall plumes, fixed between their ears, wave in the wind like trees; and they springily jolt the shell-shaped chariots driven by charioteers clothed in some sort of multicoloured cuirass, their sleeves worn loose on the arm and tight at the wrist, their legs bare, their beards full, their hair shaved above the forehead in the style of Huns.

Antony is at first deafened by the babble of voices. From the top tier downwards he sees nothing but painted faces, motley garments, plaques of wrought jewellery; and the sand on the arena, pure white, winks like a mirror.

The Emperor entertains him. He divulges important, secret matters to him, tells him confidentially of the assassination of his son Crispus, even asks him for advice about his health.

Meanwhile Antony notices the slaves at the rear of the stalls. They are the Fathers of the Council of Nicaea, in abject rags. Paphnutius the martyr combs a horse's mane, Theophilus washes the legs of another, John paints the hooves of a third, Alexander collects dung in a basket.

Antony walks among them. They line his progress, they beg him to intercede, they kiss his hands. The whole crowd boos them; and he relishes their degradation beyond all measure. So here he is, a magnate of the Court, the Emperor's confidant, the prime minister! Constantine places his diadem on Antony's forehead. And Antony keeps it, treating the honour as a matter of course.

Presently a huge hall is revealed in the gloom, lit by golden candelabra.

Ranked columns half lost in the shadows, so great is their height, stand beside tables which stretch to the horizon – where in a luminous vapour appear superimposed flights of steps, series of arcades, colossi, towers, and beyond these a vague palatial border, above which the blacker masses formed by cedars soar into the dark.

Fellow-diners crowned with violets rest their elbows on very low couches. Wine is dispensed from tilting amphorae placed along the two rows – while at the very end, topped by his tiara and rich in carbuncles, King Nebuchadnezzar eats and drinks alone.

To his right and left two files of priests in pointed bonnets swing censers. On the ground beneath him, without hands or feet, crawl the captive kings, to whom he throws bones to gnaw; lower still come his brothers, bandaged round the eyes – all of them blind.

A continuous plaint rises from the depths of the slaves' prison. The sweet slow sounds of a hydralic organ alternate with the chorus of voices; and one senses all around the hall a boundless town, an ocean of men whose surges batter the walls.

Running slaves carry dishes. Women come round with drinks, baskets creak under the weight of bread, and a dromedary loaded with pierced goatskins passes to and fro, sprinkling verbena to cool the tiles.

Keepers bring in lions. Dancers with their hair caught up in nets gyrate on their hands, spitting fire through their nostrils; negro conjurers juggle, naked infants pelt each other with snowballs which shatter against the clear silverware. So fearful is the uproar that it might be a storm, and a cloud floats above the feast, what with all the meats and steamy breath. Occasionally a brand from one of the big torches, snatched off by the wind, crosses the night like a shooting star.

The King wipes the perfumes from his face with his arm. He eats from sacred vessels, then breaks them; and he makes a mental count of his fleets, his armies, his peoples. Shortly, out of caprice, he will burn down his palace together with his guests. He intends to rebuild the tower of Babel and to dethrone God.

On his brow, from a distance, Antony reads all his thoughts. They penetrate him – and he becomes Nebuchadnezzar.

He is instantly sick of excesses and exterminations, and seized with a craving to wallow in filth. Indeed, the degradation of whatever is horrifying to men consists of an outrage on their minds, a further means of stupefying them; and since nothing is more vile than a brute beast, Antony drops down on all fours on the table and bellows like a bull.

He feels a pain in his hand – a pebble, as it happens, has hurt him – and he finds himself once again before his cabin.

The enclosure of rocks lies empty. Stars shine. All is quiet.

I've fooled myself yet again ! Why all this? It comes from the urge of the flesh. Ah, wretch!

He rushes into his cabin, fetches a bundle of cords tipped with metallic hooks, strips to the waist, and gazing up at the sky:

Accept my penance, O my God! Don't scorn it for its feebleness. Make it sharp, long-drawn-out, excessive! Now then! to work!

He inflicts a vigorous lashing on himself.

Ouch! no! no! no mercy!

He begins again.

Oh! oh! oh! Each blow rips my skin, slits my arms and legs. It burns horribly!

Ah! It's not so bad! One gets used to it. I almost feel . . .

Antony stops.

Go on, coward! Go on! Good! good! on the arms, across the back, on the chest, in the stomach, all over! Whistle down on me, thongs! Bite and tear! I want drops of my blood to spurt up to the stars, to split my bones, to bare my nerves! Pincers, racks, melted lead! The martyrs put up with plenty besides! didn't they, Ammonaria?

The shadow of the Devil's horns reappears.

What if I'd been tied to the column next to yours, face to face, under your very eyes, answering your screams with my moans, and our pains had become confused, our souls been pooled together!

He lashes himself furiously.

There, there! Take that! and again! . . . But there's a tickling all over me. Such agony! Such bliss! It's like being kissed. I'm melting to the marrow! I could die!

And in front of him he sees three riders mounted on wild asses, clothed in green robes, holding three lilies in their hands, and all alike in their features.

Antony turns round, and sees three other similar riders, also on asses, in the same posture.

He draws back. And the asses, all together, take a step forward and rub their noses against him, trying to bite his clothing. Voices shout: 'This way, this way, over here!' And standards appear between the clefts of the mountain, with camels' heads in red silk halters, mules loaded with baggage, and women covered with yellow veils mounted astride piebald horses.

The panting beasts lie down, the slaves hurry to the packs, gaudy carpets are unrolled, shining objects are spread out on the ground.

A white elephant caparisoned with cloth of gold runs up, shaking the bouquet of ostrich feathers attached to its head-piece.

On its back, among blue woollen cushions, cross-legged, with eyelids half closed and with swaying head, sits a woman so magnificently dressed that she radiates light. The crowd bows down, the elephant bends at the knees, and

THE QUEEN OF SHEBA,

sliding down along its shoulder, steps onto the carpets and advances toward Saint Antony.

Her gown of golden brocade, cut across at regular intervals by falbalas of pearl, jet, and sapphire, pinches her waist in a tight bodice, enriched with coloured appliqué to represent the twelve signs of the Zodiac. She wears very high pattens, one of them black with a sprinkling of silver stars, and a crescent moon – while the other, which is white, is covered in golden droplets with a sun in the middle.

Her wide sleeves, garnished with emeralds and birds' feathers, allow a bare view of her little round arm, ornamented at the wrist by an ebony bracelet, and her ring-laden hands are tipped with nails so sharp that her fingers finish almost like needles.

A flat golden chain passing under her chin runs up along her cheeks, spirals around her blue-powdered hair, and then dropping down grazes past her shoulder and clinches over her chest on to a diamond scorpion, which sticks out its tongue between her breasts. Two large blonde pearls pull at her ears. The edges of her eyelids are painted black. On her left cheek-bone she has a natural brown fleck; and she breathes with her mouth open, as if her corset constricted her.

In her progress she waves a green parasol with an ivory handle, hung round with silver-gilt bells; and twelve frizzy little negroes carry the long tail of her gown, held at the very end by a monkey who lifts it up from time to time.

She says:

Ah! Fine hermit! Fine hermit! My heart swoons!

I've fidgeted so impatiently on my feet that I've got calluses on my heels, and I've broken one of my nails! I sent shepherds who stood on the mountains with their hands shading their eyes, and huntsmen who shouted your name in the woods, and spies who scoured the roads asking every passer-by: 'Have you seen him?'

At night I wept, turning my face to the wall. My tears eventually made two small holes in the mosaic, like pools of sea water in the rocks, because I love you! Oh! yes! very much!

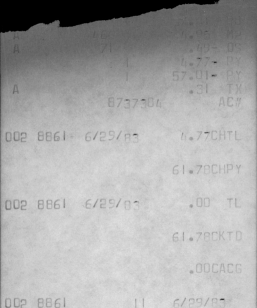

```
 A                            4.95  M2
 A            71               .49  OS
                1            4.77  PY
                1           57.01  PY
 A                            .31  TX
             8737304               AC#

002  8861   6/29/83          4.77CHTL

                            61.78CHPY

002  8861   6/29/83           .00  TL

                            61.78CKTD

                             .00CACG

002  8861          11    6/29/83
```

She catches hold of his beard.

Now laugh, fine hermit! Laugh! I'm very gay, you'll see! I play the lyre, I dance like a bee, and I have a fund of stories to tell, each more amusing than the last.

You can't imagine what a long way we've come. There, the green couriers' asses have died of fatigue!

The wild asses are stretched out on the ground, unmoving.

For the whole of the last three moons they've run at an even pace, with a pebble between their teeth to cut the wind, their tails always straight, their knees always bent, and always at a gallop. Their like will not be found again! They came to me from my maternal grandfather, the Emperor Saharil, son of Iakhschab, son of Iaarab, son of Kastan. Ah! If they were still alive, we'd yoke them to a litter and quickly make our way home! But . . . what is it? . . . what are you thinking of?

She inspects him.

Ah! When you become my husband, I'll dress you, I'll perfume you, I'll depilate you.

Antony stays quite still, stiff as a rod, and as pale as death.

You look sad; is it at leaving your cabin? As for me, I've left everything for you, even King Solomon himself – for all his great wisdom, his twenty thousand chariots of war, and his beautiful beard! I've brought you my wedding presents. Now choose.

She promenades between the rows of slaves and the merchandise.

Here's balm from Genezareth, incense from Cape Gardefan, ladanum, cinnamon, and silphium, so good in sauces. In there are embroideries from Assur, ivories from the Ganges, purple from Elissa; and that snow-box contains a goatskin full of chalybon, the wine reserved for kings of Assyria –

drunk neat from the horn of a unicorn. Here are necklaces, nets, clasps and parasols, powder of gold from Baasa, cassiterite from Tartessus, blue wood from Pandion, white furs from Issidonia, carbuncles from the island of Palaesi-mundum, and tooth-picks made of the hairs of the tacha – an underground animal now vanished. These cushions are from Emathia, and these coat fringes from Palmyra. On this Babylonian carpet, there are . . . but come along! Come along!

She plucks Saint Antony by the sleeve. He resists. She continues:

This fine tissue, which crackles under your fingers with a sound of sparks, is the famous yellow cloth brought by merchants from Bactria. They require forty-three interpreters on their journey. I'll have it made into robes for you, which you can wear at home.

Press the clasps on the sycamore case, and fetch me the ivory box from the withers of my elephant!

Something round wrapped in a veil is taken from a chest, and a little casket covered with carvings is brought.

Would you like the shield of Dgian-ben-Dgian, builder of the Pyramids? Here it is! It consists of seven dragons' skins laid on top of each other, joined by diamond screws and tanned in parricide's bile. All the wars which have been fought since the invention of arms are pictured on one side, and on the other are all the wars which will be fought before the end of the world. Lightning bounces off it like a ball of cork. I'll slip it over your arm and you can wear it hunting.

But if you knew what I have in my little box! Turn it over, try to open it! Nobody can; kiss me; I'll tell you.

She takes Saint Antony by both cheeks; he pushes her off at arm's length.

It was a night when King Solomon lost his head. Anyway we struck a bargain. He got up, tiptoeing out . . .

She performs a pirouette.

Ah! ah! Fine hermit! You shan't be told! You shan't be told!

She waves her parasol, and all its little bells tinkle.

And I have plenty of other things besides, so there! I have treasures locked in galleries which are like woods to wander through. I have summer palaces of trellised reeds, and winter palaces of black marble. In the middle of lakes as large as seas I have islands as round as coins, covered in mother-of-pearl, where the shores make music to the beat of warm waters rolling up the sand. The slaves in my kitchens take birds from my aviaries, they fish from my fish-ponds. I have engravers permanently seated to hollow my portrait out of hard stone, and panting smelters who cast my statues, and perfumers who blend plant juices with vinegars and grind pastes. I have seamstresses cutting cloths for me, jewellers chiselling gems for me, hairdressers designing new styles for me, and careful painters who sluice my walls with boiling resins, cooling them off with fans. I have women servants enough for a harem, eunuchs enough for an army. I have armies, I have peoples! In my lobby I have a guard of dwarfs shouldering ivory trumpets.

Antony sighs.

I have teams of gazelles, elephants harnessed in fours, hundreds of pairs of camels, mares with manes so long that they tangle with their galloping hooves, and herds with horns so huge that the woods are chopped down in front of them as they graze. I have giraffes which walk about my gardens and stick their heads over the edge of my roof when I take the air after dinner.

Sitting in a cockle-shell and drawn by dolphins, I go wandering through grottoes, listening to the water running off the stalactites. I visit diamond country, where my friends the magicians allow me to choose the finest; then I come up to earth and go back home.

She lets out a shrill whistle – and a big bird, dropping down from the sky, lands on the crest of her coiffure, dislodging some of the blue powder.

His plumage, orange in colour, seems to consist of metallic scales. His little head, decked with a silvery comb, presents a human face. He has four wings, vulture's claws, and an immense peacock's tail which he fans out behind him.

Seizing the queen's parasol in his beak, he teeters a little before settling plumb, then puffs out all his feathers, and remains motionless.

Thank you, beautiful Simorg-anka! you who discovered where my lover was hiding! Thank you! thank you, my heart's messenger!

He flies like desire. Each day he circles the world. In the evening he comes back; he perches at the foot of my bed; he tells me what he has seen, the seas which swept under him with the fishes and the boats, the big empty deserts which he viewed from the height of heaven, and all the harvests curving across the countryside, and the plants pushing up on the walls of abandoned towns.

Languorously she twists her arms.

Oh, if you would, if you would! . . . I have a pavilion on a promontory, in the middle of an isthmus, between two oceans. The walls are panelled with glass, the floor inlaid with tortoise-shell, and it opens onto the four winds of heaven. From above, I see my fleets returning and people climbing up the hill with loads on their shoulders. We'd sleep on quilts softer than clouds, we'd drink cold drinks from the rinds of fruit, and we'd stare at the sun through emeralds! Come! . . .

Antony backs away. She draws nearer, speaking with irritation:

What? A woman's not to be rich, or coquettish, or in love? You're after something else, hm? Seductive, fat, with a husky voice, hair the colour of fire, and swelling curves. Or would you prefer a body as cold as snakeskin, or big black eyes darker than mystic caverns? Look me in the eyes!

Despite himself, Antony looks.

All the women you ever met, from the girl at the crossroads singing under her lantern to the patrician high on her litter, plucking rose petals, all the shapes half seen or imagined by your desire, ask for them every one! I am not a woman, but a world. My clothes need only fall away for you to discover in my person one continuous mystery!

Antony's teeth are chattering.

If you laid your finger on my shoulder, it would affect you like fire running through your veins. The possession of the least place on my body will give you sharper joy than the conquest of an empire. Offer your lips! My kisses taste like fruit ready to melt into your heart! Ah! how you'll lose yourself in my hair, breathing the scent of my sweet-smelling breasts, marvelling at my limbs, and scorched by the pupils of my eyes, between my arms, in a whirlwind ...

Antony crosses himself.

You scorn me! Farewell!

She moves away crying, then she turns:

Are you sure? Such a beautiful woman!

She laughs, and the monkey holding the edge of her gown lifts it up.

You'll regret it, fine hermit, you'll be sorry! and bored! But I don't care! La! la! la! oh! oh! oh!

She goes off with her hands over her face, hopping on one foot.

The slaves file past Saint Antony, the horses, the dromedaries, the elephant, the women servants, the reloaded mules, the little negroes, the monkey, the green couriers, each with a broken lily in the hand – and the Queen of Sheba withdraws, letting out a sort of convulsive hiccup, not unlike a sob or a snigger.

III

When she has disappeared, Antony notices a child on the threshold of his cabin.

It must be one of the Queen's servants,

he thinks.

This child is as small as a dwarf and yet as stocky as a Cabirus, misshapen, miserable-looking. White hairs cover his prodigiously large head; and he shivers under a mean tunic, while clasping in his hand a roll of papyrus.

The light of the moon, grazed by a passing cloud, falls on him.

ANTONY

observes him at a distance and is scared of him.

Who are you?

THE CHILD

answers:

Your old disciple Hilarion!

ANTONY

You're lying! For many years now Hilarion has been living in Palestine.

HILARION

I've come back! It is I!

ANTONY

comes closer, considers him.

But his face was as bright as dawn, open, happy. This other looks quite dull and aged.

HILARION

Long labours have tired me out!

ANTONY

The voice besides is different. It has an icy ring.

HILARION

Because I feed on bitter things!

ANTONY

And this white hair?

HILARION

I've had so many sorrows!

ANTONY

aside:

Is it possible?...

HILARION

I wasn't as far away as you suppose. Paul the hermit paid you a visit this year during the month of Schebar. It's just twenty days since the Nomads brought you bread. Yesterday you told a sailor to forward you three marlin spikes.

ANTONY

He knows everything!

HILARION

Know also that I've never left you. But there are long periods when you fail to notice me.

ANTONY

How is that? It's true that my head is so confused! Tonight especially...

HILARION

All the Deadly Sins have been. But their pitiful snares can't survive against a saint such as you!

ANTONY

Oh, no!... no! I weaken every minute! If only I were one of those who are always intrepid of soul and firm in spirit – like the great Athanasius, for instance.

HILARION

He was illegally ordained by seven bishops!

ANTONY

What then! If his virtue...

HILARION

Come, come! An arrogant man, and cruel, forever intriguing, finally exiled as a racketeer.

ANTONY

Slander!

HILARION

You won't deny that he tried to corrupt Eustathius, treasurer of the bounty?

ANTONY

So it's claimed, I'll admit.

HILARION

He burnt down the house of Arsenius in revenge!

ANTONY

Alas!

HILARION

At the Council of Nicaea he said, referring to Jesus: 'the Lord's man'.

ANTONY

Ah! That's blasphemy!

HILARION

So limited a man, besides, that he confesses to understanding nothing about the nature of the Word.

ANTONY

smiling with pleasure:

Indeed, his intelligence is not very ... outstanding.

HILARION

If you'd been put in his place, that would have been a great blessing for your brothers as well as for you. This life apart from others is bad.

ANTONY

On the contrary! Man, being spirit, must withdraw from mortal things. All action degrades him. I could wish not to be attached to the earth – not even by the soles of my feet!

HILARION

Hypocrite, sinking into solitude the better to license your outbreaks of greed! You abstain from meat, wine, baths, slaves and honours; but you let your imagination provide you with banquets, perfumes, naked women and applauding crowds! Your chastity is only a more subtle corruption, and this scorn of the world nothing but your impotent hatred of it! This is what makes your sort so gloomy, or perhaps it's because they doubt. Possession of the truth gives joy. Was Jesus sad? He would walk surrounded by friends, rest in the shade of an olive tree, go into the publican's, multiply the cups, forgiving the sinful woman, healing all pains. You, you pity only your own misery. It's as if remorse were fretting you, and a demented fierceness, to the point of rebuffing a dog's caress or the smile of a child.

ANTONY

bursts into tears:

Enough! enough! You move me too much!

HILARION

Shake the vermin from your rags! Get up from your filth! Your God is no Moloch demanding flesh in sacrifice!

ANTONY

But suffering is blessed. The cherubim bend down to receive the blood of confessors.

HILARION

Admire the Montanists then! They surpass all the others.

ANTONY

But it's the truth of the doctrine that makes martyrdom!

HILARION

How can it be a proof of excellence when it testifies equally to error?

ANTONY

Be quiet, viper!

HILARION

It's perhaps not so very difficult. The exhortations of friends, the pleasure of causing popular outrage, the vow once made, a certain vertigo, a thousand circumstances come to their help.

Antony moves away from Hilarion. Hilarion follows him.

Besides, this manner of death induces great disturbances. Denys, Cyprian and Gregory avoided it. Peter of Alexandria censured it, and the Council of Elvira...

ANTONY

stops his ears.

I won't listen!

HILARION

raising his voice:

There you go falling into your usual sin, sloth. Ignorance is the froth of pride. One says: 'My mind is made up, why argue?' and one scorns doctors, philosophers, tradition, the very text of the Law of which one is ignorant. Do you think you hold wisdom in your hand?

ANTONY

I can still hear him. His noisy words fill my head.

HILARION

Efforts to understand God are superior to your mortifications aimed at moving him. Our merit lies only in our thirst for the True. Religion alone cannot explain everything; and the solution of those problems which you won't recognise can make it higher and more unassailable. Therefore one must, for one's own good, communicate with one's brothers – otherwise the Church, the congregation of the faithful, would be nothing but a word – and one must listen to every reason, despising nothing and nobody. The sorcerer Balaam, the poet Aeschylus and the Sibyl of Cumae had announced the Saviour. Denys the Alexandrian received an order from Heaven to read every book. Saint Clement orders us to cultivate Greek letters. Hermas was converted through the apparition of a woman he had loved.

ANTONY

What an air of authority! It seems to me that you're growing...

Hilarion's height has indeed progressively increased; and Antony, so as not to see him any more, shuts his eyes.

HILARION

Take it easy, my good hermit!

Let's sit down here, on this big stone – just like old times, when I used to greet you with the first light of day, calling you 'bright morning star': and you would at once begin my lessons. They have yet to be finished. The moon gives us light enough. I'm listening.

He has pulled a calamus from his belt; and cross-legged on the ground with his roll of papyrus in his hand, he lifts his face towards Antony, seated beside him with head still bowed.

After a moment's silence Hilarion begins again:

The word of God is confirmed for us, is it not, by miracles? And yet the Pharaoh's sorcerers performed them; other imposters can do so; one can be mistaken. What then is a miracle? An event which to us appears outside nature. But do we know the whole power of nature? And because a thing normally does not astonish us, does it follow that we understand it?

ANTONY

No matter! One must believe in the Scriptures!

HILARION

Saint Paul, Origen and many others did not take them literally; but if one explains them by allegories, they become the shared property of a small number and the evidence of the truth disappears. What is to be done?

ANTONY

One must trust in the Church!

HILARION

So the Scriptures are unnecessary?

ANTONY

Not at all! although the Old Testament, I must admit, has ... obscurities ... But the New shines with a pure light.

HILARION

And yet the angel of the annunciation appears in Matthew to Joseph, whereas in Luke it's to Mary. The anointing of Jesus by a woman happens according to the first Gospel at the beginning of his public ministry, but according to the three others only a few days before his death. The drink offered to him on the cross is in Matthew wine with gall, in Mark wine and myrrh. According to Luke and Matthew, the apostles must take neither money nor packs, not even sandals or a stick; in Mark, on the contrary, Jesus forbids them to carry anything except for sandals and a stick. I'm lost! ...

ANTONY

quite dumbfounded:

Indeed ... indeed ...

HILARION

At the contact of the haemorrhoidal woman, Jesus turned round saying: 'Who has touched me?' Did he then not know who was touching him? That contradicts the omniscience of Jesus. If the tomb was under the guards' surveillance, there was no point in the women worrying about who would help lift the stone from this tomb. Therefore there were no guards, or else the saintly women were not there. At Emmaus he eats with his disciples and makes them feel his wounds. This is a human body, a ponderable material object, and yet it passes through the walls. Is this possible?

ANTONY

It would take a lot of time to answer you!

HILARION

Why, being the Son, did he receive the Holy Ghost? What need had he of baptism if he was the Word? How could he, God, be tempted by the Devil?

Have these thoughts never occurred to you?

ANTONY

Yes! ... often! Sleeping or rampaging they persist in my mind. I stamp them out, they reappear, smother me; and sometimes I think that I'm cursed.

HILARION

Well then, there's little sense in your serving God?

ANTONY

I still need to worship him!

After a long silence,

HILARION

begins again:

But apart from dogma, full freedom of research is allowed us. Do you wish to know the hierarchy of Angels, the virtue of Numbers, the reason for germinations and metamorphoses?

ANTONY

Yes! yes! My thought struggles to leave its prison. It seems to me that by gathering my strength I'll succeed. From time to time even, for a lightning moment, I feel as if suspended; then I fall back!

HILARION

The secret you would like to hold is guarded by sages. They live in a far country, seated under gigantic trees, dressed in white and as calm as gods. The air that nourishes them is hot. Leopards stalk about them on the grass. Murmuring springs and the whinnying of unicorns mix with their voices. You shall listen to them: and the face of the Unknown will be unveiled!

ANTONY

sighing:

The road seems long, and I'm old!

HILARION

Oh! oh! Wise men are not rare! There are even some quite close to you. Here – In we go!

IV

And Antony sees in front of him an immense basilica.

Light is projected from the far end, as if from a marvellous multi-coloured sun, to fall on the countless heads of the crowd filling the nave and flowing back between the columns, towards the aisles – where in wooden compartments can be distinguished altars, beds, chainlets of small blue stones, and constellations painted on the walls.

In the middle of the crowd, here and there, groups have formed. Men up on stools harangue with lifted finger; others pray with their arms spread crosswise, lie on the ground, chant hymns, or drink wine; around a table some worshippers celebrate agapae; martyrs unbandage their limbs to show their wounds; old men, leaning on sticks, tell the story of their journeys.

There are men from the land of the Germans, from Thrace and from Gaul, from Scythia and from the Indies – snow on their beards, feathers in their hair, thorns in the fringes of their garments, sandals black with dust, skins burnt by the sun. Their costumes are a confusion of purple mantles and linen robes, embroidered dalmatics, fur sayons, sailors' caps, bishops' mitres. Their eyes fulgurate extraordinarily. They look like executioners or like eunuchs.

Hilarion advances among them. They all greet him. Pressing close to his shoulder, Antony observes them. He notices a lot of women. Several are dressed as men, their hair shaved; they frighten him.

HILARION

These are Christian women who have converted their husbands. Women, indeed, even the idolatrous, are always for Jesus – to judge by Pilate's wife Procula, and Poppaea, Nero's concubine. Stop trembling! move forward!

And more are continually arriving.

They multiply, split into two, as airy as shades, while producing a great clamour in which are mixed howls of rage, cries of love, canticles and objurgations.

ANTONY

in a low voice:

What do they want?

HILARION

The Lord said: 'I have yet many things to say unto you.' They possess those things.

And he pushes him towards a golden throne with five steps, where surrounded by ninety-five disciples all rubbed with oil, all thin and very pale, the prophet Mani sits – beautiful as an archangel, still as a statue, wearing an Indian robe, carbuncles in his plaited hair, in his left hand a book of painted images, under his right a globe. The images represent the creatures who lay sleeping within chaos. Antony leans over to see them. Then

MANI

revolves his globe; and timing his words to the crystalline sounds coming from a lyre:

The celestial earth is at the upper extremity, the mortal earth at the lower extremity. It is upheld by two angels, the Splenditenens and the six-faced Omophore.

At the top of the highest heaven dwells the impassible Divinity; beneath, face to face, are the Son of God and the Prince of Darkness.

When the darkness had advanced up to his kingdom, God drew from his essence a virtue which produced the first man; and he set the five elements about him. But the demons of darkness robbed him of one portion, and that portion is the soul.

There is one soul only, universally poured out, like the water of a river divided into several branches. This it is that sighs in the wind, grates in marble when it is hewn, howls in the voice of the sea; and weeps milky tears when you pull leaves from the figtree.

Souls departed from this world migrate to the stars, which are animate beings.

ANTONY

starts to laugh.

Ha! ha! What an absurd imagination!

A MAN

beardless, austere in appearance:

In what respect?

Antony is about to answer. But Hilarion tells him softly that this man is the prodigious Origen; and

MANI

begins again:

First they stop in the moon, where they are purified. Then they ascend to the sun.

ANTONY

slowly:

I know nothing . . . to prevent us . . . from believing it.

MANI

The aim of every creature is to release the celestial ray locked in matter. It escapes more easily through perfumes, spices, the aroma of cooked wine, light things resembling thoughts. But the actions of life hold it fast. A murderer will be reborn in the body of a leper; he who kills an animal will become that animal; if you plant a vine, you will be bound in its branches. Nourishment absorbs it. Therefore abstain! Fast!

HILARION

They show temperance, as you see!

MANI

There is much of it in meats, less in vegetables. In any case the Pure, thanks to their merits, strip the luminous part from vegetables and it reascends to its source. Animals, in procreation, imprison it in flesh. Therefore, avoid women!

HILARION

Admire their continence!

MANI

Or rather, ensure that they are not fertile. – Better the soul should fall to earth than languish in carnal shackles!

ANTONY

Ah! Abomination!

HILARION

Why worry about the hierarchy of obscenities? The Church has truly made marriage a sacrament!

SATURNINUS

in Syrian costume:

He propagates a pernicious order of things! The Father, to punish the angels in revolt, ordered them to create the world. Christ came, so that the God of the Jews who was one of these angels...

ANTONY

An Angel? He! the Creator!

CERDO

Didn't he want to kill Moses, deceive his prophets, seduce the people, spread lies and idolatry?

MARCION

Certainly, the Creator was not the true God!

SAINT CLEMENT OF ALEXANDRIA

Matter is eternal!

BARDESANES

dressed as a Babylonian mage:

It was formed by the Seven Planetary Spirits.

THE HERBIANS

Souls were made by the angels!

THE PRISCILLIANISTS

It's the Devil who made the world!

ANTONY

reels backwards:

The horror!

HILARION

holding him up:

You despair too quickly! You misunderstand their

doctrine! Here's one who has received his from Theodas, the friend of Saint Paul. Listen to him!

And, at a sign from Hilarion,

VALENTINE

in a tunic of silver cloth, with a hissing voice and a pointed skull:

The world is the work of a delirious God.

ANTONY

hangs his head.

The work of a delirious God...

After a long silence:

How is that?

VALENTINE

The most perfect of beings, of Eons, the Abyss, lay in the bosom of the Deep together with Thought. From their union came Intelligence, whose companion was Truth.

Intelligence and Truth begot the Word and Life, who in their turn begot Man and the Church – and that makes eight Eons!

He counts on his fingers:

The Word and Truth produced ten more Eons, that's to say five couples. Man and the Church had produced twelve more, among which the Paraclete, Faith, Hope, Charity, Perfection, and Wisdom – Sophia.

These thirty Eons together constitute the Pleroma, or Universality of God. And so, like the echoes of a voice receding, like the effluvia of a perfume evaporating, like the fires of the sun as it sets, the Powers emanating from the Principle grow forever weaker.

But Sophia, longing to know the Father, leapt out of the Pleroma – and the Word then made another couple, Christ and the Holy Spirit, who had linked all the Eons to each other; and all together they formed Jesus, flower of the Pleroma.

However, Sophia's attempt to flee had left in the void an image of her, a bad substance, Acharamoth. The Saviour took pity on her, delivered her from the passions; and from the smile of the delivered Acharamoth was born light; her tears made the waters, her sadness begot black matter.

From Acharamoth came the Demiurge, fabricator of the worlds, the heavens and the Devil. He dwells far beneath the Pleroma, without even catching sight of it, and thus he thinks himself the true God, and repeats through the mouth of his prophets: 'There is no other God but I!' Then he made man, and cast into his soul the immaterial seed, which was the Church, reflection of that other Church placed in the Pleroma.

One day Acharamoth, reaching the highest region, will unite herself to the Saviour; the fire hidden in the world will annihilate all matter, will devour its own self, and men changed into pure spirits will wed angels!

ORIGEN

Then the Demon will be conquered, and the reign of God will begin!

Antony stifles a cry; and at once

BASILIDES

taking him by the elbow:

The supreme Being with the infinite emanations is called Abraxas, and the Saviour with all his virtues Kaulakau, otherwise line-upon-line, rectitude-upon-rectitude.

One obtains the strength of Kaulakau with the help of certain words, inscribed on this chalcedony to facilitate memory.

And he points to a little stone engraved with bizarre lines hanging from his neck.

Then you will be uplifted into the Invisible; and superior to the law, you will scorn everything, even virtue!

We others, the Pure, we must flee from pain, following the example of Kaulakau.

ANTONY

What! and the Cross?

THE ELKHASAITES

in hyacinth robes, answer him:

The sadness, the debasement, the condemnation and oppression of my fathers are blotted out, thanks to the mission which has come!

One can repudiate the inferior Christ, Jesus the man; but one must adore the other Christ, blossoming in person under the wing of the Dove.

Honour marriage! The Holy Spirit is female!

Hilarion has disappeared; and Antony pushed by the crowd arrives before

THE CARPOCRATIANS

stretched out with women on scarlet cushions:

Before you rejoin the One, you will pass through a series of conditions and actions. To free yourself from darkness, at once perform its works! Husband will say to wife: 'Show charity to your brother', and she will take you to bed.

THE NICOLAITANS

gathered round steaming food:

Here is meat offered to idols; take some! Apostasy is allowed when the heart is pure. Gorge your flesh with what it wants. Try to exterminate it by downright debauchery! Prounikos, mother of Heaven, wallowed in degradation.

THE MARCOSIANS

gold-ringed, dripping with balm:

Come in with us to be united to the Spirit! Come in with us to drink immortality!

And one of them shows him, behind a tapestry, the body of a man ending in an ass's head. It represents Sabaoth, father of the Devil. As a mark of hatred, he spits on it.

Another uncovers a very low bed, heaped with flowers, saying that

The spiritual nuptials are about to be performed.

A third holds a glass cup, makes an invocation; blood appears in it.

Ah! There! there! the blood of Christ!

Antony turns away. But he is splattered by the water leaping from a tub.

THE HELVIDIANS

throw themselves in head first, mumbling:

Man regenerated by baptism is impeccable!

Then he passes by a big fire at which the Adamites warm themselves, completely naked to imitate the purity of paradise, and he comes up against

THE MESSALIANS

sprawled across the flagstones, half asleep, stupid:

Oh! crush us if you like, we won't move! Work is a sin, occupations are all bad!

Behind these, the abject

PATERNIANS

men, women and children, pell-mell on a pile of garbage, lift up their hideous faces smeared with wine:

The lower parts of the body made by the Devil belong to him. Eat, drink, fornicate!

AETIUS

Crimes are natural needs beneath the notice of God!

But suddenly

A MAN

dressed in a Carthaginian coat comes bounding among them, with a bunch of thongs in his hand; and hitting out at random right and left, violently:

Ah! Imposters, brigands, simoniacs, heretics and demons! Vermin of the schools, dregs of hell! That one there, Marcion, he's a sailor from Sinope excommunicated for incest; Carpocrates has been banished as a magician; Aetius robbed his concubine; Nicolas prostituted his wife; and Mani who calls himself the Buddha and whose name is Cubricus, was flayed alive with the tip of a reed, so that his tanned skin blows at the gates of Ctesiphon!

ANTONY

has recognised Tertullian, and rushes to meet him.

Master! Here! here!

TERTULLIAN

continuing:

Let images be broken! virgins veiled! Pray, fast, weep, mortify yourselves! No philosophy! No books! After Jesus, science is pointless!

All have fled; and Antony sees, where Tertullian was, a woman sitting on a stone bench.

She sobs, leaning her head against a pillar, her hair hanging down, her body collapsed under a long brown chimere.

Then the two find themselves beside each other, far from the crowd – and a silence, an extraordinary calm has come, as in the woods when the wind stops and the leaves are quite suddenly still.

This woman is very lovely, faded though she appears, and sepulchral in her paleness. They gaze at each other; and their eyes seem to carry a flood of messages, a thousand age-old thoughts, confused and deep. At last

PRISCILLA

begins:

I was in the last room of the baths, and I was falling asleep to the sound of the buzzing streets.

Suddenly I heard an uproar. They were shouting: 'He's a magician! he's the Devil!' And the crowd stopped outside our house, opposite the temple of Esculapius. I pulled myself up by the wrists to the level of the ventilator.

On the peristyle of the temple, there was a man wearing an iron collar round his neck. He took live coals from a brazier, and he was scoring great streaks on his chest, calling out 'Jesus, Jesus!' People were saying: 'That's not allowed! Stone him!' Still he went on. It was indescribable, ecstatic. Flowers as big as the sun revolved in front of my eyes, and I heard a golden harp vibrating in space. Light waned. My arms let go of the bars, my body gave way, and when he had taken me to his house...

ANTONY

But who are you talking about?

PRISCILLA

Why, Montanus!

ANTONY

He's dead, Montanus.

PRISCILLA

That's not true!

A VOICE

No, Montanus is not dead!

Antony turns round; and next to him on the bench, on the other side, a second woman is sitting – blonde, even paler than the first, with a puffiness under the eyelids as if she has spent a long time crying. Without his questioning her, she says:

MAXIMILLA

We were coming back from Tarsus across the mountains, when at a turning in the road we saw a man under a figtree.

He cried from a distance: 'Stop!' and bore down on us, shouting abuse. The slaves rushed up. He burst out laughing. The horses reared. The mastiffs were all howling.

He stood upright. Sweat ran from his face. The wind made his coat flap.

Calling us by our names, he scolded us for the vanity of our works, the vileness of our bodies – and he raised his fist towards the dromedaries because of the silver bells they wear under their jaws.

His fury filled me with deep and physical dread; but it was also like something voluptuous rocking and intoxicating me.

First, the slaves came forward. 'Master,' they said, 'our beasts are tired;' then it was the women: 'We're frightened,' and the slaves went away. Then the children began to cry: 'We're hungry!' And as the women had got no answer, they disappeared.

He talked on. I sensed someone next to me. It was my husband; I was listening to the other. He dragged himself among the stones crying out: 'You abandon me?' and I answered: 'Yes! Go away!' – in order to go with Montanus.

ANTONY

A eunuch!

PRISCILLA

Ah! You're surprised, you man of coarse feeling! But Magdalene, Joanna, Martha and Susan never went into the Saviour's bed. Souls, better than bodies, can deliriously embrace. To keep Eustolium with impunity, Bishop Leontius mutilated himself – preferring his love to his virility. Besides, it's not my fault. A spirit compels me to it. Sotas couldn't cure me, cruel though he is. What does it matter! I am the last of the prophetesses; and after me, the end of the world will come.

MAXIMILLA

He has plied me with presents. No woman, indeed, loves him better, or is better loved in return!

PRISCILLA

You're lying! I come first!

MAXIMILLA

No, I do!

They fight.
Between their shoulders appears the head of a negro.

MONTANUS

covered in a black cloak fastened with two human bones:

Quiet now, my doves! Incapable of earthly happiness, through this union we enjoy spiritual plenitude. After the Father's era, the era of the Son; and I inaugurate the third, that of the Paraclete, whose light came to me during the forty nights that the celestial Jerusalem shone in the firmament, above my house, at Pepuza.

Ah! How wildly you scream when the thongs flog you! How your sore limbs are bared to my vigorous strokes! How you pant on my chest, with a love that cannot be realised! It's so strong that worlds have been opened to you, and you can now perceive souls with your eyes.

Antony makes a gesture of astonishment.

TERTULLIAN

back again beside Montanus:

No doubt, since the soul has a body – what has no body having no existence.

MONTANUS

To make it more subtle, I have instituted a number of mortifications, three Lenten fasts a year, and nightly prayers in which the mouth is kept shut – for fear the escaping breath might tarnish the thought. One must abstain from second weddings, or rather from all marriage! Angels have sinned with women.

THE ARCHONTICS

in hair cilices:

The Saviour said: 'I have come to destroy the works of Woman.'

THE TATIANIANS

in rush cilices:

She is the tree of evil – she! The skin clothing is our body.

And, as he goes on in the same direction, Antony meets

THE VALESIANS

stretched on the ground, with red patches at the base of their stomachs, under their tunics.
They present him with a knife:

Do like Origen and like us! Is it the pain you fear, coward? Is it love of your own flesh that holds you back, hypocrite?

And while he stands staring at them as they flounder, stretched on their backs in puddles of blood,

THE CAINITES,

their hair knotted by a viper, pass close to him vociferating in his ear:

Glory to Cain! Glory to Sodom! Glory to Judas!
Cain made the race of the strong. Sodom appalled all earth with its punishment; and it was through Judas that God saved the world – yes, Judas! without him, no death and no redemption!

They disappear under a horde of

CIRCUMCELLIONS

dressed in wolf-skins, crowned with thorns, and carrying iron clubs:

Crush the fruit! Muddy the spring! Drown the child! Plunder the rich man who sits back happily and eats his fill! Beat the poor man who covets the donkey's blanket, the dog's food, the bird's nest, and who whines because others are not wretches like himself.

We Saints, to hurry the end of the world, we go poisoning, burning, massacring!

Martyrdom is the only salvation. We make each other martyrs. We pull the skin off our scalps with pincers, we stretch ourselves under the plough, we fling ourselves into the oven mouth!

Curse baptism! Curse the eucharist! Curse marriage! Universal damnation!

And now, across the whole basilica, redoubled frenzy breaks out.

The Audians shoot arrows at the Devil; the Collyridians toss blue veils up to the ceiling; the Ascites bow down before a wine-skin; the Marcionites baptise a dead man with oil. Next to Apelles a woman, the better to explain her idea, exhibits a round loaf in a bottle; another in the middle of the Sampsenes distributes, as if it were the host, the dust from her sandals. On the Marcosians' rose-strewn bed two lovers embrace. The Circumcellions cut each other's throats, the Valesians lie gasping, Bardesanes chants, Carpocrates dances, Maximilla and Priscilla moan resoundingly – and the false prophetess of Cappadocia, quite naked, resting her elbows on a lion and waving three torches, howls the Terrible Invocation.

The columns sway like tree-trunks, the amulets round the heretics' necks criss-cross in fiery lines, the constellations in the chapels quiver, and the walls give way to the coming and going of the crowd, whose every head is a wave which leaps and roars.

But then – from the very heart of the uproar, with bursts of laughter – a song rises in which the name of Jesus recurs.

These are plebeian folk, all beating their hands to mark time. In the middle of them is

ARIUS

in deacon's costume.

The fools who rail against me claim to explain the absurd; and to leave them quite at a loss I've composed some little poems, so funny that people know them off by heart in the mills and the taverns and the ports.

A thousand times no! The Son is not co-eternal with the Father, nor of the same substance! Otherwise he would not have said: 'Father, take this cup away from me! – Why do you call me good? God alone is good! – I go to my God, to your God!' and other words bearing witness to his creaturely quality. This is proved, besides, by all his names: lamb, shepherd, fountain, wisdom, son of man, prophet, true way, cornerstone!

SABELLIUS

But I maintain that the two are identical.

ARIUS

The Council of Antioch decided to the contrary.

ANTONY

What then is the Word?... What was Jesus?

THE VALENTINIANS

He was the bridegroom of the repentant Acharamoth!

THE SETHIANS

He was Shem, son of Noah!

THE THEODOTIANS

He was Melchisedech!

THE MERINTHIANS

He was nothing but a man!

THE APOLLINARISTS

He assumed the appearance of man! He simulated the Passion.

MARCELLUS OF ANCYRA

He develops from the Father!

POPE CALIXTUS

Father and Son are the two modes of a single God!

METHODIUS

He was first in Adam, then in man!

CERINTHUS

And he will rise again!

VALENTINE

Impossible – since his body is celestial!

PAUL OF SAMOSATA

He is God only since his baptism!

HERMOGENES

He lives in the sun!

And all the heretics encircle Antony, who is crying, his head in his hands.

A JEW

with a red beard, his skin spotted with leprosy, steps up close to him – sniggering horribly:

His soul was Esau's soul! He suffered from the Bellero-phontian disease; and his mother, the perfume-seller, gave herself to Pantherus, a Roman soldier, on some sheaves of maize, one evening in harvest-time.

ANTONY

sharply lifts his head, looking at them without speaking; then walking straight up to them:

Doctors, magicians, bishops and deacons, men and ghosts, back with you! back! You are all lies!

THE HERETICS

We have martyrs more martyrs than yours, we have harder prayers, higher flights of love, ecstasies quite as long.

ANTONY

But no revelation! no proofs!

At that they all brandish in the air rolls of papyrus, wooden tablets, pieces of leather, strips of cloth – jostling against each other:

THE CERINTHIANS

Here is the Gospel of the Hebrews!

THE MARCIONITES

The Saviour's Gospel!

THE MARCOSIANS

The Gospel of Eve!

THE ENCRATITES

The Gospel of Thomas!

THE CAINITES

The Gospel of Judas!

BASILIDES

The treatise of the soul's advent!

MANES

The prophecy of Barcouf!

Antony struggles, breaks free from them—and he sees, in a shadowy corner,

THE OLD EBIONITES

desiccated like mummies, dull-eyed, their eyebrows white.
In a shaky voice they say:

We knew him, we did, we knew him, the carpenter's son! We were the same age as him, we lived in his street. He used to play at modelling little birds out of mud, and without fear of the cutting edges helped his father with his work, or put together balls of dyed wool for his mother. Then he made a journey to Egypt from which he brought back great secrets. We were in Jericho when he came to find the locust-eater. They talked in hushed voices, and no one could overhear them. But it was from that time on that he made a stir in Galilee and that so many stories were spread about him.

Doddering they repeat:

We knew him, we did, we knew him!

ANTONY

Ah! Tell me more! Tell me! What was his face like?

TERTULLIAN

Fierce and forbidding – for he had taken upon himself all the crimes, all the pains, and all the deformities of the world.

ANTONY

Oh, no! no! I imagine him, on the contrary, filled with superhuman beauty.

EUSEBIUS OF CAESAREA

There is actually at Paneas, close to an old hovel, in a tangle of grasses, a stone statue – put up, so it's claimed, by the haemorrhoidal woman. But time has eaten away the face, and the rains have spoilt the inscriptions.

A woman emerges from the group of Carpocratians.

MARCELLINA

I was once a deaconess at Rome in a little church, where I would let the faithful see silver images of Saint Paul, Homer, Pythagoras and Jesus Christ.

I've kept only his.

She pulls open her cloak.

Would you like it?

A VOICE

He reappears, he himself, when we call him! This is the time! Come!

And Antony feels on his arm the pressure of a brutal hand, dragging him along.

He climbs a completely dark stairway – and after many steps, he arrives before a door.

Then the man leading him (is it Hilarion? he can't tell) whispers in another's ear: 'The Lord will come' – and they are shown into a room, low-ceilinged and bare of furniture.

What first impresses him is a long blood-coloured chrysalis just opposite, with a man's head from which light-rays are streaming, and the word *Knouphis*, written all around in Greek. It rises above the shaft of a column placed in the middle of a pedestal. On the other walls of the room there are polished iron medallions representing animals' heads: those of an ox, a lion, an eagle, a dog, and the ass's head – again!

The clay lamps hanging underneath these images cast a flickering light. Through a hole in the wall Antony catches sight of the moon, shining far away on the water, and he even distinguishes the little regular lappings and the dull sound of a ship's keel tapping against the stones of a pier.

Men squatting with their faces in their cloaks let out at intervals a sort of muffled bark. Women sleep with their foreheads laid on both arms and with their knees propping them up, so lost in their veils that they could be taken for heaps of rags along the wall. Beside them half-naked children, quite eaten up by vermin, stare idiotically at the burning lamps. No one does anything – except wait for something.

They talk in low voices about their families, or pass on to each other cures for their diseases Several will embark at first light, the persecution having become too severe. The pagans, all the same, are not hard to hoodwink. 'They believe, the fools, that we worship Knouphis!'

But one of the brothers, suddenly inspired, sets himself in front of the column, where a loaf of bread has been put on top of a basket filled with fennel and birthwort.

The others have taken their places, standing in three parallel lines.

THE INSPIRED MAN

unrolls a placard covered with intertwined cylinders, and begins:

On the darkness the ray of the Word descended, and there was loosed a violent cry, like the voice of light.

ALL

with swaying bodies answer:

Kyrie eleison!

THE INSPIRED MAN

And afterwards, man was created by the infamous God of Israel, with the help of these:

Indicating the medallions,

Astophaios, Oraios, Sabaoth, Adonai, Eloi, Lao!

And he lay on the mud, hideous, feeble, shapeless, without thought.

ALL

in a plaintive tone:

Kyrie eleison!

THE INSPIRED MAN

But tender-hearted Sophia quickened him with a particle of her soul.

Then, seeing that man was so beautiful, God was seized with anger. He imprisoned him in his kingdom, forbidding him the tree of knowledge.

The other, once again, came to his help! She sent the serpent, who by long roundabout ways made him disobey that law of hate.

And man, when he had tasted knowledge, understood heavenly things.

ALL

strongly:

Kyrie eleison!

THE INSPIRED MAN

But Ialdabaoth, to revenge himself, precipitated man into matter, and the serpent with him!

ALL

very low:

Kyrie eleison!

They shut their mouths and are then silent.

The smells of the port mix in the hot air with the smoke from the lamps. Their wicks, which splutter, are about to go out; long mosquitoes circle. And Antony chokes with anguish; he senses some kind of monstrosity floating around him, some awful crime about to be committed.

But

THE INSPIRED MAN

tapping his heel, snapping his fingers, shaking his head, intones in a furious rhythm, to the sound of cymbals and a high-pitched flute:

Come! come! come! come out of your cavern!

Swift runner without feet, firm captor without hands!

Sinuous as the rivers, orbicular as the sun, black with gold spots like the star-scattered firmament! Like twists of the vine and like convoluting entrails!

Unbegotten! eater of earth! for ever young! perspicacious! honoured at Epidaurus! beneficial to man! healer of King Ptolemy, the soldiers of Moses and Glaucus son of Minos!

Come! come! come! come out of your cavern!

ALL

repeat:

Come! come! come! come out of your cavern!

However, there is nothing to be seen.

Why? what's the matter with him?

There is consultation, means are proposed.

One old man offers a piece of turf. An upheaval now occurs in the basket. The greenery quivers, flowers fall – and the head of a python appears.

It passes slowly along the edge of the bread, as if a circle were rotating around an immobile disc, and then stretches, uncoils; it is enormous and of great weight. To stop it from brushing the ground, men hold it against their chests, women over their heads, children at arms' length – and its tail, emerging through the hole in the wall, reaches down indefinitely to the bottom of the sea. Its coils multiply, fill the room; they enclose Antony.

THE WORSHIPPERS

glue their mouths to its skin, grabbing from each other the bread it has bitten.

It's you! it's you!

Set up first by Moses, broken by Hezekiah, restored by the Messiah. He had drunk you in the waves of baptism; but you left him in the Garden of Olives, and then he felt all his weakness.

Twisted round the arms of the cross, up above his head, you slavered on the crown of thorns, you watched him die. For you are not Jesus, not you – you are the Word! you are the Christ!

Antony faints with horror, and falls on the splinters of wood in front of his cabin, where the torch which has slipped from his hand is gently burning.

The shock makes him open his eyes, and he sees the Nile, clear and undulating in the white moonshine, like a great serpent in the middle of the sands – so much so that hallucination again grips him, he has never left the Ophites; they surround him, call to him, cart baggage along, go down to the port. He embarks with them.

An uncertain time passes.

And then a prison vault shuts him round. Bars face him, black lines on a blue background – and close by, in the shadows, people crying and praying are surrounded by others who exhort and console them.

One might guess at the buzz of a crowd outside, and the gorgeousness of a summer day.

Strident voices hawk melons, water, iced drinks, grass cushions on which to sit. From time to time comes a burst of clapping. He hears steps overhead.

Suddenly there starts up a prolonged roaring, loud and cavernous like the noise of water in an aqueduct.

And opposite him, caged behind more bars, he sees a lion walking about – then a line of sandals, naked legs and purple fringes. Beyond come gradually widening rings of people in symmetrical tiers, from the lowest enclosing the arena to the highest where masts rise up to support a hyacinth sail, taut in the air on its ropes. Stairs radiating towards the centre cut into the great circles of stone at regular intervals. Their steps disappear under seated people, knights, senators, soldiers, plebeians, vestals and courtesans, in woollen hoods, silk maniples, tawny tunics, with jewelled aigrettes, plumy panaches, lictor's fasces; and all this – swarming, shouting, tumultuous and furious, like a huge bubbling cauldron, makes him giddy. In the middle of the arena, on an altar, a vase of incense smokes.

So the people who surround him are Christians condemned to the beasts. The men wear the red coat of pontiffs of Saturn, the women the fillets of Ceres. Their friends share out any shreds of their clothing, any rings. To gain entry to the prison they had to give away, they say, a lot of money. Never mind! they mean to stay to the end.

Among these consolers Antony notices a bald man in a black tunic whose face is already familiar from somewhere; he tells them of the nullity of the world and the felicity of the elect. Antony is carried away with love. He longs for the chance to pour out his life for the Saviour, not knowing whether he may not himself be one of these martyrs.

But all of them, except for a long-haired Phrygian who keeps his arms raised, are looking sad. An old man sobs on a bench and a young man stands and dreams, hanging his head.

THE OLD MAN

was unwilling to pay up, at the angle of a crossroads, before a statue of Minerva; and he considers his companions with a look which means:

You should have helped me! Communities do sometimes manage to be left alone. Several of you have even got hold of those letters falsely declaring that a person has sacrificed to idols.

He asks:

Wasn't it Peter of Alexandria who ruled what you must do if you break down under torture?

Then, to himself:

Ah! it's very hard at my age! my infirmities make me so weak! All the same, I could still have lived until next winter!

The memory of his little garden touches him – and he looks towards the altar.

THE YOUNG MAN

who has disturbed a feast of Apollo with his blows, murmurs:

After all, it was up to me, I could have run away into the mountains!

– The soldiers would have caught you,

says one of the brothers.

– Oh! I'd have done what Cyprian did; I'd have come back; and the second time, I'd have had more strength, of course!

And now he thinks about the countless days he should have lived, about all the joys he won't have known – and he looks towards the altar.
But

THE MAN IN THE BLACK TUNIC

hurries up to him:

It's a scandal! What, you, an elected victim? All those women looking at you, think of that! And then God, just sometimes, performs a miracle. Pionius made the hands of his executioners go numb, the blood of Polycarp put out the flames of his pyre.

He turns to the old man:

Father, father! you must edify us by your death. To put it off would no doubt mean committing some bad action, which would spoil the fruit of the good ones. God's power, besides, is infinite. Perhaps your example will convert the whole people.

And in the opposite cage, the lions walk up and down without stopping, in continuous rapid movement. The largest suddenly looks at Antony – and roars, with steaming throat.

The women are huddled against the men.

THE CONSOLER

goes from one to the other.

What would you say, or you, if you were to be burnt with iron plates, if horses were to drag you into four quarters, if your body smeared with honey were eaten up by flies! You'll merely die like a hunter surprised in a wood.

Antony would rather all that than the horrible wild beasts; he thinks he can feel their teeth, their claws, can hear his bones cracking under their jaws.

A keeper comes into the prison; the martyrs tremble.

Only one is impassive: the Phrygian, who has been praying apart. He has burnt down three temples; and he goes forward with raised arms, open-mouthed and his head in the air, seeing nothing, like a somnambulist.

THE CONSOLER

cries out:

Keep back! keep back! The spirit of Montanus might seize you.

ALL

recoil, clamouring:

Damnation to the Montanist!

They insult him, spit on him, want to beat him.

The lions rear and bite their manes. The people howl: 'To the beasts! to the beasts!'

Bursting into sobs, the martyrs hold each other tight. A cup of narcotic wine is offered to them. They pass it from hand to hand, eagerly.

Another keeper waits for the signal by the door of the cage. It opens; a lion comes out.

It crosses the arena, with big oblique steps. Behind it, in single file, the other lions appear, then a bear, three panthers, some leopards. They disperse like a herd in a meadow.

The crack of a whip echoes. The Christians falter – and, to put an end to it, their brothers give them a push. Antony shuts his eyes.

Opening them, he is wrapped in deep shadows.

But soon they lighten; and he makes out an arid plain with nipple-like hillocks, similar to those that are seen around abandoned quarries.

Here and there, a clump of shrubs grows low among the flagstones; and white forms, hazier than clouds, hover over them.

Others softly appear. Eyes shine in the slits of long veils. By the nonchalance of their step and their wafting scents, Antony identifies these women as patricians. There are also men, but of inferior rank, for their faces are at once naïve and coarse.

ONE OF THE WOMEN

breathing deeply:

Ah! how good the cold night air is, here among the graves! I'm so tired of soft beds, bustling days, oppressive sun!

Her maid-servant takes a torch from a cloth bag and sets it alight. Other torches are lit from it, and the faithful go and place them on the tombs.

A WOMAN

panting:

Ah! here I am at last! But what a nuisance to have married an idolator!

ANOTHER

Prison visits, meetings with our brothers, all of it is suspect to our husbands! We even have to hide when we cross ourselves – they might take it for a magical spell.

ANOTHER

With mine, it was quarrels every day; I wouldn't submit to his constant abuse of my body – and to revenge himself, he has had me prosecuted as a Christian.

ANOTHER

Do you remember Lucius, such a beautiful young man, whom they dragged by the heels behind a chariot, like Hector, from the Esquilean door to the mountains of Tibur – and the blood stained the bushes on either side of the road! I've collected drops of it. Here!

She pulls from between her breasts a blackened sponge, covers it with kisses, then throws herself on the flagstones, screaming:

Ah! my friend! my friend!

A MAN

It's just three years today since Domitilla died. She was stoned at the far end of the woods of Proserpina. I've collected her bones which shone like glow-worms in the dark. Now the earth covers them!

He throws himself on a tomb.

O my betrothed! my betrothed!

AND ALL THE OTHERS

across the plain:

O sister! O brother! O daughter! O mother!

They are on their knees, their heads in their hands, or lying flat on the ground, both arms stretched out – and their heaving chests almost burst with the sobs they stifle. They look up to the sky, saying:

Pity their souls, O God! They pine in the dwelling-place of shades; grant them admission to the Resurrection, let them enjoy your light!

Or, their eyes fixed on the flagstones, they murmur:

Be still now, don't suffer! I've brought you wine, and meat!

A WIDOW

Here is some pultis I've made just to his liking, with plenty of eggs and a double measure of flour! We'll eat it together, as we used to, won't we?

She lifts a little to her lips; and suddenly she starts to laugh in an extravagant, frenetic way.

The others, like her, snatch a mouthful, take a sip or two.

They tell each other their own stories of martyrdom; grief becomes exalted, the libations redouble. Their swimming eyes fasten on each other. They stutter with drunkenness and desolation; little by little, their hands touch, their lips join, the veils fall open, and they come together on the tombs between the cups and the torches.

The sky begins to whiten. Mist dampens their clothes; and they part – looking as if they had never met, going cross-country along different paths.

The sun shines; the grass has grown taller, the plain is transformed.

And through bamboos Antony distinctly sees a forest of columns, bluish grey. These are tree-trunks all stemming from a single trunk. From each of its branches, down come more, burying themselves in the soil; and this mass of horizontal and vertical lines, indefinitely multiplied, might be likened to some monstrous construction, were it not for a small fig here and there, between blackish leaves not unlike a sycamore's.

He glimpses clusters of yellow flowers among the forking branches, as well as violet-coloured flowers and ferns like birds' feathers.

Under the lowest boughs can be seen every so often a hartebeest's horns, or the bright eyes of an antelope; parrots perch, butterflies flutter, lizards slither, flies buzz; and within the silence, deep down, there seems to sound a palpitating life.

At the entrance of the wood, on a kind of pyre, is something strange – a man – smeared with cowdung,. completely naked, drier than a mummy; his joints form knots at the ends of his stick-like bones. He has bunches of shells in his ears, a very long face, and a nose like a vulture's beak. His left arm points straight into the air, ankylosed, stiff as a rod – and he has been there for so long that birds have built a nest in his hair.

Four fires are alight at the four corners of his pyre. The sun is exactly opposite. He gazes at it with wide open eyes. And without a glance at Antony:

Brahman of the banks of the Nile, what do you say?

Flames shoot out on all sides from the gaps between the timbers; and

THE GYMNOSOPHIST

goes on:

Like the rhinoceros I have sunk into solitude. I once lived in the tree behind me.

Indeed, the grooves in the large figtree afford a natural man-sized cavity.

And I fed on flowers and fruit, with such observance of the precepts that not even a dog ever saw me eat.

Since existence stems from corruption, corruption from desire, desire from sensation, sensation from contact, I fled all action, all contact. And keeping as still as the stele of a tomb – letting my breath out through both nostrils, looking fixedly at my nose, considering the ether in my spirit, the world in my limbs, the moon in my heart – I reflected on the essence of the great Soul from which continually stream, like sparks of fire, the principles of life.

At last I grasped through all beings the supreme Soul, and

through the supreme Soul all beings; and I managed to fit my own soul – within which I had shut my senses – into it.

I receive science straight from the sky, like the Chataka bird which quenches its thirst only in streams of rain.

By the very fact that I know a thing, that thing ceases to exist.

For me there is now no hope and no anxiety, no happiness, no virtue, neither night nor day, nor you, nor me – absolutely nothing.

Through my appalling austerities I have surpassed the Powers. One contraction of my thought can kill a hundred kings' sons, dethrone the gods, cause the world's upheaval.

All this he has said in a monotonous voice.

The surrounding flowers curl up on themselves. Rats on the ground run off.

He slowly lowers his eyes towards the now mounting flames, and adds:

I have become disgusted with form, disgusted with perception, disgusted with knowledge itself – because thought does not survive the fleeting impulse that causes it, and mind is an illusion like the rest.

Everything begotten will die, everything dead must live again; beings now vanished will inhabit still unformed matrixes and will come back to earth, in pain, to serve other creatures.

But as I have revolved through an infinite quantity of existences in the guise of gods, men and animals, I renounce the journey, I want no more of this exhaustion! I am abandoning the dirty inn of my body walled up with flesh, red with blood, covered with hideous skin, full of filth – and as my reward I shall at last sleep in the depth of the absolute, in Annihilation.

The flames reach up to his chest – then wrap round him. His head protrudes as if through a hole in a wall. His staring eyes never blink.

ANTONY

rises.

The torch has set fire to the splinters of wood on the ground; and the flames have singed his beard.

Screaming, Antony tramples on the fire – and when there is nothing left but a heap of cinders:

But where is Hilarion? He was here just now.

I saw him!

Oh, no, it's impossible! I'm mistaken!

Why? . . . My cabin, these stones, the sand, perhaps they are all just as unreal. I'm going mad. Steady now! Where was I? What was it?

Ah! the gymnosophist! . . . That's a common death among Indian sages. Kalanos set fire to himself in front of Alexander; another did the same in Augustus's time. What a hatred of life one must have! Or are they driven by pride? . . . In any case, it's the dauntlessness of martyrs . . . And as for them, I now believe everything I was told about the debauchery they provoke.

And before that? Yes, I remember! the crowd of heretics . . . What screams! What eyes! But why such licence of the flesh, such aberrations of mind?

It's towards God they claim to travel, by all those paths! What right have I to condemn them, stumbling as I am on mine? When they disappeared I was perhaps about to learn something more. It was all whirling round too fast; I had no time to answer. Now it's as if there were more space and light in my brain. I'm calm. I feel able . . . What's that? I thought I'd put out the fire!

A flame flutters between the rocks; and soon a staccato voice is heard far off on the mountain.

Is it a hyena yelping, or some lost traveller's howls?

Antony listens. The flame draws nearer.

And he sees a woman coming forward crying, leaning on the shoulder of a white-bearded man.

She is covered in a tattered purple dress. Bare-headed like her, he wears a tunic of the same colour and carries a bronze vase from which leaps a little blue flame.

Antony is scared – and wonders who this woman is.

THE STRANGER (SIMON)

She's a young girl, a poor child, whom I take everywhere with me.

He raises the brazen vase.
Antony considers her, in the light of the flickering flame.
On her face are bite-marks, and along her arms traces of blows; her loose hair catches in her torn rags; her eyes seem insensitive to light.

SIMON

Sometimes she stays like this for a very long time, without talking or eating; then she wakes up – and comes out with marvellous things.

ANTONY

Really?

SIMON

Ennoia! Ennoia! Ennoia! tell us what you have to say!

She rolls her eyeballs as if emerging from a dream, slowly passes her fingers over both her eyebrows, and in a doleful voice:

HELEN (ENNOIA)

I remember a far land, the colour of emerald. One single tree is there.

Antony gives a start.

On each plane of its wide boughs a spirit-couple balances in the air. The branches around them intertwine, like the veins of the body; and they watch how eternal life circulates from the roots plunging into the shade to the peak that soars beyond the sun. I, on the second branch, lit up the summer nights with my face.

ANTONY

touching his forehead:

Ah! ah! I understand! in the head!

SIMON

his finger to his lips:

Shsh!...

HELEN

The sail was billowing, the keel cut the foam. He was saying: 'What do I care if I bring trouble to my country, if I lose my kingdom! You shall belong to me, in my own house!'

How enchanting the high room in his palace was! He would lie on the ivory bed stroking my hair and singing lovingly. At the end of the day I could pick out the two camps, the watch-lights being lit, Ulysses at the edge of his tent, Achilles fully armed driving a chariot along the seashore.

ANTONY

But she's totally mad! Why?...

SIMON

Shsh!...shsh!

HELEN

They greased me with ointments, and sold me to the people for their entertainment.

One evening I was standing with my cittern in my hand, making Greek sailors dance. The rain was like a cataract, hitting the tavern, and the cups of hot wine steamed. A man came in, though no door was open.

SIMON

It was I! I found you!

Here she is, Antony, she who is known as Sigeh, Ennoia, Barbelo, Prounikos! The Spirits governing the world were jealous of her and they fastened her in a woman's body.

She has been the Trojans' Helen, whose memory was cursed by the poet Stesichorus. She has been Lucretia, the patrician raped by three kings. She has been Delilah, cutting Samson's hair. She has been that daughter of Israel who gave herself to goats. She has loved adultery, idolatry, lies and folly. She has prostituted herself to every nation. She has sung at every crossroads. She has kissed every face.

At Tyre, a Syrian, she was mistress to thieves. She drank with them during the nights and hid assassins among the vermin of her warm bed.

ANTONY

So! what's that to me? ...

SIMON

furiously:

I bought her back, I tell you – and set her up again in her splendour; so much so that Caius Caesar Caligula fell in love with her, since he wanted to sleep with the Moon!

ANTONY

Well?...

SIMON

But she herself is the Moon! Didn't Pope Clement write that she was imprisoned in a tower? Three hundred people made a ring round the tower; and at each loophole at the same time the moon was seen to appear – although there are neither several moons in the world, nor several Ennoias!

ANTONY

Yes...I seem to remember...

And he falls into a reverie.

SIMON

Innocent as Christ, who died for men, she devotes herself to women. Jehovah's impotence is indeed demonstrated by Adam's transgression, and one must shake off the old law, antipathetic to the order of things.

I have preached renewal in Ephraim and in Issachar, along the torrent of Bizor, in the valley of Mageddo, even beyond the mountains in Bostra and Damascus! Let them come to me, those who are daubed with wine, those who are daubed with mud, those who are daubed with blood; and I shall wipe out their stains with the Holy Spirit called Minerva by the Greeks! She is Minerva! She is the Holy Spirit! I am Jupiter, Apollo, Christ, the Paraclete, the great power of God incarnate in the person of Simon!

ANTONY

Ah! so that's who you are! You!... But I know your crimes!

You were born at Gitta, near Samaria. Dositheus, your first master, expelled you! You loathe Saint Paul for having converted one of your women; and defeated by Saint Peter, you flung into the water, in rage and terror, your sackful of tricks!

SIMON

Would you like them?

Antony looks at him – and an inner voice whispers deep down: 'Why not?'

Simon goes on:

He who knows the forces of Nature and the substance of the Spirits will perform miracles. Such is the dream of all wise men – and your consuming desire; admit it!

Surrounded by Romans, I flew so high in the circus that I wasn't seen again. Nero ordered me to be beheaded; but it was a lamb's head that fell to the ground instead of mine. At last I was buried alive; but I came to life again on the third day. For proof, here I am!

He offers his hands to be sniffed. They smell of corpse. Antony recoils.

I can make bronze serpents move, marble statues laugh, and dogs talk. I shall show you a huge quantity of gold; I shall set up kings, you shall see nations adoring me! I can walk on clouds and water, pass through mountains, appear as a young man or an old, a tiger or an ant, take your face, give you mine, conduct lightning. Do you hear it?

There are rolls of thunder, repeated flashes.

The voice of the Most High! 'For your God, the Eternal, is fire', and all creation is performed in spurts from this fire.

You shall thence receive your baptism – that second baptism announced by Jesus, which descended upon the apostles one stormy day when the window was open!

And shaking the flame with his hand, slowly, as if to sprinkle Antony:

Mother of mercy, you who uncover secrets, so that rest may befall us in the eighth house...

ANTONY

cries out:

Ah! if only I had some holy water!

The flame goes out, producing much smoke.
Ennoia and Simon have disappeared.

An extremely cold, opaque and fetid fog fills the atmosphere.

ANTONY

stretching out his arms like a blind man:

Where am I? . . . I'm frightened of falling into the abyss. And the cross, of course, is too far away from me . . . Ah, what a night! what a night!

A gust of wind makes the fog break open – and he sees two men, clothed in long white tunics.

The first is tall, with a gentle face and a grave bearing. His fair hair, parted like Christ's, falls regularly down over his shoulders. He has thrown away a cane which he held in his hand, and his companion has caught it while making a bow in Oriental fashion.

The latter is short, fat, snub-nosed, thick-set, with frizzy hair and a naïve expression.

Both of them are barefoot, bare-headed and dusty, like people returning from a journey.

ANTONY

with a start:

What do you want? Speak up! Go away!

DAMIS

(This is the short man.)

There, there! . . . my good hermit! What do I want? I haven't a clue! Here's the Master.

He sits down; the other remains standing. Silence.

ANTONY

begins again:

So you've come? . . .

DAMIS

Oh, a long way – a very long way!

ANTONY

And you're going? . . .

DAMIS

pointing to the other:

Wherever he wants!

ANTONY

But who is he?

DAMIS

Look at him!

ANTONY

aside:

He looks like a saint! If I dared . . .

The smoke has gone. There is very clear weather. The moon shines.

DAMIS

What is it you're thinking, why don't you say something?

ANTONY

I was thinking ... Oh, nothing.

DAMIS

goes up to Apollonius and walks round him several times with bent back, without lifting his head.

Master! It's a Galilean hermit who asks to know the origins of wisdom.

APOLLONIUS

Let him approach!

Antony hesitates.

DAMIS

Go on, approach him!

APOLLONIUS

in a booming voice:

Approach! You would like to learn who I am, what I do, what I think? isn't that so, child? ·

ANTONY

. . . If these things, that is, could contribute to my salvation.

APOLLONIUS

Rejoice! I shall tell them to you.

DAMIS

softly to Antony:

Who would have thought it! He must have recognised in you at first sight an extraordinary bent for philosophy. And I shall profit as well!

APOLLONIUS

I shall first tell you of the long road that I travelled to obtain the doctrine; and if you find in all my life one bad action, you must stop me – for he who has transgressed in his deeds will scandalise in his speech.

DAMIS

to Antony:

What a just man! eh?

ANTONY

Certainly, I believe he is sincere.

APOLLONIUS

On the night of my birth, my mother thought she saw herself picking flowers on the edge of a lake. There was a flash of lightning and she brought me into the world to the sound of swans singing in her dream.

Until I was fifteen I was plunged three times a day into the Asbadean fountain, whose water gives dropsy to perjurers; and my body was rubbed with cnyza leaves, to make me chaste.

One evening a Palmyrian princess came to find me, offering

me treasures which she knew to be in tombs. A hierodule from the temple of Diana cut her throat in despair with the sacrificial knife; and the governor of Cilicia, at the end of all his promises, cried out in front of my family that he would make me die; but it was he who died three days later, assassinated by the Romans.

DAMIS

to Antony, prodding him with his elbow:

Eh? didn't I tell you! what a man!

APOLLONIUS

For four years on end I kept the perfect silence of the Pythagoreans. The most unexpected pain drew not a gasp from me; and at the theatre, as I came in, people shunned me as if I were a ghost.

DAMIS

Would you too have done that?

APOLLONIUS

Once my time of trial was over I undertook to instruct the priests, who had lost the tradition.

ANTONY

What tradition?

DAMIS

Let him carry on! Be quiet!

APOLLONIUS

I have chatted with the Samaneans of the Ganges, with the astrologers of Chaldea, with the mages of Babylon, with the Gaulish Druids, with the sacerdotal negroes! I have scaled the fourteen mounts of Olympus, plumbed the lakes of Scythia, measured the size of the desert!

DAMIS

But it's true, all this! I was there!

APOLLONIUS

First I went as far as the Hyrcanian sea. I travelled all round it; and passing through the land of the Baraomats, where Bucephalus is buried, I came down to Niniveh. At the town gates I saw a man approaching.

DAMIS

Me – me! Good Master! I loved you at once! You were gentler than a girl and handsomer than a god!

APOLLONIUS

without hearing him:

He wanted to accompany me to act as an interpreter.

DAMIS

But you answered that you understood all languages and divined all thoughts. So then I kissed the hem of your coat, and started walking behind you.

APOLLONIUS

After Ctesiphon, we reached the territory of Babylon.

DAMIS

And the satrap screamed, seeing such a pale man!

ANTONY

aside:

What can it mean...

APOLLONIUS

The King received me standing, near a silver throne in a round hall studded with stars – and from the cupola there hung on hidden wires four great birds of gold, with both wings outstretched.

ANTONY

dreaming:

Are there such things on earth?

DAMIS

What a town it is, that Babylon! everybody there is rich! The houses, painted blue, have bronze doors as well as a stairway leading down to the river.

Drawing on the ground, with his stick,

Like that, you see? And then the temples, the squares, the baths, the aqueducts! The palaces are covered with copper! and the interiors, if you only knew!

APOLLONIUS

On the northern wall rises a tower which supports another, and a third, a fourth, a fifth – and there are still three more! The eighth is a chapel with a bed. No one goes into it except the woman chosen by the priests for the god Belus. The King of Babylon made it my lodging.

DAMIS

Nobody took any notice of me! So I was left on my own walking around the streets. I inquired about customs; I visited workshops; I inspected the big machines which bring water into the gardens. But it distressed me to be separated from the Master.

APOLLONIUS

At last we left Babylon; and by the light of the moon, suddenly we saw an empusa.

DAMIS

It's a fact! She jumped on her iron hoof; she neighed like a donkey; she galloped across the rocks. He shouted abuse at her; she vanished.

ANTONY

aside:

What are they driving at?

APOLLONIUS

At Taxilla, capital of five thousand fortresses, the King of the Ganges, Phraortes, showed us his guard of black men five cubits high, and in his palace gardens, under a green brocade pavilion, an enormous elephant which the queens were perfuming for fun. It was Porus's elephant, which had run away after the death of Alexander.

DAMIS

And which was found in a forest.

ANTONY

They talk as freely as if they were drunk.

APOLLONIUS

Phraortes made us sit down at his table.

DAMIS

Such an odd country! While they drink, the lords entertain themselves by shooting arrows under the feet of a dancing child. But I don't approve...

APOLLONIUS

When I was ready to leave, the King gave me a parasol and he said to me: 'I have on the Indus a stud of white camels. When you no longer need them, blow in their ears. They will come back.'

Down by the river we went, walking at night by the glimmer of glow-worms shining in the bamboos. The slave whistled a tune to scare off snakes; and our camels had to crouch as they passed under the trees, as if under doors too low-set.

One day a black child holding a golden caduceus in his hand led us to the college of sages. Iarchas, their chief, talked to me of my ancestors, and of all my thoughts, all my actions, all my existences. He had been the river Indus, and he reminded me that I had steered boats on the Nile in the time of King Sesostris.

DAMIS

As for me, nothing was told me, so I don't know who I've been.

ANTONY

They look as vague as shadows.

APOLLONIUS

On the edge of the sea we met the Cynocephales gorged with milk, on their way back from their expedition to the island of Taprobane. Lukewarm waves dropped blonde pearls in front of us. Amber crackled under our feet. Skeletons of whales whitened in the cliffs' crevasses. The earth, in the end, became narrower than a sandal – and having thrown some drops of the Ocean at the sun, we turned right, to come back.

We came back through the Aromatic Country, the land of the Gangarides, the Comarian promontory, the district of the Sachalites, the Adramites and the Homerites – then, crossing the Cassanian mountains, the Red Sea and the island of Topazos, we penetrated into Ethiopia through the kingdom of the Pygmies.

ANTONY

aside:

How big the earth is!

DAMIS

And when we reached home, all the people we used to know were dead.

Antony hangs his head. Silence.

APOLLONIUS

goes on:

Then I began to be talked about in the world.

The plague was ravaging Ephesus; I had an old beggar stoned.

DAMIS

And the plague went!

ANTONY

Indeed! he drives away diseases?

APOLLONIUS

At Cnidos, I cured the man in love with the Venus.

DAMIS

Yes, a madman, who had even promised to marry her.— It's one thing to love a woman – but a statue, what nonsense! The Master laid a hand on the man's heart; his love was snuffed out at once.

ANTONY

What! he drives out demons?

APOLLONIUS

At Tarentum, a young girl who had died was being carried to the funeral pyre.

DAMIS

The Master touched her lips, and she sat up calling for her mother.

ANTONY

Indeed! he brings the dead to life?

APOLLONIUS

I predicted Vespasian would come to power.

ANTONY

What! he sees into the future?

DAMIS

There was at Corinth . . .

APOLLONIUS

Sitting at table with him, at the waters of Baia . . .

ANTONY

Strangers, excuse me, it's late!

DAMIS

A young man called Menippus.

ANTONY

No! no! go away!

APOLLONIUS

A dog came in, carrying in its mouth a severed hand.

DAMIS

One evening, in a suburb, he met a woman.

ANTONY

Don't you hear me? please leave!

APOLLONIUS

It prowled vaguely around the beds.

ANTONY

Enough!

APOLLONIUS

People chased it away.

DAMIS

So Menippus went to her house; they became lovers.

APOLLONIUS

Beating the mosaic with its tail, it deposited this hand on Flavius's knees.

DAMIS

But in the morning, in lessons at school, Menippus was pale.

ANTONY

umping up:

Still more! Oh, let them carry on, since there isn't...

DAMIS

The Master said to him: 'O beautiful young man, you caress a serpent; a serpent caresses you! When will you wed?' We all went to the wedding.

ANTONY

I'm wrong, of course, to listen to this!

DAMIS

From the entrance hall onwards, there were servants moving about and doors opening; but one could hear neither the sound of footsteps nor the sound of doors. The Master placed himself next to Menippus. At once the fiancée broke out in anger against philosophers. But the golden plate, the cup-bearers, the cooks, the pantlers disappeared; the roof flew off, the walls collapsed; and Apollonius was left standing on his own, with this woman at his feet all in tears. She was a vampire, who satisfied beautiful young men so as to eat their flesh – because nothing is better for these sorts of phantoms than lovers' blood.

APOLLONIUS

If you want to know the art ...

ANTONY

I don't want to know anything!

APOLLONIUS

The night we arrived at the gates of Rome ...

ANTONY

Oh, yes! tell me about the city of popes!

APOLLONIUS

A drunkard accosted us, singing in a soft voice. It was an epithalamion of Nero's; and he had the right to make anyone die who listened carelessly. He carried in a box on his back a string taken from the Emperor's cithara. I shrugged my shoulders. He threw mud in our faces. I undid my belt and placed it in his hand.

DAMIS

Well now, that was quite wrong of you!

APOLLONIUS

During the night the Emperor had me summoned to his house. He was playing at knuckle-bones with Sporus, his left elbow propped on an agate table. He turned round, drawing his fair eyebrows into a frown: 'Why don't you fear me?' he asked. – 'Because God who made you terrible made me intrepid,' I answered.

ANTONY

aside:

Something I can't explain appals me.

Silence.

DAMIS

begins again in a shrill voice:

The whole of Asia, for that matter, will tell you ...

ANTONY

with a start:

I'm ill! Leave me alone!

DAMIS

Listen to this. He saw, from Ephesus, the killing of Domitian, who was at Rome.

ANTONY

trying to laugh:

Who would have thought it!

DAMIS

Yes, in the theatre, in broad daylight, on the fourteenth of the October calends, he suddenly cried out: 'Caesar is being slaughtered!' and from time to time he added: 'He's rolling on the ground; oh! how he struggles! He's up; he's trying to run away; the doors are shut; ah! it's over! he's dead now!' And that very day, in fact, Titus Flavius Domitianus was assassinated, as you know.

ANTONY

Without the Devil's help ... certainly ...

APOLLONIUS

He wanted to make me die, this Domitian! On my orders Damis had fled, and I was left by myself in prison.

DAMIS

It was terribly bold, you must admit!

APOLLONIUS

At about the fifth hour, the soldiers took me to the tribunal. I had my harangue tucked under my coat, quite ready.

DAMIS

We were on the shore at Pozzuoli, the rest of us! We thought you were dead; we were crying. When at the sixth hour suddenly you appeared, and said to us: 'It is I!'

ANTONY

aside:

Like Him!

DAMIS

out loud:

Absolutely!

ANTONY

Oh no! you're lying, aren't you? you're lying!

APOLLONIUS

He came down from Heaven. I myself am ascending there – thanks to my virtue which has raised me to the height of the Principle!

DAMIS

Tyana, his native city, has instituted in his honour a temple with priests!

APOLLONIUS

comes closer to Antony and shouts in his ears:

Of course I know all the gods, all the rites, all the prayers, all the oracles! I have penetrated the cave of Trophonius, son of Apollo! I have kneaded the cakes for the Syracusan women to carry on the mountains! I have undergone the eighty ordeals of Mithra! I have pressed to my heart the serpent of Sabasius! I have received the scarf of the Cabiri! I have washed Cybele in the waters of the Campanian gulfs, and spent three moons in the caverns of Samothrace!

DAMIS

with a silly laugh:

Ah! ah! ah! among the mysteries of the Good Goddess!

APOLLONIUS

And now we must start the pilgrimage again!

We go north, to the land of swans and snow. On the white plain, the blind hippopods are breaking the ultramarine plant with the ends of their feet.

DAMIS

Come! it's dawn. The cock has crowed, the horse has neighed, the sail is ready.

ANTONY

The cock has not crowed! I hear the cricket in the sands, and I see the moon still in its place.

APOLLONIUS

We go south, behind the mountains and the great tides, to find in perfumes the reason for love. You will inhale the smell of the myrrhodion which causes the weak to die. You will bathe your body in the lake of rosy oil on the island of Junonia. You will see, asleep on primulas, the lizard which wakes every century when the carbuncle on its forehead matures and falls. Like eyes the stars pulsate, like lyres the cascades are in song, and intoxicating scents float up from the flowers; in the airy open your spirits will expand, within your heart and on your face.

DAMIS

Master! it's time! The wind is rising, the swallows wake, the myrtle leaf has blown away.

APOLLONIUS

Yes! we must go!

ANTONY

No! I shall stay!

APOLLONIUS

Shall I teach you where the Balis plant grows, which resuscitates the dead?

DAMIS

Ask him rather for the androdamas, which attracts silver, iron and bronze!

ANTONY

Oh! how I suffer! how I suffer!

DAMIS

You'll understand the voices of all creatures, the roaring and the cooing!

APOLLONIUS

I will make you ride on unicorns, on dragons, on hippocentaurs and dolphins!

ANTONY

is in tears.

Oh! oh! oh!

APOLLONIUS

You shall know the demons who live in the caverns, and those who talk in the woods, who move the waves, who drive the clouds.

DAMIS

Tighten your belt! Fasten your sandals!

APOLLONIUS

I will explain to you the reasons for the divine forms, why Apollo stands, Jupiter sits, why Venus is black at Corinth, square at Athens, conical at Paphos.

ANTONY

clasping his hands:

Let them leave! let them leave!

APOLLONIUS

I will tear off the armour of the gods in front of you, we will force the sanctuaries, you shall violate the Pythia!

ANTONY

Help me, Lord!

He makes a rush for the cross.

APOLLONIUS

What is your desire? your dream? In the time it takes for a wish...

ANTONY

Jesus, Jesus, come to my aid!

APOLLONIUS

Shall I make him appear, Jesus?

ANTONY

What! How?

APOLLONIUS

It will be he and none other! He will throw off his crown, and we shall talk face to face.

DAMIS

softly:

Say you're willing! Say you're willing!

Antony, at the foot of the cross, murmurs orisons. Damis circles round him, with wheedling gestures.

Come now, good hermit, dear Saint Antony! you man of purity, you illustrious man! a man who can't be too much praised! Don't be frightened; it's an exaggerated manner of speech, borrowed from the Orientals. It doesn't at all prevent...

APOLLONIUS

Let him be, Damis!
He believes, like a brute, in the reality of things. His terror of the gods prevents him from understanding them; and his own he degrades to the level of a jealous king!
You, my son, do not leave me!

He backs away towards the edge of the cliff, overshoots it, and stays suspended.

Above all forms, beyond earth, further than heaven, lies the world of Ideas, quite full of the Word! In one leap we shall cross the other space; and you shall grasp in its infinity the

Eternal, the Absolute, pure Being! – Come! give me your hand! move on!

The pair of them, side by side, lift into the air, quite gently.
Antony, embracing the cross, watches them rise.
They disappear.

V

ANTONY

walking about slowly:

He outdoes all hell!

Nebuchadnezzar dazzled me less. Not even the Queen of Sheba could charm me so profoundly.

His way of speaking about the gods makes one long to know them!

I recollect seeing several hundreds of them together on the island of Elephantine, in the time of Diocletian. The Emperor had granted a large land to the Nomads on condition they should guard the frontiers; and the treaty was concluded in the name of the 'Invisible Powers' – because each people was ignorant of the other's gods.

The Barbarians had brought theirs. They were occupying the sand-hills bordering the river. And there they could be seen holding their idols in their arms like big paralytic children; or steering between cataracts in a palm-trunk, showing off from a distance the amulets round their necks, the tattoos on their chests – all of which is no more criminal than the religion of the Greeks, the Asiatics and the Romans!

When I lived in the temple of Heliopolis, I used to examine everything on the walls: vultures holding sceptres, crocodiles plucking lyres, faces of men with snakes' bodies, cowheaded women bowing in front of ithyphallic gods; and their supernatural shapes carried me away to other worlds. I would have liked to know what they look at with those quiet eyes.

For matter to have so much power, it must contain a spirit. The souls of the gods are attached to their images ...

Those with seeming beauty might well seduce one. But the others . . . the abject or the terrible, how can one believe in them? ...

Just grazing the ground as they pass, he sees leaves, stones, shells, branches of trees, vague animal figures, and then what look like dropsical dwarfs; these are gods. He bursts out laughing.

More laughter starts up behind him; and Hilarion presents himself – dressed as a hermit, very much larger than before, colossal.

ANTONY

is not surprised to see him again.

How dumb one must be to worship all this!

HILARION

Oh, yes! extremely dumb!

Now idols of all nations and all ages file past them, made of wood, of metal, of granite, of feathers, of sewn skins.

The oldest ones, earlier than the Deluge, are hidden under seaweed which hangs down like a mane. A few, too tall for their bases, creak at the joints and break their backs as they walk. Others let sand trickle out through holes in their bellies.

Antony and Hilarion are enormously amused. They split their sides laughing.

Next follow sheep-shaped idols. They teeter on their knock-kneed legs, half-open their eyes and stammer like mutes: 'Bah! bah! bah!'

The more they approximate to human form, the more they irritate Antony. He hits out with his fists, kicks them, pitches into them.

They become quite frightful – with tall plumes, bulging ball-eyes, arms ending in claws, sharks' jaws.

And before these gods, men are slaughtered on stone altars; others are mashed in vats, crushed under chariots, nailed up in trees. One in particular, all of red-hot iron and with bull's horns, devours children.

ANTONY

The horror!

HILARION

But the gods always demand torture. Your own indeed wanted...

ANTONY

in tears:

Oh! don't go on, be quiet!

The enclosure of rocks changes into a valley. A herd of oxen grazes on the cropped grass.

The shepherd who drives them observes a cloud – and shrilly launches into the air some words of command.

HILARION

Since he needs rain, he tries with incantations to coerce the sky-god into opening the fertile clouds.

ANTONY

laughing:

What silly arrogance!

HILARION

Why do you perform exorcisms?

The valley becomes a lake of milk, immobile and limitless.

In the middle floats a long cradle, composed of the coils of a serpent whose heads all curve down together, shading a god asleep on its body.

He is young, beardless, lovelier than a girl and covered in diaphanous veils. The pearls on his tiara shine as softly as moons, a chaplet of stars makes several turns on his chest – and with one hand under his head, the other arm outstretched, he lies resting with a dreamy, intoxicated look.

A woman squatting at his feet waits for him to wake.

HILARION

It's the primordial duality of the Brahmans – no form being fit to express the Absolute.

From the god's navel a lotus stem has sprouted; and in the calyx there appears another god, with three faces.

ANTONY

Well, how ingenious!

HILARION

Father, Son and Holy Spirit likewise make up a single person!

The three heads move apart, and three large gods appear.

The first, who is pink, bites the end of his big toe.

The second, who is blue, waves four arms.

The third, who is green, wears a necklace of human skulls.

Opposite them three goddesses immediately spring up, the first wrapped in a net, the next offering a cup, the last brandishing a bow.

And these gods and goddesses proliferate and multiply. Their shoulders sprout arms, their arms end in hands holding banners, axes, shields, swords, parasols and drums. Fountains gush from their heads, grasses dangle from their nostrils.

Riding on birds, rocked in palanquins, enthroned on gold seats, upright in ivory niches, they dream, journey, command, drink wine, smell flowers. Dancers whirl, giants pursue monsters; at grotto entrances are solitaries, meditating. One cannot tell stars from eyeballs, clouds from banderoles; peacocks find refreshment in streams of gold dust, the embroidery of pavilions mixes with leopards' spots, coloured beams criss-cross on blue air together with arrows in flight and swinging censers.

And all this unfolds like a tall frieze – resting firmly against the rocks, and mounting up into the sky.

ANTONY

dazzled:

How many there are! What do they want?

HILARION

The one who scratches his abdomen with his elephant's trunk is the solar god, inspirer of wisdom.

That one with towers on his six heads and javelins in his fourteen arms is the prince of armies, the devouring Fire.

The old one astride a crocodile is going off to wash the souls of the dead on the shore. They will be tormented by that black woman with rotten teeth who rules the inferno.

The chariot drawn by red mares, driven by a legless coachman, is taking the master of the sun for a ride into the blue. The Moon-god accompanies him in a litter harnessed to three gazelles.

Kneeling on a parrot's back, the goddess of Beauty presents her round breast to Love, her son. There she is again, jumping for joy in the meadows. Look! look! With a dazzling mitre on her head she runs across corn and water, rises into the air, spreads herself everywhere!

Between these gods preside the genii of the winds, the planets, the months, the days, a hundred thousand besides! And they go under all manner of guises and are rapidly transformed. This one changes from a fish into a tortoise; he assumes a boar's head, a dwarf's shape.

ANTONY

What for?

HILARION

To re-establish equilibrium, to fight evil. But life exhausts itself, forms wear out; and they must progress in their metamorphoses.

Suddenly there appears

A NAKED MAN

sitting in the middle of the sand, cross-legged.

Poised behind him, a large halo quivers. The small curls of his hair, black with blue lights, cluster symmetrically around a protuberance on top of his skull. His very long arms run straight down his sides. His two hands rest, palms up, flat on his thighs. The undersides of his feet offer the image of two suns; and he stays completely still – facing Antony and Hilarion, with all the gods arranged in echelons around him on the rocks, as if on the steps of a circus.

His lips part; and in a deep voice:

I am the master of all alms, the helper of all creatures, and to believers and profane alike I expound the law.

To free the world I wished to be born among men. The gods wept when I left.

First I looked for a fitting woman: of military race, wedded to a king, very good, extremely beautiful, deep-navelled, with a body as firm as diamond; and at the time of the full moon, without the assistance of any male, I entered her belly.

I came out through the right side. The stars stopped.

HILARION

murmurs between his teeth:

'And when they saw the star stop, they were filled with great joy!'

Antony pays closer attention to

THE BUDDHA

who goes on:

From the depths of the Himalayas, a holy centenarian hurried to see me.

HILARION

'A man named Simeon, who should not see death, before he had seen the Christ!'

THE BUDDHA

They led me to the schools. I knew more than the doctors.

HILARION

'. . . In the midst of the doctors; and all that heard him were amazed at his wisdom.'

Antony makes a sign to Hilarion to be quiet.

THE BUDDHA

I meditated never-endingly in the gardens. The shadows of the trees circled; but the shadow of that which sheltered me did not.

No one could match me in knowledge of the scriptures, in enumerating atoms, in managing elephants, in wax-work, astronomy, poetry, pugilism, every exercise and every art!

To conform to custom, I took a wife – and I spent my days in my kingly palace, dressed in pearls, under a rain of perfumes, fanned by the fly-whisks of thirty-three thousand women, looking at my people from up high on my terraces ornamented with echoing bells.

But the sight of the world's miseries turned me away from pleasure. I fled.

I begged on the roads, covered in rags picked up from among the graves; and as there existed a very wise hermit, I wished to become his slave; I guarded his door, I washed his feet.

Every sensation was wiped out, every joy, every weakness.

Then, concentrating my thought in larger meditation, I came to know the essence of things, the illusion of forms.

I made short work of the science of the Brahmans. They are eaten up with greedy longing under their apparent austerity, rubbing themselves with filth and lying on thorns, expecting to reach happiness by way of death!

HILARION

'Pharisees, hypocrites, whited sepulchres, race of vipers!'

THE BUDDHA

I too have done astonishing things – eating no more than a single grain of rice a day, and the grains of rice in those days were no bigger than now: my hair fell out, my body turned black; my eyes, sunken into their sockets, looked like stars glimpsed at the bottom of a well.

For six years I never moved, exposed to flies, lions and snakes; fierce sun, floods of rain, snow, lightning, hail and wind, all this I surrendered to, without so much as sheltering myself with my hand.

Passing travellers thought me dead, and used to fling clods of earth at me from a distance!

The Devil had yet to tempt me.

I called him.

His sons came – hideous, covered in scales, with the stench of charnel-houses, howling and whistling and bellowing, clashing together pieces of armour and dead men's bones. Some of them spit flames through their nostrils, some make darkness with their wings, some wear strings of chopped-off fingers, some drink snake's venom from the hollow of their hands; their heads are those of pigs, rhinoceroses and toads, all kinds of shapes inspiring disgust and terror.

ANTONY

aside:

I once had to endure all that!

THE BUDDHA

Then he sent me his daughters – beautiful, well painted, with golden belts, teeth as white as jasmine, thighs as round as an elephant's trunk. Some of them yawningly stretch their arms, to show the dimples in their elbows; some wink, some start to laugh, some pull open their clothes. There are blushing virgins, matrons full of pride, queens with a big retinue of baggage and slaves.

ANTONY

aside:

Ah! he too?

THE BUDDHA

Having conquered the demon, I spent twelve years living exclusively on perfumes – and as I had acquired the five virtues, the five faculties, the ten forces, the eighteen substances, and penetrated into the four spheres of the invisible world, Understanding was mine! I became the Buddha!

All the gods bow down; those with several heads bend them simultaneously.

He raises a hand high in the air and resumes:

With a view to freeing all creatures, I have made hundreds and thousands of sacrifices! To the poor I have given robes of silk, beds, carriages, heaps of gold and diamonds! I have given my hands to the maimed, my legs to the lame, my eyes to the blind; I have cut off my head for the beheaded. At the time when I was king, I distributed provinces; at the time when I was a brahman, I despised nobody. When I was a solitary, I spoke kind words to the thief who cut my throat. When I was a tiger, I allowed myself to die of hunger.

And in this last existence, having preached the law, I have nothing more to do. The great period is accomplished! Men, animals, gods, bamboos, oceans, mountains, the grains of sand of the Ganges with the myriads and myriads of stars, all of it will die – and until the coming of fresh births, a flame will dance on the ruins of worlds laid waste!

Now the gods are seized with vertigo. They stagger, fall into convulsions, vomit out their existence. Their crowns shatter, their banners blow away. They tear off their attributes, their sexual parts, they throw over their shoulders the cups in which they drank immortality, strangle themselves with their snakes, faint away in smoke. And once everything has vanished...

HILARION

slowly:

You have just witnessed the belief of several hundred million men!

Antony is on the ground, his face in his hands. Standing next to him, turning his back on the cross, Hilarion watches him.
Time passes.
There then appears a singular being, with a man's head on a fish's body. He moves upright in the air, beating the sand with his tail – and this patriarch's figure with tiny arms makes Antony laugh.

OANNES

in a plaintive voice:

Respect me! I am coeval with all origins.

I have inhabited the amorphous world where hermaphrodite beasts lay slumbering in an atmosphere heavy and opaque, in the depths of dark waters – when finger, fin, and

wing were confounded, and headless eyes floated like mol-
luscs, among bulls with human faces and serpents with dogs'
paws.

Omoroca, bent like a hoop, stretched her woman's body
over this mass of creatures. But Belus cut her clean in two,
made the earth with one half, the sky with the other; and the
two matching worlds are in mutual contemplation.

I, first consciousness of Chaos, rose from the abyss to
harden matter, to define forms; and I taught humans the
history of the gods and how to fish, to sow, to write.

Since then I have lived in the pools left over from the
Deluge. But the desert encroaches all around them, the
wind scatters them with sand, the sun eats them up – and I am
dying on my bed of ooze, watching the stars through the
water. I must go back.

He jumps, and disappears into the Nile.

HILARION

An ancient god of the Chaldeans!

ANTONY

ironically:

What then were those of Babylon?

HILARION

You can see them!

And they find themselves on the platform of a quadrangular tower
overlooking six more towers, all narrowing as they rise so as to form a
monstrous pyramid. At the bottom can be detected a great black mass –
the town, no doubt – stretched across the plains. The air is cold, the sky
a sombre blue; stars in great profusion pulsate.

In the middle of the platform a white stone column stands erect.
Linen-robed priests come and go all around, their paths effectively
describing a moving circle; and with heads high they gaze at the stars.

HILARION

points out several to Saint Antony.

There are thirty principal ones. Fifteen face the earth's upper side, fifteen its lower. At regular intervals, one of them shoots from the upper regions to the lower, while another abandons the lower regions for the sublime.

Of the seven planets, two are benign, two bad, three ambiguous; here in the world, everything depends on these eternal fires. Omens can be drawn from their positions and their movements. And you are treading the most notable spot on earth – where Pythagoras and Zoroaster met. For twelve thousand years now, these men have been observing the stars so as better to know the gods.

ANTONY

The stars are not gods.

HILARION

Yes, say they! Because things pass away around us; while the sky, like eternity, is immutable!

ANTONY

But it must have a master.

HILARION

indicating the column:

Over there, Belus, the first ray, the Sun, the Male! – the Other, whom he impregnates, is under him!

Antony catches sight of a lamp-lit garden. He is in the middle of a crowd, in an avenue of cypresses. To right and left, little paths lead to cabins set up in a pomegranate wood fenced off by a trellis of reeds. Most of the men have pointed caps and robes as gaudy as peacocks' feathers. There are people from the North dressed in bearskins, nomads in brown woollen cloaks, pale Gangarides with long earrings; and ranks as well as nations have become confused, for sailors and stone-cutters are elbowing princes who sport carbuncled tiaras and tall canes with carved knobs. They all walk with dilated nostrils, drawn by the same desire.

From time to time, they step aside to make way for a long covered chariot pulled by oxen: or it's a donkey jolting on its back a woman bundled up in veils which vanishes likewise in the direction of the cabins.

Antony is scared; he would like to turn back. Nameless curiosity, however, drags him on.

At the foot of the cypresses, women are squatting in line on deer-skins, all wearing diadems of braided cords. A few of them, gorgeously dressed, call out aloud to passers-by. The more timid hide their faces under their arms, while behind them a matron, doubtless their mother, urges them on. Others with their heads wrapped in a black shawl, their bodies entirely naked, would seem from a distance to be statues of flesh. As soon as a man tosses some money into their laps, they get up.

Kisses are heard under the foliage – and sometimes a sharp scream.

HILARION

These are the virgins of Babylon prostituting themselves to the goddess.

ANTONY

What goddess?

HILARION

There she is!

And he shows him, right at the end of the avenue, on the threshold of an illuminated grotto, a block of stone representing a woman's sex-organ.

ANTONY

For shame! what an abomination to give a sex to God!

HILARION

You yourself picture him as a living person!

Antony finds himself in the dark.

He notices, up in the air, a luminous circle resting on horizontal wings.

This peculiar hoop passes like a loose belt around the waist of a little man who has a mitre on his head and carries a crown in his hand, the lower part of his body vanishing under large feathers spread out like a skirt.

This is

ORMUZ

the god of the Persians.

Hovering, he screams:

I'm frightened! I can see his jaws.

I had conquered you, Ahriman! But you begin again!

First you rebelled against me and put to death the eldest of creatures, Kaiomortz, the Man-Bull. Then you seduced the first human couple, Meschia and Meschiana; and you flooded hearts with darkness, you drove your battalions into the sky.

I had my own, the throng of stars; and I contemplated all the astral echelons spread out beneath my throne.

My son Mithra lived in a remote region. There he received souls and sent them out and rose each morning to dispense his riches.

The splendour of the firmament was reflected on earth. Fire flashed on the mountains – image of the other fire with which I had created all beings. To keep it unsoiled, the dead were not burnt. They were taken to heaven on the beaks of birds.

I had regulated the pastures, the ploughland, the wood for sacrifice, the shape of the cups, the words to be spoken in insomnia – and my priests were continually at prayer, so that their homage should be as eternal as divinity. Water was used for purification, loaves were offered on altars, crimes were confessed out loud.

Homa gave himself as a drink to men, to communicate his strength to them.

While the genii of the sky fought demons, the children of Iran pursued serpents. The King, whom an innumerable court served on its knees, represented my person and wore my head-dress. His gardens had the magnificence of a heavenly land; and his tomb pictured him slaughtering a monster – emblem of Good exterminating Evil.

For one day, thanks to limitless time, I was definitively to conquer Ahriman.

But the interval between the two of us is disappearing; night rises! Hurry, my Amschaspands, my Izeds, my Ferouers! Help me, Mithra! Take your sword! Caosyac, you who must come back to deliver the universe, defend me! What? ... No one!

Ah! I'm dying! Ahriman, you are master!

Hilarion, behind Antony, holds back a shout of joy – and Ormuz plunges into the dark.
Now comes

THE GREAT DIANA OF EPHESUS

black and enamel-eyed, her elbows by her sides, her forearms turned out, her hands open.

Lions crouch on her shoulders; fruits, flowers and stars criss-cross on her chest; below are three rows of breasts; and from her stomach to her feet she is caught in a narrow sheath, its whole length leaping with bulls, stags, griffins and bees. – She can be seen by the white glimmer of a silver disc, as round as the full moon, set behind her head.

Where is my temple?
Where are my amazons?

What is it I feel . . . I, the incorruptible, overcome with faintness!

Her flowers fade. Her fruits, overripe, drop off. The lions and bulls droop at the neck; the stags slaver with exhaustion; the bees die humming on the ground.

One after the other, she squeezes her breasts. Empty, all of them! But in a despairing effort her sheath splits. She lifts it up, like the panel of a dress, flings into it her animals and blooms – then retreats into obscurity.

And in the distance, voices are murmuring, rumbling, roaring, belling and bellowing. The night grows thick and breathy. Warm drops of rain are falling.

ANTONY

The fragrance of palm-trees, the rustling of green leaves, the transparency of spring-water – how good it is! I'd like to lie down flat, feeling the earth against my heart; and my life would be reimmersed in its eternal youth!

He hears a noise of castanets and cymbals – and in the middle of a rustic crowd come men dressed in white tunics with red bands, leading a richly harnessed donkey, its tail ornate with ribbons and its hooves painted.

A box covered with a yellow linen blanket joggles on its back between two baskets; one of these holds the offerings placed in it: eggs, grapes, pears and cheeses, poultry, small coins; and the second is full of roses, whose petals are scattered in front of the donkey by the drivers as they go.

They have pendants in their ears, large cloaks, plaited hair, painted cheeks; over each forehead an olive crown is fastened by means of a medallioned figurine; daggers are thrust into their belts; and they wave ebony-handled whips, whose three thongs are garnished with knuckle-bones.

The last in the cortege lower to the ground a great pine, straight as a candelabrum, which burns at the crown and whose nethermost boughs shelter a small sheep.

The donkey has stopped. The blanket is pulled off. Underneath is another wrapping of black felt. And now one man in his white tunic starts to dance, playing the crotals; another on his knees in front of the box beats the tambourine, and

177

THE OLDEST OF THE TROOP

begins:

Here is the Good-Goddess, Idean of the mountains, great Mother of Syria: Come close, honest folk!

She brings joy, cures the sick, sends bequests, and satisfies lovers.

Our task is to take her cross-country in good weather and bad.

Often we sleep in the open, and it's not every day that our table is well spread. Thieves live in the woods. Wild beasts leap from their caves. Slippery paths run alongside precipices. Here she is! here she is!

They take off the covering; and a box is revealed, encrusted with little stones.

Higher than the cedars, she soars in blue ether. Vaster than the wind, she surrounds the world. She breathes out through the nostrils of tigers; her voice growls under volcanoes, her anger is the storm; the paleness of her face has blanched the moon. She ripens the harvest, swells the rinds, makes your beards grow. Give her something, because she hates misers!

The box opens; and under a blue silk canopy can be glimpsed a little image of Cybele – glittering with spangles, crowned with towers and sitting in a red stone chariot drawn by two lions with raised paws.

The crowd pushes to see.

THE ARCHIGALLUS

continues:

She loves reverberating tympani, stampeding feet and howling wolves, echoing mountains and deep gorges, almond blossom, green figs and pomegranates, wild dancing, warbling flutes, sugary sap, salt tears – and blood! Here then, here! Mother of the mountains!

They flog themselves with their whips, landing smacking blows on their chests; the skin of the tambourines vibrates fit to burst. They take their knives and slash their arms.

She mourns; we must mourn! It is her pleasure that we should suffer! That way your sins will be forgiven. Blood washes all; fling drops of it, like flowers! She claims the blood of this other – who is pure!

The archigallus draws his knife on the sheep.

ANTONY

horrified:

Don't slaughter the lamb!

A crimson flood gushes out.
The priest sprinkles the crowd with it; and gathered round the burning tree all of them – including Antony and Hilarion – observe in silence the last palpitations of the victim.
From among the priests emerges a Woman – exactly resembling the image contained in the little box.
She stops at the sight of a Young Man wearing a Phrygian cap.
His thighs are clothed in tight breeches, pulled open here and there in regular lozenges knotted off by coloured bows. In a languorous pose he leans his elbow against a branch of the tree, holding a flute in his hand.

CYBELE

putting both arms round his waist:

I have scoured every district to find you again – and the countryside was ravaged by famine! You deceived me! It doesn't matter, I love you! Warm my body! Be one with me!

ATYS

Spring will not return, O everlasting Mother! For all my love, I cannot penetrate your essence. I wish I could put on a painted dress, like yours. I envy your breasts swollen with milk, the length of your hair, your broad hips from which come more beings. If only I were you! if only I were a woman! – No, never! Go away! My manhood makes me sick!

With a sharp stone he emasculates himself, then starts to run around furiously, waving in the air his severed organ.

The priests copy the god, the worshippers copy the priests. Men and women exchange their clothes, cling together – and this swirl of bleeding flesh moves away, while the voices, persisting, become shriller and more discordant, like those heard at funerals.

A large catafalque hung with purple carries aloft an ebony bed, surrounded by torches and silver filigree baskets full of green sprouting lettuces, mallow and fennel. On the steps, from top to bottom, sit women all dressed in black, their belts undone and their feet bare, looking melancholy as they hold big bunches of flowers.

On the ground at the corners of the platform alabaster urns full of myrrh slowly smoke.

Visible on the bed is the corpse of a man. Blood flows from his thigh. He lets his arm dangle – and a dog, howling, licks his fingernails.

The row of close-set torches hides his face from view; and Antony is gripped with anxiety. He is frightened he might recognise somebody.

The sobs of the women stop; and after an interval of silence,

ALL

together intone:

Beautiful! Beautiful! He is beautiful! Sleep no more, raise your head! Stand up!

Smell our flowers! they are narcissi and anemones picked in your gardens to please you. Come to yourself, don't frighten us!

Speak! What do you need? Will you drink wine? Will you lie in our beds? Will you eat honey loaves shaped like little birds?

Hug his hips, kiss his chest! There! there! Don't you feel

them, our fingers laden with rings running across your body, and our lips searching for your mouth, and our hair brushing your thighs, god in a swoon, deaf to our prayers!

They let out screams, tearing their faces with their fingernails, then fall silent – and the howls of the dog are still audible.

Alas! alas! Black blood flows across his snowy flesh! See how his knees are twisting, his ribs caving in. The flowers of his face have moistened the purple. He is dead! Weep! Mourn!

One after another they come and deposit between the torches their long tresses of hair, which from afar seem like black or blond snakes – and the catafalque is slowly lowered to the level of a grotto, a dark grave which yawns behind.

And now

A WOMAN

leans over the corpse.

Her hair, which she has not cut, wraps her round from head to foot. She sheds so many tears that her grief must be unlike that of the others, more than human, infinite.

Antony is reminded of the mother of Jesus.

She says:

Escaping from the East, you would take me all quivering with dew in your arms, O Sun! Doves fluttered on the blue of your cloak, our kisses made a breeze in the leaves; and I abandoned myself to your love, taking pleasure in my weakness.

Alas! alas! Why would you go coursing across the mountains?

A boar wounded you at the autumn equinox!

You are dead; and the springs weep, the trees bow down. The winter wind whistles in the bare brushwood.

My eyes shall close, now that darkness covers you, now that you live on the other side of the world near my more powerful rival.

O Persephone, all that is beautiful goes down to you, and does not come back!

While she has been talking, her companions have taken the corpse to lower it into the grave. It rubs off on their hands. It was nothing but wax.

Antony feels a sense of relief.

Everything vanishes – and the cabin, the rocks, and the cross are again visible.

Meanwhile he distinguishes on the other side of the Nile a Woman – standing upright in the desert.

In her hand she holds the lower edge of a long black veil which hides her face, while on her left arm she carries a little child which she suckles. Beside her a large ape squats on the sand.

She lifts her head towards the sky – and despite the distance her voice can be heard.

ISIS

O Neith, beginning of all things! Ammon, lord of eternity, Ptha the demiurge, Thoth his intelligence, gods of the Amenthi, distinct triads of the Nomes, sparrow-hawks in the blue, sphinx at the edge of the temples, ibis upright between the horns of oxen, planets, constellations, shores, murmuring winds, mirrored lights, tell me where I can find Osiris!

I have searched for him across every channel and every lake – and further still, as far as Phoenician Byblos. With pricked ears Anubis bounded around me, yapping and rummaging with his muzzle in the tamarind clumps. Thank you, good Cynocephalus, thank you!

She amicably gives the ape two or three little taps on the head.

The hideous red-haired Typhon had killed him, cut him up! We found all his parts. But I don't have the one which made me fertile!

She breaks out in shrill lamentations.

ANTONY

is suddenly furious. He flings stones at her, shouting abuse.

Shameless woman! clear off! clear off!

HILARION

Respect her! It was the religion of your forebears! you wore her amulets in your cradle.

ISIS

Long ago, when summer returned, the floods would drive unclean beasts into the desert. The dams gave way, boats were dashed together, the panting earth drank the river rapturously. You lay, bull-horned god, between my breasts – and the lowing of the everlasting cow was heard!

Sowing, reaping, threshing and vintage followed in regular succession, according to the alternation of the seasons. Great stars gave a radiance to nights permanently pure. The days were all bathed in equal splendour. Like a royal couple, the Moon and the Sun were visible on either side of the horizon.

We two were enthroned in a sublimer world, twin-monarchs married in the womb of eternity – he with a coucoupha sceptre in his hand, I with a lotus-flower sceptre, each of us upright, our hands joined – and the crumbling of empires could not change our attitude.

Egypt lay beneath us, monumental and serious, long as a temple corridor, with her obelisks on the right, her pyramids on the left, her labyrinth in the middle – and everywhere avenues of monsters, forests of columns, heavy pylons flanking gates always crowned with the earth's globe set between two wings.

The animals of her zodiac reappeared in her pastures, her

mysterious script was filled with their shapes and colours. Partitioned into twelve regions like the year into twelve months, each month and day having its god, she reproduced the immutable order of heaven; and man when he died did not disintegrate; but soaked with perfumes, made indestructible, he went and slept for three thousand years in a silent Egypt.

This one, larger than the other, stretched underground.

It was reached by stairways leading down to halls in which were pictured the joys of the good, the tortures of the wicked, and everything that takes place in the third invisible world. Ranged along the walls, the dead in painted coffins waited their turn; souls exempt from migrations continued in deep drowsiness until the stirring of another life.

Osiris, however, returned sometimes to see me. His shade made me mother of Harpocrates.

She contemplates the child.

This is he! These are his eyes; this is his hair, plaited into ram's horns! You shall re-enact his works. We shall bloom again like lotuses. I am still Isis the great! None has yet lifted my veil! My fruit is the sun!

O spring sun, clouds are obscuring your face! Typhon's breath devours the pyramids. Just now I saw the Sphinx on the run. He galloped like a jackal.

I am searching for my priests – my linen-robed priests with large harps and bearing a mystical nacelle ornamented with silver paterae. No more feasts on the lakes! No more illuminations in my delta! No more vessels of milk at Philae! Apis has long since ceased to reappear.

Egypt! Egypt! Your great unmoving gods have their shoulders blanched by bird-droppings, and the wind passing over the desert rolls the ashes of your dead! – Anubis, guardian of the dead, don't leave me!

The cynocephalus has fainted.

She shakes her child.

But . . . what is it? . . . your hands are cold, you hang your head!

Harpocrates has just died.

At this she lets out so piercing, desolate and harrowing a cry that Antony responds with another cry, opening his arms to hold her up.

She is no longer there. He bows his face, crushed with shame.

All that he has just seen is confused in his mind. It feels like the dizziness of travel, or a sick drunkenness. He wishes he could hate; and yet a blurred pity softens his heart. He starts to weep freely.

HILARION

Who makes you so sad?

ANTONY

after searching, for a long time, in himself:

I'm thinking of all the souls lost by those false gods!

HILARION

Don't you feel they have . . . sometimes . . . some likeness to the true one!

ANTONY

That's a trick of the Devil's, the better to seduce the faithful. He attacks the strong through the mind, the others by means of the flesh.

HILARION

But lust, in its frenzy, is as disinterested as penitence. The body's frantic love accelerates its destruction – proclaiming by its feebleness the extent of the impossible.

ANTONY

What does it matter to me! My stomach heaves with disgust at all these bestial gods, for ever busy with carnage and incest!

HILARION

Remember all those things in the Scriptures which scandalise you, because you don't know how to understand them. Just so, beneath their criminal shapes, these gods may conceal the truth.

There are still more to see. Turn round!

ANTONY

No! no! it's a snare!

HILARION

A short time ago you wanted to know them. Would your faith waver on account of lies? What do you fear?

The rocks facing Antony have become a mountain.

A line of clouds cuts it half-way up; and above appears another mountain, enormous, quite green, irregularly hollowed into valleys and which bears aloft, in a laurel wood at the top, a bronze palace with golden tiles and ivory capitals.

Enthroned in the centre of the peristyle, JUPITER, colossal and with naked torso, holds victory in one hand, thunder in the other; and between his legs his eagle raises its head.

Beside him, JUNO rolls her great eyes, beneath a tall diadem from which streams a vapourish veil floating in the wind.

Further back, MINERVA, standing on a pedestal, leans on her lance. The gorgon's skin covers her breast; and a linen peplos falls in regular folds down to her toe-nails. Shining under her visor, her sea-green eyes look into the distance attentively.

To the right of the palace, old NEPTUNE bestrides a dolphin beating its fins on an azure expanse which could be sky or sea, for the perspective of the Ocean follows on from the ether's blue; the two elements merge.

On the other side PLUTO, fierce and in a night-coloured cloak, with a diamond tiara and an ebony sceptre, is at the centre of an island surrounded by the coils of the Styx. And this shadowy river runs to throw itself into the gloom which makes a great black hole under the cliff, a formless abyss.

MARS, ironclad, brandishes with a furious look his wide shield and his sword.

HERCULES contemplates him from below, leaning on his club.

With a radiant face APOLLO, his right arm outstretched, drives four galloping white horses; and CERES, in a chariot drawn by oxen, advances towards him with a sickle in her hand.

BACCHUS comes behind her on a very low chariot lazily pulled by lynxes. Fat, beardless and with vine branches on his forehead, he goes past, holding a crater overflowing with wine. Next to him on a donkey reels Silenus. Pointed-eared Pan blows into his syrinx; the Mimalloneids beat drums, the Maenads toss flowers, the Bacchantes whirl with heads flung back, hair loose.

DIANA, her tunic tucked up, comes out of the wood with her nymphs.

At the far end of a cavern VULCAN strikes the iron between the Cabiri; here and there the old Rivers, leaning their elbows on green stones, tip their urns; the Muses stand singing in the valleys.

Equal in build, the Hours hold each other by the hand; and MERCURY is obliquely perched on a rainbow with his caduceus, his talaria and his petasus.

But at the top of the stairway of the Gods, among clouds as soft as feathers and whose spiralling scrolls let fall roses, VENUS ANADYOMENE looks at herself in a mirror; her pupils slide languorously under her slightly heavy lids.

She has thick blonde hair uncoiling on her shoulders, small breasts, a narrow waist, hips curving like the outline of a lyre, both thighs very rounded, dimples around the knees and delicate feet; not far from her mouth flutters a butterfly. The splendour of her body creates a halo of pearly brilliance around her; and all the rest of Olympus is bathed in a ruddy dawn which imperceptibly reaches the heights of the blue sky.

ANTONY

Ah! I can breathe freely. A happiness quite new to me
spreads to the depths of my soul! How beautiful this is! how
beautiful!

HILARION

They leant from the cloud-tops to guide men's swords; you
met them at the roadside, you owned them in the home – and
this familiarity helped to make life divine.

Its only aim was to be free and beautiful. Wide clothes made
noble attitudes come easily. The orator's voice, trained by the
sea, beat in resonant waves against marble porticoes. Rubbed
with oil, each ephebe would wrestle stark naked in the hot
sun. To reveal purity of form was the holiest of actions.

And these men respected wives, old men, suppliants.
Behind the temple of Hercules there was an altar to Pity.

Victims were immolated with flowers around their
fingers. Memory itself stood exempt from the decay of the
dead. There was left of them only a few ashes. The soul,
blending with boundless ether, had gone to the gods!

Bending towards Antony's ear:

And they still live! The Emperor Constantine worships
Apollo. You can find the Trinity again in the mysteries of
Samothrace, find baptism with Isis, redemption with Mithra,
a god's martyrdom in the feasts of Bacchus. Proserpina is the
Virgin!... Aristeas, Jesus!

ANTONY

keeps his eyes lowered; then suddenly he repeats the symbol of Jeru-
salem – as he remembers it – letting out with each phrase a long sigh:

I believe in one God, the Father – and in one Lord, Jesus

Christ – first-begotten son of God – who was incarnate and was made Man – who was crucified – and buried – who ascended into heaven – who shall come to judge the quick and the dead – whose kingdom shall have no end – And in one Holy Ghost – and in one baptism of repentance – and in one holy catholic Church – and in the resurrection of the flesh – and in life eternal!

At once the cross grows taller and piercing the clouds casts a shadow on the sky of the gods.

All turn pale. Olympus has moved.

Against its base, half lost in the caverns or with their shoulders upholding the boulders, Antony makes out vast enchained bodies. These are the Titans, the Giants, the Hecatonchyres, the Cyclopes.

A VOICE

arises, indistinct and formidable – like the roaring of waves, or the sound of storm-tossed woods, or wind soughing in precipices:

All this we knew! The gods must come to an end. Uranus was mutilated by Saturn, Saturn by Jupiter. He himself will be obliterated. To each his turn; this is destiny!

and, little by little, they sink into the mountain, disappear.

Meanwhile the tiles of the golden palace fly off.

JUPITER

has come down from his throne. Like a brand about to go out, the thunder smokes at his feet – and his eagle, craning its neck, pecks up its moulting feathers.

No longer am I lord of things, almighty, all-good, god of the phratries and of the Greek people, forebear of all kings, Agamemnon of the sky!

Eagle of apotheoses, what gust from Erebus drove you here to me? Or have you, flying from the Camp of Mars, brought me the soul of the last of the emperors?

I have no more use for those of men! Let the Earth keep them, let them busy themselves on a level with its baseness. For now they live like slaves, oblivious of insults, of ancestors, of vows; and on all sides what triumphs is the mob's imbecility, the meanness of the individual, the hideousness of every race!

His breathing swells his ribs to bursting, and he wrings his hands. Hebe in tears hands him a cup. He seizes it.

No! no! While anywhere there remains one head which can entertain thought, can hate disorder and conceive Law, the spirit of Jupiter will live!

But the cup is empty.
He tilts it slowly over the tip of his finger.

Not a drop! When the ambrosia fails, the Immortals go too!

It slips from his hands; and he leans against a pillar, dying.

JUNO

You should have had fewer loves! Eagle, bull, swan, golden rain, cloud and flame, you took every shape, frittered your light in every element, lost your hair in every bed! This time divorce is irrevocable – and our dominion, our existence dissolved!

She moves away in the air.

MINERVA

no longer has her lance; and crows which were nesting in the sculptures of the frieze are circling around her, biting her helmet.

Let me see whether my ships, ploughing the shiny sea, have returned to my three ports, and why it is that the countryside is deserted, and what is now happening to the daughters of Athens.

In the month of Hecatombeon my entire people would surge towards me, led by their magistrates and their priests. Forward came the long files of virgins in white robes with golden chitons, holding bowls, baskets, parasols; next the three hundred oxen for the sacrifice, old men waving green boughs, soldiers in clashing armour, ephebes chanting hymns, flute-players, lyrists, rhapsodes, dancers – and at last, on the mast of a trireme rolling on wheels, my great veil embroidered by virgins, who had been fed on a special diet for a year; and when it had been shown in all the streets, in all the squares and before all the temples, amid the still psalm-odising procession it ascended, step by step, the hill of the Acropolis, brushed the Propylaea, and entered the Parthenon.

But I feel suddenly troubled – I, the industrious! How now, how now, not one idea! Here I am, trembling worse than a woman.

She sees a ruin behind her, lets out a scream, and struck on the forehead falls backward to the ground.

HERCULES

has thrown off his lionskin; and gripping with his feet, arching his back, biting his lips, he makes frantic efforts to uphold Olympus as it crumbles.

I conquered the Kerkopes, the Amazons and the Centaurs. I killed a lot of kings. I broke the horn of Achelous, a great river. I cut up mountains, I joined oceans. I freed enslaved countries; empty countries I peopled. I travelled all over Gaul. I crossed the thirsty desert. I defended the gods, and made my escape from Omphale. But Olympus is too heavy. My arms are giving way. I shall die!

He is crushed under the debris.

PLUTO

The fault is yours, Amphitryonades! Why did you go down into my empire?

The vulture which eats the entrails of Tityos lifted its head, Tantalus wetted his lip, Ixion's wheel stopped.

Meanwhile the Keres dug their claws in, holding back souls; the Furies in despair contorted the snakes of their hair; and Cerberus, whom you tied up with a chain, was choking, drooling from his three mouths.

You had left the door open. Others came. The light of men has penetrated Tartarus!

He collapses into the gloom.

NEPTUNE

My trident no longer raises storms. The monsters which spread fear have rotted at the bottom of the water.

Amphitrite, with her white feet running on the foam, the green Nereids once sighted on the horizon, the scaly Sirens who stopped the ships to tell stories, the old Tritons blowing in their shells, all dead! The gaiety of the sea has gone!

I shall not survive it! Let the vast Ocean cover me!

He faints into the blue.

DIANA

dressed in black, among her dogs now turned into wolves:

I have grown drunk with the independence of the great woods, with the smell of wild animals and the breath from the marshes. Women, whom I protected in pregnancy, are giving birth to dead children. The moon trembles under the incantations of witches. I have longings for violence and vastness. I want to drink poisons, to lose myself in mists, in dreams!...

And a passing cloud carries her off.

MARS

bare-headed, bloody:

First I fought alone, provoking a whole army with my insults, indifferent to countries and for the pleasure of the carnage.

Later I had comrades. They marched to the sound of flutes, in good order, evenly in step, breathing above their shields with plumes high and lances tilted. Men rushed into battle with great eagles' cries. War was as joyful as a feast. Three hundred men withstood the whole of Asia.

But they are coming back, the Barbarians! and by the myriad, by the million! Since numbers, machines and ruse are the strongest, better finish bravely!

He kills himself.

VULCAN

wiping the sweat from his body with a sponge:

The world is getting colder. We must warm the springs and volcanoes and rivers which roll the metals underground! Strike harder – full-blast! with all your might!

The Cabiri hurt themselves with their hammers, blind themselves with sparks, and groping their way are lost in the dark.

CERES

standing in her chariot, which is carried away by wheels with wings on the hubs:

Stop! stop!

How wise it was to debar strangers, atheists, epicureans and christians! The mystery of the basket is unveiled, the sanctuary profaned, everything lost!

She careers down a steep slope – desperate, screaming, tearing her hair.

Ah! lies! Daira is not restored to me! I am tolled towards the dead. Here is another Tartarus – from which there is no return. Horror!

The abyss swallows her.

BACCHUS

laughing frenetically:

Who cares? The Archon's wife is mine! Law itself falls drunk. I have a new song and countless new shapes!

The fire which consumed my mother runs in my veins. Let it burn more fiercely, though I perish!

Male and female, good for all, I am yours, Bacchantes! I am yours, Bacchants! and the vine shall twist round the tree-trunks! Howl, dance, writhe! Untie the tiger and the slave! Sink your savage teeth into flesh!

And Pan, Silenus, the Satyrs, the Bacchantes, the Mimalloneids and the Maenads, with their snakes and their torches and their black masks, all fling flowers, uncover a phallus, kiss it – brandish tambourines, beat their thyrses, pelt each other with shells, gobble raisins, strangle a he-goat, and tear Bacchus apart.

APOLLO

whipping his steeds, his whitened hair flying:

Stony Delos I have left behind me, so pure that now everything there seems dead; and I am trying to reach Delphi before the mist of its inspiration should be quite lost. Mules browse on its laurel. The wandering Pythia cannot be found.

Through harder concentration I shall have sublime poems, eternal monuments; and all matter will be penetrated by the vibrations of my cithara!

He plucks its strings. They snap, stinging his face. He throws it aside; and furiously lashing his quadriga:

No! finish with forms! Further still! To the very top! Into the pure idea!

But the horses balk, rear up, break the chariot; and snarled in the pieces of the shaft, the harness's tangle, he falls head first into the abyss.

The sky has darkened.

VENUS

shivers, purple with cold.

I traced with my belt the whole horizon of Hellas.

Her fields shone with the roses in my cheeks, her shores were cut in the shape of my lips; and her mountains, whiter than doves, palpitated under the hands of statuaries. My spirit could be recognised in the ordering of feasts, the styling of hair, the dialogue of philosophers, the constitution of the republics. But I've been too fond of men! Love has dishonoured me!

In tears, she trips up.

The world is abominable. I want air to breathe!

O Mercury, inventor of the lyre and conductor of souls, carry me away!

She puts a finger to her mouth, and describing an immense parabola falls into the abyss.

Not a thing can be seen. It is pitch dark.

But from Hilarion's eyes there seem to flash two red arrows.

ANTONY

at last notices how tall he is.

Several times already, while you were talking, you have

seemed to grow – and it wasn't an illusion. How? tell me . . .
I find you terrifying!

Steps draw nearer.

What's that?

HILARION

stretches out his arm.

Look!

And now under a pale beam of moonlight Antony distinguishes an
interminable caravan filing past on the crest of the rocks – and one
after another each traveller topples from the cliff into the pit.

First come the three great gods of Samothrace – Axieros, Axiokeros,
Axiokersa, bunched together, masked in scarlet and raising their arms.

Esculapius advances in a melancholy manner without even seeing
Samos and Telesphorus, who anxiously question him. Sosipolis the
Elean python-shaped, rolls his coils towards the abyss. Despoina
giddily throws herself in. Britomartis, howling with fright, clings
to the meshes of her net. The centaurs arrive at a stiff gallop, and
bowl pell-mell into the black hole.

Behind them limp the pathetic troop of Nymphs. Those of the
meadows are covered in dust, those of the woods moan and bleed,
wounded by the woodmen's axes.

The Gelludes, the Striges, the Empusas, all the infernal goddesses
mixing their fangs and torches and vipers form a pyramid – and up on
top, on a vulture's skin, Eurynome, blue as a blowfly, devours her own
arms.

Then in an eddy vanish all at once: bloodthirsty Orthia, Hymnia of
Orchomenus, the Patreans' Laphria, Aphaea of Aegina, Bendis of
Thrace, bird-thighed Stymphalia. Instead of three eyes Triopas has
nothing but three orbits. Erichtonius, his legs flabby, crawls like a
cripple on his wrists.

HILARION

What a pleasure, don't you think, to see them all abject and
in agony! Climb up with me onto this stone; and you'll be
like Xerxes reviewing his army.

Over there, in the far distance, through the mist, can you see that giant with the fair beard who lets fall a blade red with blood? It's Zalmoxis the Scythian, between two planets: Artimpasa – Venus, and Orsiloche – the Moon.

Further off, emerging from pale clouds, are the gods once worshipped by the Cimmerians, beyond Thule itself!

Their large halls were kept warm; and by the gleam of naked swords lining the roof they drank hydromel from ivory horns. They fed on whale's liver in copper dishes wrought by demons; or they listened to captive sorcerers passing their hands over harps of stone.

They are tired! and cold! Snow makes their bearskins heavy, and their feet show through the tears in their sandals.

They mourn the prairies, where grassy knolls allowed them to take breath in battle, the long boats whose bows would cut through cliffs of ice, and the skates with which they used to follow the orbit of the poles, keeping the whole firmament turning with them at the ends of their arms.

A frosty squall shrouds them.

Antony lets his gaze fall elsewhere.

And he sees – showing up black against a red background – strange personages with chin-pieces and gauntlets who are volleying balls, leaping over each other, making grimaces, frenetically dancing.

HILARION

These are the gods of Etruria, the numberless Aesars.

Here is Tages, inventor of auguries – trying with one hand to increase the divisions of the sky, leaning with the other on the earth. Let him get back in!

Nortia is considering the wall into which she drove nails to mark the count of the years. Its surface is covered, the last period accomplished.

Like two storm-beaten travellers, Kastur and Pulutuk are sheltering all of a tremble under the same cloak.

ANTONY

shuts his eyes.

Enough! enough!

But there pass in the air with a great sound of wings all the Victories of the Capitol – hiding their faces behind their hands, and letting fall the trophies hung about their arms.

Janus – the master of dusk – flees on a black ram; of his two faces, one is already putrefied, the other dropping with sleep.

Summanus – god of gloomy skies, now minus his head – presses to his heart an old wheel-shaped cake.

Beneath a ruined cupola Vesta tries to revive her lamp, gone cold.

Bellona slashes her cheeks but cannot spurt the blood which purified her devotees.

ANTONY

Mercy! they make me tired!

HILARION

They were once amusing!

And in a grove of service-trees he shows him a Woman stark naked, on all fours like an animal – whom a black man covers, holding a light in either hand.

This is the goddess of Aricia with the demon Virbius. Her priest, the king of the wood, had to be an assassin – and runaway slaves, corpse-strippers, brigands from the Salarian Way, cripples from the Pons Sublicius, all the vermin from the hovels of Subura knew no dearer devotion!

The patrician women of Mark Antony's time preferred Libitina.

And under cypresses and rose-bushes he shows him another Woman – clothed in gauze. She smiles, while around her lie picks, stretchers, black hangings, all the funeral utensils. Her diamonds shine from far off beneath spiders' webs. Like skeletons, the Larvae show their bones between the branches, and the Lemures, which are ghosts, stretch their bat-like wings.

On the edge of a field the god Terminus leans uprooted, all covered in filth.

In the middle of a furrow the great cadaver of Vertumnus is devoured by red dogs.

The rustic gods move away from it in tears – Sartor, Sarrator, Vervactor, Collina, Vallona, Hostilinus, all covered with little hooded cloaks and each carrying mattock, pitchfork, wattles or stake.

HILARION

It was their spirit that made the villa prosper, with its dovecots, its pens full of dormice and snails, its safely netted poultry-yards, its warm cedar-scented stables.

They protected all that wretched population which dragged its leg-irons on the stones of Sabina, those who called the pigs with a blast on the horn, who picked the high clusters of hops, who drove the donkeys loaded with dung along the by-ways. Panting over the handle of his plough, the ploughman prayed them to give him stronger arms; and cowherds in the shade of lime-trees, by calabashes of milk, took turns with their praises on reed flutes.

Antony sighs.

And in the middle of a room, on a platform, is revealed an ivory bed, round which are people holding pine torches.

These are the gods of marriage. They are expecting the bride!

Domiduca was to lead her in, Virgo to undo her belt, Subigo to lay her in the bed – and Praema to open her arms, saying sweet things in her ear.

But she will not come! and the others are being dismissed: Nona and Decima the sick-nurses, the three Nixii who delivered the child, the wet-nurses Educa and Potina – and lullabying Carna, whose sprig of hawthorn kept the child free from bad dreams.

Ossipago would later have consolidated his knees, Barbatus would have given him a beard, Stimula his first desires, Volupia his first enjoyment of them, Fabulinus would have taught him to speak, Numera to count, Camoena to sing, Consus to think.

The room is empty; at the bedside only Naenia is left – a centenarian mumbling to herself the lament she howled at the death of old men.

But soon her voice is drowned by shrill cries. These come from

THE DOMESTIC LARES

squatting at the far end of the atrium, clothed in dogskins and with flowers about their bodies, holding their clenched hands against their cheeks and crying for all they are worth.

Where is the share of food we were given at each meal, the maid-servant's good offices, the matron's smile, and the gaiety of the little boys who played knuckle-bones on the mosaics in the courtyard? When they grew up they used to hang their bullas of gold or leather on our chests.

What a pleasure when the master came home on the evening of a triumph, and turned his wet eyes towards us! He recounted his battles; and the narrow house was prouder than a palace and as sacred as a temple.

How blest the family meals were, especially the day after the Feralia! Tenderness for the dead calmed down all disagreements; and everyone embraced, drinking to the glories of the past and the hopes for the future.

But the painted wax forebears shut away behind us are gradually growing mouldy. New races, to punish us for their disappointments, have broken our jaws; chewed by rats' teeth our wooden bodies crumble.

And the countless gods watching by the doors, the kitchen, the cellar, the wash-rooms, scatter in all directions – in the guise of enormous ants trotting off or big butterflies flying away.

CREPITUS

makes himself heard.

I too was honoured once. Libations were made to me. I was a god!

An Athenian would greet me as a lucky omen, while a devout Roman would curse me with raised fists, and the pontiff of Egypt, abstaining from beans, quailed at my voice and paled at my odour.

When the army vinegar ran down unshaven beards and people tucked into acorns, peas and raw onions, and the goat was chopped up and cooked in shepherds' rancid butter, no one was bothered – never mind your neighbour. Solid foods made for ringing digestions. In the sunlight of the countryside, men relieved themselves at leisure.

So I got by without scandal, like the other natural necessities, like Mena the virgins' affliction and like Rumina, who protects the nurse's breasts swollen with bluish veins. I was happy. I raised a laugh! And gladly distended on my account, a guest would let all his gaiety out through the apertures of his body.

I had times to boast of. Good Aristophanes put me on the stage, and the Emperor Claudius Drusus had me sitting at his table. In the patricians' laticlaves I moved majestically! Gold pots echoed under me like tympani – and when, full of eels and truffles and paté, the master's intestine noisily disgorged itself, the attentive universe learnt that Caesar had dined!

But now I'm confined to the populace – and people object to my very name!

And Crepitus moves off with a groan.
Next a clap of thunder:

A VOICE

I was the Lord, the Lord of Hosts, the Lord God!

I set up Jacob's tents on the hills and I fed my fleeing people in the sands.

It was I who burnt Sodom! I who engulfed the earth under the Deluge! I who drowned Pharaoh, with the princely sons of kings, the war chariots and the drivers.

A jealous God, I execrated other gods. I crushed the impure; I cut down the proud – and my devastation ran from right to left, like a dromedary let loose in a field of maize.

To deliver Israel, I chose simple people. Angels with flaming wings spoke to them from bushes.

Scented with nard, cinnamon and myrrh, transparently robed and in high-heeled shoes, women of intrepid spirit went to slaughter captains. The passing wind bore away prophets.

My law I engraved on stone tablets. It enclosed my people as if in a citadel. They were my people. I was their God! The earth was mine and men were mine, with their thoughts, their works, their tools for tillage and their posterity.

My ark rested in a triple sanctuary, behind scarlet curtains and lighted candelabra. To serve me I had a whole tribe swinging censers, and the high priest in a hyacinth robe, wearing on his breast precious stones arranged in symmetric order.

Rue the day! The Holy-of-Holies has been laid bare, the veil torn, and the perfumes of the holocaust have been scattered to the four winds. The jackal screeches in the graveyard; my temple is destroyed, my people dispersed!

The priests were strangled with the cords of their robes. The women are captive, the vases are melted down!

The voice grows distant:

I was the Lord, the Lord of Hosts, the Lord God!

Now comes an enormous silence, and deep night.

ANTONY

All of them have vanished.

SOMEONE

All but I!

And in front of him is Hilarion – but transfigured, lovely as an archangel, luminous as a sun – and so tall that to see him

ANTONY

tilts his head back.

Who then are you?

HILARION

My kingdom has the dimensions of the universe; and my desire knows no bounds. I go on forever, freeing the spirit, weighing up worlds, without hate, without fear, without pity, without love and without God. I am called Science.

ANTONY

reels backwards:

You're more likely ... the Devil!

HILARION

fixes him with his eyes:

Do you want to see him?

ANTONY

can no longer detach himself from this gaze; he is seized with the Devil's own curiosity. His terror increases, his longing becomes extravagant.

Suppose I see him, though ... suppose I do?

Then in a spasm of anger:

The horror I'll feel will rid me of him for ever. — Yes!

A cloven hoof appears.
Antony has regrets.
But the Devil has tossed him on his horns, and carries him off.

VI

Underneath Antony he flies like an elongated swimmer – and cloudlike, his two wide-open wings wholly conceal him.

ANTONY

Where am I going?

Just now I glimpsed the shape of the Evil One. No! I'm carried on a cloud. Perhaps I'm dead, and going up to God?

Ah! how well I can breathe! The stainless air buoys my spirit. No more weight! No more suffering!

Down there beneath me the thunder breaks, the horizon widens, rivers intersect. That blonde patch is the desert, that pool of water the Ocean.

Other oceans too appear, huge regions that I didn't know. Here are the black lands smoking like braziers, and the snow zone always smothered in mists. I'm looking out for the mountains where each night the sun goes down.

THE DEVIL

The sun never does go down!

Antony is not surprised by this voice. It strikes him as an echo of his thoughts – his memory's answer.

Meanwhile the earth becomes ball-shaped; and he observes how it turns in the blue on its poles, while turning around the sun.

THE DEVIL

So it doesn't form the centre of the world? Human arrogance, humble yourself!

ANTONY

I can barely make it out any more. It's confused with the other fires.

The firmament is just a tissue of stars.

They are still climbing.

No noise! not even the croaking of eagles! Nothing! . . . and I'm beginning to strain my ears for the harmony of the planets.

THE DEVIL

You won't hear them! Nor will you see Plato's antichtone, Philolaus's central fire, Aristotle's spheres, nor the Jews' seven heavens with the great waters above the crystal vault!

ANTONY

From down there it looked as solid as a wall. While on the contrary I penetrate it, I plunge through!

And he arrives before the moon – which looks like a piece of ice, quite round and full of still light.

THE DEVIL

It was once the home of souls. Worthy Pythagoras had even furnished it with magnificent birds and flowers.

ANTONY

I see only dreary plains there, and extinct craters, under an all-black sky.

Steer towards those stars which shine more gently, so that we can gaze at the angels holding them at the ends of their arms like tapers.

THE DEVIL

brings him among the stars.

They attract and at the same time repel each other. Each one's action results from the others and makes its contribution – without means of any auxiliary, by the force of law, the single virtue of order.

ANTONY

Yes!... yes! I grasp it in my mind! This joy is superior to the pleasures of tenderness! I'm breathless and dumbfounded at the enormousness of God!

THE DEVIL

Like the firmament which rises the more you climb, it will grow as your thought reaches higher – and you will experience increasing joy from this discovery of the world, this widening of the infinite.

ANTONY

Ah! higher! higher! higher still!

The stars multiply and glitter. The Milky Way unravels on high like an enormous belt, set with holes at intervals; within these rents in its clarity, dark tracts reach out. There are star-rains, trails of gold dust, luminous vapours which float and dissolve.

Sometimes a comet suddenly passes – and then the countless lights resume their tranquillity.

Antony leans with outstretched arms on the Devil's two horns, occupying their whole span.

Scornfully he remembers the ignorance of the old days, the mediocrity of his dreams. So here they are beside him, those luminous globes he stared at from down there! He traces their intersecting paths, their complex directions. He watches how they come from far off – balanced like stones in a sling – to describe their orbits and draw out their hyperbolas.

With a single glance he takes in the Southern Cross and the Great Bear, the Lynx and the Centaur, the nebula of the Swordfish, Jupiter with its four satellites and monstrous Saturn's triple ring! All the planets and stars which men will later discover! He feasts his eyes on their lights, he strains his mind with calculations regarding their distance; then his head falls forward.

What is the purpose of all this?

THE DEVIL

There is no purpose!
How should God have a purpose? By what experience could he be taught, by what reflections determined?
Before the beginning he would not have acted, and now he would be useless.

ANTONY

Yet he created the world, all at once, by his word!

THE DEVIL

But the beings which populate the earth do so in succession. In the sky, just so, new stars spring up – different effects of varied causes.

ANTONY

The variety of causes is the will of God!

THE DEVIL

But to admit several acts of will in God is to admit several causes, and to destroy his unity!
His will is inseparable from his essence. He cannot have had another will, since he could have no other essence – and since he exists eternally, he acts eternally.

Observe the sun! From its edges shoot high flames, flinging sparks which scatter to become worlds – and beyond the last of these, beyond those depths where you discern nothing but night, further suns are whirling, and beyond these are more, and still more, indefinitely...

ANTONY

Enough! enough! I'm frightened! I shall fall into empty space.

THE DEVIL

stops; and rocking him softly:

There is no emptiness! there is no void! There are everywhere bodies moving in the immutable depths of Extension – and since, if it were bounded by anything, it would no longer be space but a body, it has no limits!

ANTONY

gaping:

No limits!

THE DEVIL

Climb up the sky for ever and ever; you'll never reach the top! Go down under the earth for billions and billions of centuries, you'll never come to the bottom – because there is no bottom, no top, nor high, nor low, no end-point whatever; and Extension is included in God, who is not a portion of space of such-and-such a size, but immensity!

ANTONY

slowly:

Might matter... then... be part of God?

THE DEVIL

Why not? Can you know where he ends?

ANTONY

On the contrary I bow, I fall prostrate before his power!

THE DEVIL

And you claim to move him! You speak to him, you even grace him with virtues – goodness, justice, mercy – instead of recognising that he possesses every perfection!

To conceive of something beyond, is to conceive of God beyond God, of Being beyond Being. Therefore he is the one Being, the one substance.

If Substance could be divided, it would lose its nature, it would not be itself, God would no longer exist. He is therefore indivisible as well as infinite. And if he had a body, he would be made up of parts, he would not be one, he would no longer be infinite. Therefore he is not a person!

ANTONY

What? my prayers, my tears, my physical suffering, my flights of passion, can all this have rushed away towards a lie . . . into space . . . uselessly – like the cry of a bird, like an eddy of dead leaves!

He weeps:

Oh, no! Above it all there must be someone, a great soul, a Lord, a father, whom I worship in my heart and who must love me!

THE DEVIL

You want God not to be God – for if he felt love, or anger,

or pity, he would pass from his perfection to a greater or a lesser perfection. He cannot descend to a feeling, nor be contained in a form.

ANTONY

One day, for all that, I shall see him!

THE DEVIL

Indeed, with the blessed? When the finite will enjoy the infinite, in a confined space confining the absolute!

ANTONY

But still, there must be both a paradise for goodness and a hell for evil!

THE DEVIL

Do the demands of your reason legislate for things? God is no doubt indifferent to evil since the earth is thick with it!

Is it through impotence that he tolerates it, or through cruelty that he conserves it?

Do you imagine him to be constantly readjusting the world like an imperfect masterpiece, and watching over every creature's every movement, from the butterfly's flight to the mind of man?

If he created the universe, his providence is superfluous. If Providence exists, creation is defective.

But good and evil concern only you – like day and night, or pleasure and pain, or birth and death, which are relative to a corner of extension, to a special milieu, to a particular interest. Since the infinite alone is permanent, there is the Infinite – and that's all!

The Devil has gradually spread his long wings; they now cover space.

ANTONY

cannot see a thing. He feels faint.

An icy cold grips my very soul. I'm past the point of pain! It's like a death deeper than death. I'm spinning in vast darkness. It's inside me. My conscious self shatters under this dilating void!

THE DEVIL

But things reach you only through the medium of your mind. Like a concave mirror it distorts objects – and you lack the means to make accurate checks.

You will never know the universe in its full extent; consequently you cannot form an idea of its cause, nor have a right notion of God, nor even say that the universe is infinite – for it would first be necessary to know Infinity!

Form is perhaps an error of your senses, and Substance an image in your mind.

Unless – the world being a perpetual flux of things – appearance on the contrary were to be all that is truest, and illusion the one reality.

But are you sure of seeing? Are you even sure of being alive? Perhaps there is nothing!

The Devil has taken Antony; and holding him at arm's length, he surveys him with open jaws, ready to devour him.

Worship me, therefore! and curse the ghost you call God!

In a last movement of hope Antony lifts up his eyes.
The Devil abandons him.

VII

ANTONY

finds himself flat on his back at the edge of the cliff.

The sky is turning white.

Is it the glimmer of dawn, or a reflection from the moon?

He tries to pull himself up, then sinks back; and with chattering teeth:

I feel so exhausted ... as if I'd broken every bone!

Why?

Ah! it's the Devil! I remember – he was even repeating to me everything I learnt from old Didymus about the opinions of Xenophanes, Heraclitus, Melissus and Anaxagoras, about infinity, creation, the impossibility of ever knowing anything!

And I'd thought I could be one with God!

Laughing bitterly:

Ah, madness! madness! Is it my fault? I find prayer intolerable. My heart is as dry as rock! It used to overflow with love! ...

In the morning the sand steamed on the horizon like dusty incense; at sunset fiery flowers bloomed on the cross; and often – in the middle of the night – it seemed as if all creatures and things, absorbed in the same silence, were worshipping the Lord with me. Enchanting orisons, ecstasies of happiness, gifts from heaven, where have you all gone?

I remember a journey I made with Ammon, in search of a

wilderness in which to found monasteries. It was the last evening; and we were quickening our pace, murmuring hymns, side by side, without talking. As the sun sank lower, the two shadows cast by our bodies lengthened like two obelisks growing for ever, apparently on the march before us. With pieces of our sticks we planted crosses here and there, to mark each place for a cell. Night was slow to come; black waves were swamping the earth while a great flush of pink still filled the sky.

When I was a child, I played at building hermitages out of pebbles. My mother would watch nearby.

She must have cursed me for abandoning her, must have torn her white hair out by the handful. And her corpse has been left lying in the middle of the hut, under the roof of reeds, between the tumbledown walls. A hyena snuffles through a hole, nosing forward!... Horrible! horrible!

He sobs.

No, Ammonaria won't have left her!

Where is she now, Ammonaria?

Perhaps she's in some hot-room taking off her clothes one by one, the cloak first, then the belt, the top tunic, the second lighter one, all her necklaces; and cinnamon vapour wreathes her nakedness. At last she lies down on the warm mosaic. Her hair comes around her hips like a black fleece – and slightly stifled by the overheated atmosphere, arching her body, she breathes, both breasts thrust out. There now!... my flesh rebels! In the middle of grief I'm plagued by lust. Two tortures at once, it's too much! I can no longer endure my own self!

He leans forward, looking into the precipice.

Anyone who fell in would be killed. Nothing easier, simply by rolling over to the left; one movement to make! just one.

There now appears

AN OLD WOMAN

Antony leaps up with a terrified start – thinking he sees his mother come back to life.

But this woman is much older, and unbelievably thin.

A shroud knotted around her head hangs with her white hair all the way down her legs, which are lean as two crutches. The brilliance of her ivory-coloured teeth makes her earthy skin duller still. The orbs of her eyes are full of darkness, and in their depths flicker two flames, like grave-lamps.

She says:

Go on. Who can stop you?

ANTONY

stuttering:

I'm frightened of committing a sin!

SHE

rejoins:

But King Saul killed himself! Razis, a just man, killed himself! Saint Pelagia of Antioch killed herself! Domnina of Aleppo and her two daughters – three more saints – killed themselves. And remember all the confessors who outstripped their executioners, impatient for death. To enjoy it the sooner, the virgins of Miletus strangled themselves with their girdles. The philosopher Hegesias, in Syracuse, preached it so effectively that people left the brothels to hang themselves in the fields. The patricians of Rome procure it for their pleasure.

ANTONY

Yes, that love is strong! Many anchorites succumb to it.

THE OLD WOMAN

To do something that makes you God's equal, think of that! He created you and you will destroy his work, you yourself, by your courage, freely. The joy of Herostratus was no greater. And besides, your body has sufficiently mocked your soul for you to take your revenge at last. You won't suffer. It will soon be over. What do you fear? A big black hole? It's empty, maybe?

Antony listens without answering; and on the other side appears:

ANOTHER WOMAN

young and lovely, marvellously so – and he takes her at first for Ammonaria.

But she is taller, blonde as honey, quite plump, with rouge on her cheeks and roses on her head. Her long dress laden with spangles gives out metallic flashes; her fleshy lips are blood-red, and her slightly heavy lids so swimming with languor that she looks blind.

She murmurs:

Flourish, live to the full! Solomon extols pleasure! Go wherever your eyes are drawn and follow your heart's desire!

ANTONY

What pleasure can I find? My heart feels tired, my eyes dim!

SHE

goes on:

Make your way to the district of Racotis, push ajar a blue-painted door; and when you are in the atrium where a water-spout murmurs, a woman will come up to you – in a white silk peplos shot with gold, her hair untied, and with a laugh like the ring of crotals. She's skilled. In her caress you shall taste the pride of initiation and the stilling of need.

You know nothing, besides, of the thrill of adultery, of the climbs, the abductions, the pleasure of seeing quite naked someone who when clothed was respected.

Have you pressed a virgin in love between your arms? Do you remember her abandoned modesty, and her feelings of remorse slipping away in a flood of gentle tears?

You can see the two of you, can't you, walking in the woods by the light of the moon? The pressure of your joined hands sends a shiver through you both; your eyes meet, pouring into each other as it were immaterial waves, and the heart fills; it bursts; here's a sweet whirlwind, a drunkenness that overflows...

THE OLD WOMAN

One needn't have these joys to be aware of their bitterness! To see them at a distance is enough to put people off. You must be sick of the same monotonous actions, the long-drawn-out days, the ugly world, the stupid sun!

ANTONY

Oh, yes, everything it lights is loathsome!

THE YOUNG WOMAN

Hermit! hermit! you'll find diamonds between the pebbles, fountains under the sand, and a delight in the hazards you despise; the earth is even so beautiful in places that we want to hug it to our hearts.

THE OLD WOMAN

Every evening, as you fall asleep on it, you hope it will soon cover you up!

THE YOUNG WOMAN

Yet you believe in the resurrection of the flesh, which is life's translation into eternity!

The Old Woman, while speaking, has grown even gaunter; and above her skull, which has lost its hair, a bat circles in the air.

The Young Woman has become still plumper. Her dress shimmers, her nostrils quiver, her liquid eyes roll.

THE FIRST

says, opening her arms:

Come! I am consolation, rest, forgetfulness, everlasting peace.

THE SECOND

offering her breasts:

I am she who lulls, I am bliss, life, inexhaustible happiness!

Antony turns on his heels to run. Each of them puts a hand on his shoulder.

The shroud pulls open to reveal the skeleton of Death.

The dress splits, exposing the entire body of Lust, who has a narrow waist with an enormous rump and long wavy hair flying out at the ends.

Antony stays stock-still between the two, studying them.

DEATH

tells him:

Now or later, what does it matter! You are mine like the suns, the nations, the towns, the kings, the snow on the peaks, the meadow grasses. I outsoar the sparrowhawk, I outrun the gazelle, I touch hope itself, I have conquered the son of God!

LUST

Don't resist; I am omnipotent! Forests echo to my sighs, waters shudder to my movements. Virtue, courage and piety dissolve in the scent of my mouth. I accompany man's every step – and on the brink of the grave he turns back to look at me!

DEATH

I shall show you what you tried to glean, by the light of tapers, from the faces of the dead – or when you vagabonded beyond the Pyramids, in those great sands composed of human remains. From time to time a fragment of skull turned beneath your sandal. You grasped some dust, you let it sift through your fingers; and your mind, mixing with it, vanished into the void.

LUST

My pit is deeper! Marble has inspired obscene desires. People rush into dread encounters. Chains are no sooner forged than cursed. Where does it come from, the courtesans' witchery, the extravagance of dreams, the immensity of my sadness?

DEATH

My irony exceeds all other! There are convulsions of pleasure at kings' funerals, at a people's extermination – and war is waged with music, plumes, flags, gold harness, a whole ceremonious display to render me greater homage.

LUST

My rage is a match for yours. I howl, I bite. I sweat like the dying and I look like a corpse.

DEATH

But I alone make you serious; Why don't we embrace?

Death sniggers, Lust roars. They take each other by the waist and together sing:

- – I hasten the decay of matter!
- – I help to scatter seeds!
- – You destroy, for my renewing!
- – You breed, for my destroying!
- – Make me more potent!
- – Impregnate me where I rot!

And their voice, whose rolling echoes fill the horizon, becomes so loud that Antony falls flat on his back.

A tremor, from time to time, makes him open his eyes; and he discerns in the darkness before him a kind of monster.

It is a death's head with a crown of roses. It rises above a woman's torso, pearly white. Beneath this, a shroud starred with dots of gold acts as a sort of tail – and the whole body undulates, as might a gigantic worm lifting upright.

The vision dims, disappears.

ANTONY

gets up.

It was yet again the Devil, and in his double guise: the spirit of fornication and the spirit of destruction.

Neither of the two can terrify me. I reject happiness, and I feel eternal.

Death is then a mere illusion, a veil, masking in places the continuity of life.

But since Substance is one, why are Forms so various?

There must be, somewhere, primordial figures whose bodies are nothing but their image. If one could see them one would discover the link between matter and thought, what Being consists of!

Those were the figures which were painted on the walls of the temple of Belus at Babylon, and they covered a mosaic in the port of Carthage. I myself have now and then seemed to see spirit-shapes in the sky. Travellers crossing the desert meet animals that beggar belief...

And opposite, on the other side of the Nile, all at once the Sphinx appears.

He stretches his paws, shakes the fillets on his brow, and lies down on his stomach.

Striking her wings with her dragon's tail, as she leaps, and flies, and spits fire from her nostrils, comes the green-eyed Chimera, wheeling, yelping.

On one side her long ringlets are tossed away to tangle with the hair on her back, and on the other they dangle down to the sand and sway with the rocking of her whole body.

THE SPHINX

is motionless, and watches the Chimera:

Stay here, Chimera; stop!

THE CHIMERA

No, never!

THE SPHINX

Don't run so fast, don't fly so high, don't yelp so loud!

THE CHIMERA

Don't call to me, don't call to me, since you're forever dumb!

THE SPHINX

Stop shooting your flames into my face and shrieking in my ear; you shan't melt my granite!

THE CHIMERA

You shan't catch me, terrible Sphinx!

THE SPHINX

You're far too mad to stay with me!

THE CHIMERA

You weigh too much to follow me!

THE SPHINX

But where are you off to, running so fast?

THE CHIMERA

I gallop through the corridors of the labyrinth, I soar above the peaks, I skim the waves, I yap at the bottom of precipices, I fasten my teeth into walls of cloud; with my trailing tail I pattern the beaches, and the slope of the hills follows the curve of my shoulders. But you, you're always to be found utterly still, or else drawing alphabets with the tip of your claw in the sand.

THE SPHINX

It's because I keep my secret! I think and I calculate.

The sea tosses in its bed, the corn waves in the wind, caravans pass, the dust flies up, cities go to ruin – and my gaze, which nothing can deflect, remains fixed across everything on an unreachable horizon.

THE CHIMERA

While I am light and happy! I show men dazzling vistas with cloudy paradises and distant bliss. I pour into their souls those eternal follies, projected felicities, plans for the future, dreams of glory, and vows of love and virtuous resolutions.

I incite to perilous voyages and great enterprises. With my paws I have chiselled architectural wonders. It was I who hung the little bells on Porsenna's tomb, and surrounded with a wall of orichalc the quays of Atlantis.

I look for new scents, larger flowers, untried pleasures. If anywhere I catch sight of a man contented and wise in spirit, I fall upon him and strangle him.

THE SPHINX

All those whom a longing for God torments I have devoured. The strongest, to scale my royal brow, climb the furrows of my fillets like a stairway. They are overcome with exhaustion; of their own accord they fall back.

Antony begins to tremble.
He is no longer in front of his cabin, but in the desert – with on either side of him these two monstrous beasts breathing down his neck.

THE SPHINX

O Fantasy, carry me off on your wings to distract me from my sadness!

THE CHIMERA

O Unknown, I am in love with your eyes! Like a hyena on heat I circle, I solicit you, eaten up with the need to be made fertile.

Open your mouth, lift your feet, mount on my back!

THE SPHINX

My feet, since they've lain flat, can no longer be lifted. Lichen has broken out on my face like a rash. I have thought so hard that I have nothing left to say.

THE CHIMERA

That's a lie, hypocritical Sphinx! How is it that you constantly call me and reject me?

THE SPHINX

It's you, untamable caprice, tearing and eddying past!

THE CHIMERA

Is it my fault? How? Let me be!

She yelps.

THE SPHINX

You're moving, you're out of reach!

He grunts.

THE CHIMERA

Try again! – you're crushing me!

THE SPHINX

No! impossible!

And little by little, he sinks down and disappears into the sand – while the Chimera, ramping with her tongue out, ranges away in widening circles.

The breath from her mouth has produced a fog.

In this mist Antony sees cloudy convolutions, inconstant curves. At last, he makes out what would appear to be human bodies.

And first comes

THE GROUP OF ASTOMI

like bubbles of air transparent to sunlight.

Don't blow too hard! Raindrops bruise us, grating sounds jar on us, darkness blinds us. Made of breezes and scents, we go rolling, floating – a little more than dreams, not altogether creatures . . .

THE NISNAS

have just one eye, one cheek, one hand, one leg, just half a body, just half a heart. And they say out loud:

We live mightily at ease in our halves of houses, with our halves of wives and our halves of children.

THE BLEMMYES

absolutely bereft of heads:

Our shoulders are all the broader – and there isn't an ox, a rhinoceros, or an elephant that can carry what we carry.

Features of sorts, and a vague kind of face imprinted on our chests, nothing more! We ponder digestive processes, we subtilise secretions. For us, God floats at peace in the chyles of our insides.

We keep to the road in front of us, crossing every quag mire, skirting every chasm – and we're the hardest-working, happiest and worthiest of folk.

THE PYGMIES

We little men swarm over the world like vermin on a dromedary's hump.

They burn us, drown us, squash us; and we always re-appear, all the livelier and more numerous – in quite terrible quantity!

THE SCIAPODES

Held to the earth by our hair as long as lianas, we vegetate beneath the shelter of our parasol-sized feet; light reaches us filtered through the thickness of our heels. Not a jot of bother or work! – keep your head well down, that's the secret of happiness!

Their raised thighs reminiscent of tree-trunks proliferate.

And a forest appears. In it large apes run round on all fours; these are dog-headed men.

THE CYNOCEPHALES

We jump from branch to branch to suck eggs, and we pluck out fledglings; then we put their nests on our heads to serve as caps.

Quick to rip the udders off cows, we also put out lynxes' eyes, we drop dung from the treetops, we flaunt our depravity in broad daylight.

Slashing flowers, crunching fruit, muddying streams and raping women, we are the masters – through the strength of our arms and the ferociousness of our hearts.

Keep it up, fellows! Snap your jaws!

Blood and milk dribble from their chops. The rain streams off their hairy backs.

Antony inhales the freshness of the green leaves.

They stir, the boughs clash together; and suddenly a great black stag appears, with a bull's head, and between his ears a thicket of white horns.

THE SADHUZAG

My seventy-four antlers are as hollow as flutes.

When I turn towards the south wind, the sounds produced by them attract the enraptured beasts to me. Snakes coil around my legs, wasps are glued to my nostrils, and parrots, doves and ibises land on my branches. – Listen!

He revolves his antlers, from which comes music ineffably sweet.
Antony presses both hands to his heart. He feels as though this melody will ravish his soul.

THE SADHUZAG

But when I turn towards the north wind, my antlers, spikier than a battalion of lances, give vent to a howling; the forests quake, the rivers run backwards, fruits burst their husks, and grasses stand on end like a coward's hair.
– Listen!

He tilts his branches, from which issue discordant cries; Antony is as if lacerated.
And his horror increases at the sight of:

THE MARTICHORAS

a gigantic red lion with a human face, and three rows of teeth.

The watery markings on my scarlet coat mimic the glinting of the great sands. My nostrils snort the dread of the wilderness. I spit the plague. I eat armies, when they venture into the desert.

My talons are twisted into gimlets, my teeth sharpened like a saw; and my tail, which lashes to and fro, bristles with darts which I fling to left and right, forwards or backwards. There! – there!

The Martichoras ejects the spines from his tail, which radiate like arrows in all directions. Drops of blood rain down, drumming on the foliage.

THE CATOBLEPAS

a black buffalo, with a hog's head which lolls on the ground and is attached to his shoulders by a narrow neck, long and flaccid like an emptied gut.

He is sprawled out flat; and his feet disappear under the enormous mane of stiff hairs covering his face.

Fat, melancholy, moody, I subsist with the constant sensation of warm mud under my belly. My skull weighs so much that to hold it up is beyond me. I roll it about, gently – and open-mouthed, I tear out with my tongue the poisonous grasses dampened by my breath. I once gobbled up my own paws unawares.

Nobody ever saw my eyes, Antony, or those who did so died. If I lifted my lids – my pink and swollen lids – you would die, straight away.

ANTONY

Oh! that one ... is ... is ... Suppose I were to want? ... His stupidity attracts me. No! no! I won't!

He stares fixedly at the ground.

But the grasses catch fire, and from the torsive flames rises

THE BASILISK

a great violet serpent with a trilobed crest and two teeth, one upper and one lower.

Watch out, you're falling into my clutches! I drink fire. Fire is my very self – and I breathe it up from everywhere: from clouds, stones, dead trees, animal fur, boggy surfaces. My temperature keeps the volcanoes going; I am the glitter in gems, the colour in metals.

THE GRIFFIN

a lion with a vulture's beak, and white wings, red paws and a blue neck.

I command the resplendent deep. I know the secret of the tombs where the old kings sleep.

A chain which runs from the wall holds their heads erect. Beside them, in porphyry basins full of black liquids, float women they have loved. Their treasures are arranged around halls, in lozenges, in little mounds, in pyramids; and lower down, well beneath the tombs, at the end of long journeys through stifling darkness, there are rivers of gold as well as forests of diamonds, fields of carbuncles, lakes of mercury.

With my back to the door of the underground way and one claw in the air, I spy with my flaming eye those who try to come near. The vast plain stretches to the horizon's end quite bare and whitened by the bones of travellers. For you the bronze panels will part, you will inhale the vapour of the mines, will go down into the caverns ... Quickly! quickly!

He digs up the ground with his paws, crowing like a cock.
A thousand voices answer him. The forest trembles.
And all sorts of frightful beasts spring out: the Tragelaphus, half stag and half ox; the Myrmecoleo, lion in front, ant at the rear, and whose genitals are back to front; the python Aksar, sixty cubits long, which dismayed Moses; the great weasel Pastinaca, which kills trees by its smell; the Presteros, whose contact induces imbecility; the Mirag, a horned hare which inhabits the isles of the sea. Phalmant the leopard splits its stomach by dint of howling; the Senad, a triple-headed bear, tears up its little ones with its tongue; Cepus the dog splashes the rocks with blue milk from its udders. Mosquitoes start to drone, toads to leap, snakes to hiss. Lightning flashes. Hail falls.

There come squalls, full of wonderful anatomies. There are alligators' heads on roe-deers' feet, owls with snakes' tails, swine with tigers' snouts, goats with donkeys' rumps, frogs as furry as bears, chameleons as big as hippopotamuses, calves with two heads, one of which weeps while the other bellows, quadruple foetuses linked by the navel and waltzing like tops, winged stomachs hovering like gnats.

They rain from the sky, they spring from the ground, they flow from the rocks. Eyeballs are everywhere flaming, and mouths roaring; there are bulging breasts, elongated claws, gnashing teeth, the smack of flesh on flesh. Some give birth, others copulate, or in a single mouthful eat each other up.

Stifled by their numbers, multiplying on contact, they crawl over one another – and they all heave around Antony with a regular movement, as if the ground were a ship's deck. Across his calves he feels the trail of snails, on his hands the chill of vipers; and spiders spinning their webs enclose him in their mesh.

But the circle of monsters opens, the sky all at once becomes blue, and

THE UNICORN

makes her appearance.

At the gallop! at the gallop!

My hooves are of ivory, my teeth of steel, my head is coloured crimson, my body snowy white, and the horn on my brow has the motley shades of the rainbow.

I journey from Chaldea to the Tartar desert, along the banks of the Ganges and through Mesopotamia. I overtake the ostriches. I run so fast that I leave the wind behind. I rub my back against palm trees. I roll in the bamboos. With one bound I jump the rivers. Doves fly above my head. I can be bridled only by a virgin.

At the gallop! at the gallop!

Antony watches her run off.

And still looking up, he catches sight of all the birds which feed on wind: the Gouith, the Ahuti, the Alphalim, the Iukneth of the mountains of Caff, the Homai of the Arabs which are the spirits of murdered men. He hears parrots pronouncing human words, then the great pelagian palmipeds which sob like children or cackle like old women.

Salt air assails his nostrils. A beach now lies before him.

In the distance rise jets of water, spouted by whales; and from the depth of the horizon

THE BEASTS OF THE SEA

round as wineskins, flat as blades, jagged as saws, advance by dragging themselves over the sand.

You shall come with us, down to our vastitudes where no one has yet been!

Various populations inhabit the countries of the Ocean. Some are at home with the tempests; others swim in the full transparence of the cold waves, graze like oxen on coral plains, inhale through their suckers the wash of the tides, or bear on their shoulders the weight of the sources of the sea.

A phosphorescence gleams around the whiskers of seals and the scales of fish. Urchins revolve like wheels, horns of Ammon uncoil like cables, oysters set their hinges creaking, polyps deploy their tentacles, jellyfish resemble balls of quivering crystal, sponges float, anemones spew water; mosses and sea-wrack have sprouted.

And all sorts of plants extend into branches, twist into gimlets, elongate into points, curve round into fans. Gourds look like breasts, lianas are interlaced like snakes.

The Dedaims of Babylon, which are trees, have human heads for their fruit; there are Mandrakes singing, the Baaras root runs in the grass.

Vegetable and animal can now no longer be distinguished. Polyparies looking like sycamores have arms on their boughs. Antony thinks he sees a caterpillar between two leaves; but a butterfly takes off. He is about to step on a pebble; a grey grasshopper leaps up. Insects resembling rose-petals adorn a bush; the remains of may-flies form a snowy layer on the ground.

And then the plants become confused with the rocks.

Stones are similar to brains, stalactites to nipples, iron flower to tapestries ornate with figures.

In fragments of ice he perceives efflorescences, imprints of shrubs and shells – so that he hardly knows whether these are the imprints of the things, or the things themselves. Diamonds gleam like eyes, minerals pulsate.

And he no longer feels any fear!

He lies flat on his stomach, leaning on both elbows; and holding his breath, he watches.

Insects having lost their insides continue to eat; dried ferns recover their freshness; missing limbs grow again.

At last, he sees little globular masses, no bigger than pin-heads and garnished with hairs all round. A vibration quivers across them.

ANTONY

deliriously:

O happiness! happiness! I have seen the birth of life, I have seen the beginning of movement. The blood in my veins is beating so hard that it will burst them. I feel like flying, swimming, yelping, bellowing, howling. I'd like to have wings, a carapace, a rind, to breathe out smoke, wave my trunk, twist my body, divide myself up, to be inside everything, to drift away with odours, develop as plants do, flow like water, vibrate like sound, gleam like light, to curl myself up into every shape, to penetrate each atom, to get down to the depth of matter – to be matter!

Day at last dawns; and like the raised curtains of a tabernacle, golden clouds furling into large scrolls uncover the sky.

There in the middle, inside the very disc of the sun, radiates the face of Jesus Christ.

Antony makes the sign of the cross and returns to his prayers.

NOTES

Abbreviations used in the Notes

Beausobre Isaac de Beausobre, *Histoire critique de Manichée et du Manichéisme*, Amsterdam, 1734–9, 2 vols.

C Flaubert, *Correspondance*, ed. Jean Bruneau, Gallimard, Bibliothèque de la Pléiade, 1973–. This edition is in progress.

Corr. Flaubert, *Correspondance*, Conard, Paris, 1926–33, 9 vols; and *Supplément*, Conard, Paris, 1954, 4 vols.

Creuzer Creuzer-Guigniaut, *Religions de l'antiquité considérées principalement dans leurs formes symboliques et mythologiques*, Treuttel et Würtz, Paris, 1825–51, 4 vols.

Life St Athanasius, *The Life of Saint Antony*, ed. Robert T. Meyer, Longmans, London, 1950.

Matter Jacques Matter, *Histoire critique du Gnosticisme*, Paris, 1828, 2 vols.

OC *Oeuvres complètes de Gustave Flaubert*, Conard, Paris, 1910, 18 vols.

OC (1971–5) *Oeuvres complètes de Gustave Flaubert*, Club de l'Honnête Homme, Paris, 1971–5, 16 vols.

Seznec Jean Seznec, *Nouvelles études sur la Tentation de Saint Antoine*, The Warburg Institute, London, 1949.

Tillemont Le Nain de Tillemont, *Mémoires pour servir à l'histoire écclésiastique des six premiers siècles*, Paris, 1701–12, 16 vols.

NOTES TO THE INTRODUCTION

1. I use this abbreviation throughout, but I refer to Flaubert's fictional figure as Antony to avoid confusion with the historical St Antony. I have preferred the spelling which is closest to the Latin *Antonius* and the French *Antoine*, despite the fact that 'Anthony' is the more familiar English spelling of the Saint's name.

2. See *C*, vol. I, pp. 884–5 and 920; and cf. the comments in Jean-Paul Sartre, *L'Idiot de la famille: Gustave Flaubert de 1821 à 1857* (Gallimard, Paris, 1971, 3 vols.), especially vol. I, pp. 66–7 and 87–9.

3. *Corr.*, vol. II, p. 412.

4. *Corr.*, vol. IV, p. 169.

5. A useful brief survey is Jean Seznec's 'The Temptation of St Anthony in Art', *Magazine of Art*, vol. XL (1947), pp. 86–93. See also Theodore Reff, 'Cézanne, Flaubert, St Anthony, and the Queen of Sheba', *Art Bulletin*, vol. XLIV (1962), pp. 113–25.

6. See Georges Dubosc, *Trois Normands* (Henri Defontaine, Rouen, 1917), p. 139, and André Dubuc, 'La Tentation de Saint Antoine', *Les Amis de Flaubert*, no. 45 (Dec. 1974), pp. 9–17; and cf. *C*, vol. I, p. 959.

7. *Corr.*, vol. III, p. 331.

8. See Benjamin F. Bart, *Flaubert* (Syracuse University Press, Syracuse, 1967), pp. 93–5, and *C*, vol. I, pp. 943–4

9. See *Corr. Supplément* (1864–71), pp. 94–5

10. *Corr.*, vol. III, p. 270.

11. See *C*, vol. I, p. 471, and *Corr.*, vol. IV, p. 180.

12. *C*, vol. I, p. 281.

13. See *C*, vol. I, p. 489, and *Corr.*, vol. III, p. 77.

14. See *C*, vol I, pp. 230, 462 and 989.

15. *OC*, *Par les champs et par les grèves*, pp. 130–1.

16. *C*, vol. I, pp. 287 and 320.

17. See *Corr.*, vol. IV, p. 233.

18. See Jean-Paul Sartre, *L'Idiot de la famille*, vol. I, p. 1018.

19. *C*, vol. I, pp. 494–5.

20. The impact of Romanticism on the young Flaubert is challengingly discussed by Sartre in *L'Idiot de la famille*, vol. II, pp. 1364 ff.

21. Albert Thibaudet, *Gustave Flaubert* (Gallimard, Paris, 1935), p. 167.

22. *Corr.*, vol. III, p. 156.

23. *Corr.*, vol. V, p. 72.

24. See Alfred Le Poittevin, *Une Promenade de Bélial et oeuvres inédites*, ed. René Descharmes (Paris, 1924), p. 47, and cf. *OC*, *Bouvard et Pécuchet*, p. 274.

25. I am indebted to the discussion of Spinoza's influence on Flaubert in *Les Débuts littéraires de Gustave Flaubert (1831–1845)* (Armand Colin, Paris, 1962), pp. 444–53 and 511–12. Cf. also A. Gyergai's argument on the close links between Flaubert's aesthetics and Spinoza's *Ethics* in 'Flaubert et Spinoza', *Les Amis de Flaubert*, no. 39 (Dec. 1971), pp. 11–22.

26. See Bruneau, *Les Débuts littéraires de Gustave Flaubert*, pp. 537–8, and E. W. Fischer, 'La Spirale: un inédit de Gustave Flaubert', *La Table Ronde* (April 1958), pp. 96–124; also *OC* (1971–5), vol. XII, pp. 229–32.

27. *C*, vol. I, p. 675.

28. See *Corr.*, vol. IV, p. 104, vol. II, pp. 362 and 461–2, and vol. VI, p. 385.

29. See the account in Maxime Du Camp, *Souvenirs littéraires*, (Paris, 1882–3), vol. I, pp. 427–35.

30. *OC*, *La Tentation de Saint Antoine*, p. 352.

31. *Ibid.*, p. 372.

32. *Ibid.*, pp. 588–9.

33. See *Corr.*, vol. II, pp. 344–5, 362 and 365, vol. III, p. 156, and VI, 31, 132, 215, 250 and 397.

34. See *OC* (1971–5), vol. IV, p. 305, and the editors' comments in vol. IX, p. 21; and cf. the fragment published at the end of *La Première Tentation de Saint Antoine (1849–1856)* (which is actually the 1856 version), ed. Louis Bertrand (Charpentier, Paris, 1908), pp. 275–7.

35. See Benjamin F. Bart's discussion in *Flaubert's Landscape Descriptions* (Ann Arbor, 1956), pp. 33–7.

36. See *C*, vol. I, p. 234, and *Corr.*, vol. IV, p. 169.

37. *Oeuvres complètes*, ed. Y.-G. Le Dantec and Claude Pichois (Gallimard, Bibliothèque de la Pléiade, 1961), p. 657.

38. See E. Esquirol, *Des Maladies mentales* (Paris, 1838), p. 9; and see note 128 below.

39. For a summary of the critics' reactions, see *OC* (1971–5), vol. I, pp. 19–20 and 34–5; see also Taine's letter quoted in *OC, La Tentation de Saint Antoine*, p. 683, and Renan's letter in *Feuilles détachées* (Paris, 1892), pp. 345–6.

40. Hugo's comment is quoted in *OC, La Tentation de Saint Antoine*, p. 682; see also J.-K. Huysmans, *A Rebours*, ed. Marc Fumaroli (Gallimard, 1977), pp. 215 and 307–10.

41. See Jean Seznec, *Nouvelles études sur la Tentation de Saint Antoine* (The Warburg Institute, London, 1949), pp. 38–43. I abbreviate subsequent mentions of this work to 'Seznec'.

42. See Francis J. Carmody, 'Rimbaud and *La Tentation de Saint Antoine*', *PMLA*, vol. LXXIX (Dec. 1964), pp. 594–603; to my mind, the most plausible textual parallels are those between *Nuit de l'Enfer* and chapter II of *Saint Antoine*.

43. See Theodore Reff's article referred to in note 5 above, and his 'Images of Flaubert's Queen of Sheba in later nineteenth-century art' in *The Artist and the Writer in France: Essays in honour of Jean Seznec*, ed. Francis Haskell, Anthony Levi and Roger Shackleton (Clarendon Press, Oxford, 1974), pp. 126–33.

44. See 'Flaubert and the Graphic Arts', *Journal of the Warburg and Courtauld Institutes*, vol. VIII (1945), pp. 186–8.

45. See Alfred Lombard, *Flaubert et Saint Antoine* (Paris, 1934), pp. 95–6, and the essay by Reff referred to in note 43 above, pp. 131–2.

46. See Jules Laforgue, *Moralités légendaires* (Paris, 1887), pp. 132 and 139–40.

47. *Flaubert und seine 'Versuchung des heiligen Antonius': Ein Beitrag zur Künstler Psychologie* (J. C. C. Bruns, Minden, 1912).

48. Quoted in Ernest Jones, *Sigmund Freud, Life and Work* (London, 1953–7), vol. I, pp. 191–2.

49. *C*, vol. I, p. 421.

50. See *C*, vol. I, pp. 605–7, and Gustave Flaubert, *Voyages*, ed. René Dumesnil (Paris, 1948), pp. 86–91 and 594–6.

51. See Bart's comments in *Flaubert*, pp. 103, 171, 220–1 and 743.

52. *C*, vol. I, p. 423.

53. See *OC, Notes de voyage*, vol. II, p. 359.

54. *Corr.*, vol. III, p. 77.

55. *Corr.*, vol. III, pp. 216–17. Cf. *The Diaries of Franz Kafka*, ed. Max Brod (Penguin, Harmondsworth, 1972), p. 481, and *Letters to Friends, Family and Editors* (John Calder, London, 1978), pp. 49 and 59.

56. *The Romantic Agony* (Oxford University Press, London, 1951), pp. 154 and 307.

57. See *Le 'Conte Oriental' de Gustave Flaubert* (Denoël, Paris, 1973), especially pp. 37–80. Cf. the hostile discussion in Edward W. Said, *Orientalism* (Routledge & Kegan Paul, 1978), pp. 184–90.

58. See *Oeuvres* (Pléiade, 1961), pp. 74, 244, 1247, 1286–7 and 1294, and the discussion in Daniel Vouga, *Baudelaire et Joseph de Maistre* (José Corti, Paris, 1957), pp. 210–19.

59. The point is emphasised by Harry Levin in 'Flaubert: Portrait of the Artist as a Saint', *Kenyon Review*, vol. X (1948), pp. 28–43.

60. *Corr.*, vol. III, p. 304.

61. See *Stendhal et Flaubert* (Seuil, Paris, 1970), especially the discussion of Flaubert's 'frenetic quest' on pp. 189–97.

62. See *OC, Notes de Voyage*, vol. II, pp. 356 and 367.

63. *C*, vol. I, p. 429.

64. See *Les Débuts littéraires de Gustave Flaubert*, pp. 462–4.

65. *C*, vol. I, p. 350.

66. See Paul Valéry, *Oeuvres*, ed. Jean Hytier (Gallimard, Bibliothèque de la Pléiade, 1965), vol. I, pp. 613–19.

67. The quotations that follow are taken from 'La Bibliothèque Fantastique', in *La Tentation de Saint Antoine*, ed. Henri Ronse (Gallimard, Livre de Poche, Paris, 1971), pp. 7–33.

68. See 'La Spirale des sept péchés', *Critique*, vol. XXVI (May 1970), pp. 387–412.

69. See *Gustave Flaubert* (Paris, 1912), pp. 117 and pp. 122–6.

70. *OC, La Tentation de Saint Antoine*, p. 327.

71. *OC, Salammbô*, pp. 412–13.

72. *OC, Trois contes*, pp. 124–5.

73. *C*, vol. I, p. 433.

74. *Histoire de la folie* (Plon, Collection 10/18, Paris, 1974), p. 302.

75. *Ibid.*, p. 97.

76. *L'Idiot de la famille*, vol. II, p. 1186.

77. *Ibid.*, vol. II, pp. 1306–8.

78. *Ibid.*, vol. II, pp. 1282–3; for Flaubert's sense of delicious involvement in the creation of this scene, see *Corr.*, vol. III, p. 405.

79. *L'Idiot de la famille*, vol. II, p. 1302, and Friedrich Nietzsche, *The Will to Power*, ed. Walter Kaufmann (Vintage Books, New York, 1968), p. 66.

80. *L'Idiot de la famille*, vol. II, p. 1372.

81. See *Flaubert: The Uses of Uncertainty* (Paul Elek, London, 1974), especially pp. 173–85.

82. *Ibid.*, p. 207.

83. *Ibid.*, p. 227.

84. *Ibid.*, p. 227.

85. *Ibid.*, p. 228.

86. *Ibid.*, p. 184.

87. See *Sade, Fourier, Loyola* (Jonathan Cape, London, 1977), p. 36.

88. See Valéry, *Oeuvres* (1965), vol. I, pp. 617–19, and Marcel Proust, 'A propos du "style" de Flaubert', in *Chroniques* (Gallimard, Paris, 1927), especially pp. 193–203.

89. See *Corr.*, vol. II, p. 411, and vol. III, p. 210, and *OC, La Tentation de Saint Antoine*, p. 417.

90. *OC, Trois Contes*, p. 56.

91. *OC, La Tentation de Saint Antoine*, p. 218.

92. See *Corr.*, vol. VI, p. 456.

93. See especially his *Nouvelles études sur la Tentation de Saint Antoine*, to which I have been greatly indebted throughout my work on Flaubert.

94. *OC, Bouvard et Pécuchet*, p. 41.

95. See *Dictionnaire historique et critique* (Rotterdam, 1720), article 'Manichéens'.

96. *Ibid.*, article 'Pauliciens'.

97. See *Histoire critique du Gnosticisme* (Paris, 1828), vol. II, p. 357.

98. *Ibid.*, vol. II, p. 315.

99. See Isaac de Beausobre, *Histoire critique de Manichée et du Manichéisme* (Amsterdam, 1734–9), vol. II, p. 471.

100. See 'Saint Irénée et les Gnostiques de son temps', *Revue des Deux Mondes*, vol. LV (Jan. 1865), p. 1027.

101. *Corr.*, vol. IV, pp. 313–14.

102. *Revue des Deux Mondes*, vol. LV, p. 1026.

103. See *OC, La Tentation de Saint Antoine*, p. 683.

104. See Robert M. Grant, *Gnosticism and Early Christianity* (Harper Torchbook, New York, 1966), pp. 142–7.

105. See Beausobre, vol. II, p. 28.

106. *Gnosticism and Early Christianity*, pp. 8–9.

107. Matter, vol. II, p. 94.

108. Creuzer-Guigniaut, *Religions de l'Antiquité* (Paris, 1825–51), vol. II, p. 915.

109. See *Introduction à l'histoire du Buddhisme Indien* (Paris, 1844), especially pp. 194, 335–6 and 339–40.

110. See *OC* (1971–5), vol. IV, p. 305.

111. See Creuzer, vol. I, pp. 408 and 494–5.

112. *C*, vol. I, p. 437.

113. Creuzer, vol. I, p. 392.

114. See p. 16 above and cf. Creuzer, vol. I, pp. 47–8, and *The Bhagavad Gita*, chapter vii, verse 7; on Flaubert's choice of translations see *C*, vol. I, p. 976 and p. 1003.

115. *Corr.*, vol. II, p. 345.

116. See *OC* (1971–5), vol. IV, p. 315.

117. *C*, vol. I, p. 551.

118. See 'Sphinx und Chimäre: Zu Einer Episode der *Tentation de Saint Antoine*', in *Aufsatze zur Themen und Motivgeschichte. Festschrift für Hellmuth Petriconi* (Hamburg, 1965), pp. 135–49.

119. See *OC* (1971–5), vol. IV, p. 363.

120. See *Flaubert et Saint Antoine*, p. 31.

121. *OC, Par les champs et par les grèves*, pp. 60–1.

122. *Corr.*, vol. V, p. 95.

123. Cf. Creuzer, vol. I, p. 503.

124. See *OC* (1971–5), vol. IV, p. 363.

125. See Seznec, pp. 76–81.

126. For my comments I am indebted to the article by J. S. Wilkie, 'Buffon, Lamarck and Darwin: The originality of Darwin's Theory of Evolution', in *Darwin's Biological Work*, ed. P. R. Bell (Cambridge University Press, 1959), pp. 262–307, 340–3.

127. See *Oeuvres Philosophiques* (Garnier Frères, Paris, 1964), pp. 268 and 302–3.

128. See Seznec, p. 81. Flaubert's bibliography on *Saint Antony* was first published in 1908 by Louis Bertrand at the end of his edition of the 1856 version, and is reproduced in *OC* (1971–5), vol. IX, pp. 521–34.

129. See *L'Hétérogénie ou Traité de la génération spontanée* (Paris, 1859), especially ch. II, 'Métaphysique', pp. 95–137.

130. *Ibid.*, p. 123.

131. Edmond et Jules de Goncourt, *Journal*, ed. Robert Ricatte (Fasquelle and Flammarion, Paris, 1956), vol. II, p. 839.

132. *OC* (1971–5), vol. IV, pp. 317, 362 and 366.

133. *Literary Essays of Ezra Pound*, ed. T. S. Eliot (Faber, London, 1960), p. 406.

134. See the discussion in Seznec, pp. 40–6.

135. *Corr.*, vol. VIII, p. 374.

136. *Pagan and Christian in an Age of Anxiety* (Cambridge University Press, 1965), p. 37.
137. *Ibid.*, p. 82.
138. See 'The Rise and Function of the Holy Man', *Journal of Roman Studies*, vol. LXI (1971), pp. 80–101.
139. See *OC, Notes de Voyage*, vol. II, p. 367, and *C*, vol. I, p. 209.
140. See *Tristes tropiques* (Plon, Paris, 1955), pp. 445–54.
141. See *The Savage Mind* (Weidenfeld & Nicolson, London, 1966), p. 256.
142. *Lévi-Strauss* (Fontana/Collins, London, 1970), p. 16.
143. *The Savage Mind*, p. 212.
144. *C*, vol. I, p. 314.
145. *Tristes tropiques*, p. 454.
146. See Matter, vol. II, pp. 362–3.
147. See *Tristes tropiques*, pp. 468 and 475–6.
148. *Ibid.*, pp. 479–80.
149. See *Gustave Flaubert*, p. 175.
150. See *Tristes tropiques*, p. 478.

NOTES TO THE TRANSLATION

I have tried to keep as closely as possible to Flaubert's rhythm and punctuation while writing modern English. Every comma has been listened to, but not quite all have survived. And I hope to have conveyed the ironic and humorous as well as the lyrical qualities of his style. These notes are intended to provide the reader mainly with a historical perspective, and to indicate occasionally how Flaubert treats his material. But they are not intended as a comprehensive survey of his sources, nor do they offer detailed comparisons between the third version and the two earlier ones. The best starting-point for scholarly study is the text of the three versions contained in volumes IV and IX of the Club de l'Honnête Homme edition of Flaubert's works (Paris, 1971–5); various manuscript drafts and documents are also published there, including Flaubert's bibliography for *Saint Antony* (see vol. IX, pp. 521–34). The most thorough account of Flaubert's sources is to be found in the books and articles by Jean Seznec which I refer to in the course of the notes.

CHAPTER I

p. 61   *The Thebaid.* The scene is set in Upper Egypt, where formerly flourished Thebes, ancient capital city and seat of the worship of Ammon, sacked c. 30 BC. Mount Colzim, St Antony's Inner Mountain, lies in the open desert about seventy-five miles east of the Nile. Flaubert has made a picturesque conflation of this site with that of the Outer Mountain, at Pispir on the east bank of the Nile; see *Life*, pp. 110 and 120. On the connections between this description and Flaubert's experience of unusual light effects in Greece, see Benjamin F. Bart, *Flaubert's Landscape Descriptions* (Ann Arbor, 1956), pp. 53–7.

The hermit's cabin. Another picturesque detail (and I have therefore opted for 'cabin' rather than the more prosaic 'hut'); St Antony is thought to have lived in a cleft in the rock.

p. 62   *My mother ... my sister ... Ammonaria.* St Antony's parents had died some years earlier, and Athanasius mentions an only sister who was then still very young; see *Life*, p. 19. Flaubert's Ammonaria, whose relation to Antony is left vague (could she be a second sister?) is a fictional character created in the final version to act as a focus for Antony's erotic and sadistic obsessions. See also note to p. 64 below.

p. 63   *Alexandria.* The Hellenic capital of Egypt, founded by Alexander the Great in 332 BC, notable for its two harbours and its lighthouse on the island of Pharos. A centre for trade between the Mediterranean and the East, the city also attracted scholars and scientists to its famous library and Museum, founded in the reign of Ptolemy Soter (323–285 BC). In Roman times, after its submission to Augustus in 30 BC, Alexandria developed a school of philosophy which drew on both Eastern and Western thought and combined Hellenic and Jewish traditions, culminating in the Neoplatonism of the third century which in turn influenced Christian theologians. The city was divided into Jewish, Greek and Egyptian quarters. The Greek or royal quarter contained the principal buildings, including the Museum, the Posidium or Temple of the sea-god, the Caesareum where divine honours were paid to past and present emperors, the Mausoleum of the Ptolemies also known as the Soma where lay the body of Alexander the Great, and the Panium, a stone mound which commanded a view of the whole city.

Didymus. St Antony visited Alexandria in about 311, at the time of the Maximinian persecution, between his period at Pispir and his retreat to the Inner Mountain; he returned to denounce the Arian heresy at a later time, identified by modern authorities as 337–8. On the latter occasion he is said to have paid three visits to Didymus the Blind (c. 313–c. 398), head of the catechetical school of Alexandria. Flaubert has transposed and expanded this detail into an earlier scholarly interlude, despite the fact that Didymus would then hardly have been born. Presumably he felt the need to justify the sophistication of some of Antony's temptations by giving him a more erudite background. See *Life*, pp. 59, 78, 118–19 and 128–9.

Cimmerians. Ancient northern people who came from south Russia to invade Asia Minor towards the end of the eighth century BC.

Gymnosophists. Literally, 'naked sages', a sect of ancient Hindu philosophers who practiced asceticism and meditation.

Mani, Valentine, Basilides. Gnostic teachers. Cf. notes to pp. 102, 106, 107 below.

Arius. Born about 256, Arius was the celebrated leader of the heretical party which taught that the son of God or Logos was an angelic creature essentially different from God the Father, who was created out of nothing, and acted as an intermediary between God and the world. The Arian doctrine was condemned, and the consubstantiality of Father and Son upheld, when Constantine called the first ecumenical council at Nicaea in 325. But the theological and political struggle continued; Constantine was gradually won over to the Arian party; and Arius himself was about to be re-admitted into the Church when he suddenly died in 336.

Colzim. It was not here but at Pispir, the Outer Mountain, that fellow anchorites gathered round St Antony. By confusing the circumstances, Flaubert turns what was deliberate isolation into Antony's state of bewildered abandonment.

Gnosticism. The nature and origins of Gnosticism are still controversial. The word is loosely used to denote various systems of belief which flourished in the second and third centuries, and which promised superior knowledge or *gnosis* to the initiated. Besides taking many elements from Christianity, these syncretic religions absorbed ideas from Greek, Semitic, and Oriental sources. Some sects were largely Christian, others almost wholly pagan, and they relied in varying degrees on philosophical mysticism and on crude magic. Flaubert's authorities, notably Jacques Matter, emphasised the pre-Christian, Oriental origins of Gnosticism, and its intuitive non-rationalistic character.

The salient feature of Gnosticism is its dualism. Believing in a supreme, transcendent God who could not be responsible for evil, Gnostics concluded that the evil principle was to be found, whether as active power or passive presence, in the cosmos. To account for this polarised state of things, they adopted the Greek concept of emanation according to which a series of divine beings or eons, often occurring in couples or syzygies, were interpolated between God and creation. The further the eons got from their original source, the less they resembled it. And at some point, so the Gnostics thought, a dislocation occurred, and particles of the divine suffered a fall into a lower state. Matter came into existence, as well as the Demiurge, who created man out of inert matter. The Demiurge was often identified with the Jewish Jehovah, so that Gnostics differed from Christians in maintaining that the God of the Old Testament was not the supreme God but an inferior creator or legislator, who acted either in ignorance or with deliberate malevolence. While they believed that matter, and above all flesh, was irreducibly evil, they also believed that a spark of divinity survived in man and might ultimately be freed from its alien prison. Through *gnosis*, the elect would realise their true, divine being. Some sects regarded Christ as one of the first of the Eons, who appeared in order to spread the saving knowledge. But they could not accept the Christian doctrine of the incarnation, or the suffering on the cross, or the resurrection of the flesh: either the divine Christ parted from the mortal Jesus before the crucifixion, or Christ's body was all along a phantom, his suffering an illusion. This mesh of beliefs could result in very various codes of behaviour. Some sects considered that only the strictest asceticism could secure salvation, others that no bodily licence could affect the soul, since spirit and matter were utterly distinct – to the pure all things are pure. Only the most fanatic sects were totally antinomian.

The persecution. The Maximinian persecution. Cf. note to p. 63 above on *Didymus*.

The temple of Serapis. The outstanding feature of the Egyptian quarter was the Serapeum. Besides its religious function, it served to house part of the library.

p. 64   *Ammonaria.* Eusebius records that two Ammonarias were martyred in Alexandria in 250, during the earlier Decian persecution. See *Ecclesiastical History*, book VI, chapter xli.

Athanasius. St Antony's biographer (c. 295–373), bishop of Alexandria in 328, a lifelong champion of the Nicene faith and enemy of the Arians. He was exiled on five separate occasions, the first time in 335, when St Antony wrote to the Emperor Constantine in his defence. Flaubert's chronology is indistinct, but this first exile seems to have been in his mind since further incidents relating to it are mentioned in chapter III.

Hilarion. Born about 293, Hilarion went as a boy of fifteen to spend some months with St Antony at his Outer Mountain, before becoming a solitary in Palestine. He exchanged letters with St Antony and visited the Inner Mountain on the first anniversary of the saint's death, spending the night in prayer, lying on the little bed, and kissing it as if St Antony had only just left. See Tillemont, vol. VII, pp. 110–11 and 138–9. Building on these indications, Flaubert imagines a subtly intellectual intimacy between Antony and his disciple. This allows Hilarion to fill the role assigned in the first version of *Saint Antony* to Logic, who appeared as a black dwarf, and Science, who appeared as a white-haired child with an outsize head.

Ammon. Egyptian monk who withdrew in about 330 to the Nitrian desert west of the Nile and founded a great cenobitic centre. He visited St Antony several times, but I find no reference to a Roman trip. Flaubert is confusing him with another Ammon or Ammonius, also a celebrated Nitrian monk, who went in about 341 with Athanasius to Rome, where he confined his sight-seeing to the church of St Peter and St Paul. Antony's nostalgia for travel is thoroughly Flaubertian.

p. 65   *Pabena.* Perhaps a conflation of Tabennesis and Pabau, two monasteries founded by Pachomius (292–346), the famous originator of cenobitic monasticism.

Canopic river. Most westerly of the three great branches of the Nile, linked by canal with Lake Mareotis and Alexandria.

p. 66   *Better be dead! ... stars pulsate.* A very similar, if more humorous, transition from suicidal impulses to religious serenity is experienced by Bouvard and Pécuchet; see *OC*, *Bouvard et Pécuchet*, pp. 296–7.

the fat book. There is doubt as to whether St Antony could read or write. Some letters of his which survive in Latin translations were probably in the first place dictated in Coptic. But Flaubert had good iconographical precedent for his scenario: in the painting then assigned to Brueghel, the saint is shown poring over a large volume. The random pinpointing of scriptural passages was normally practised as a method of divination, but here Flaubert uses it to provide a springboard for Antony's revealing reverie. According to Michel Foucault, this open book is the key to the organisation of the whole work. Cf. pp. 27ff. above.

'*He saw ... and eat*'. See Acts X, 11.

p. 67   '*So the Jews ... whom they hated.*' See Esther IX, 5. Flaubert owned an edition of the Bible de Sacy, but I have not identified any single French version of the Bible as his source, nor found any precedent for his 'ceux qu'ils haïssaient' or 'those whom they hated', which replaces the normal 'those who hated them', thus adding a vindictive twist to what is already a notoriously godless story. My own translation of the texts is partly based on the Revised Version.

'*Nebuchadnezzar ... Daniel.*' See Daniel II, 46.

'*Hezekiah ... house.*' See 2 Kings XX, 13.

p. 68   '*Now when ... questions.*' See 1 Kings X, 1.

immutable order. Antony is talking as a faulty Plotinian.

Flaubert has based the passage closely on an account of the cosmology of Plotinus, who apparently frowned upon just such a magical tinkering with the 'immutable order' as appeals to Antony; see Etienne Vacherot, *Histoire critique de l'école d'Alexandrie* (Paris, 1846), vol. I, p. 519.

an illusion. Flaubert aimed at 'gradations of distinctness' in Antony's illusions, noting that 'at first he knows they are visions, he rebels, wants to chase them away, cannot do so. Then accepts them as realities.' See *OC* (1971–5), vol. IV, p. 335.

p. 69   *Constantine.* Constantine the Great (274–337), who became Emperor in 306, and in 313 published the edict of toleration which made possible the eventual adoption of Christianity as the State's official religion. He was baptised on his death-bed. On his correspondence with St Antony, see *Life*, pp. 86 and 133.

Balacius. Arian sympathiser and military commander in the province of Egypt, 340–45. St Antony wrote to him, warning him not to persecute orthodox Christians. See *Life*, pp. 91 and 135.

Eusebius. Abbot of Corypha in Syria, who loaded himself with chains as penance for a moment's irreligious absorption in the sight of some labourers in the fields.

Macarius. Macarius the Alexandrian, who condemned himself to months of nakedness in marshy country after he had killed one mosquito in a moment of irritation.

Pachomius. See note to p. 65 above on *Pabena*.

one long martyrdom. Antony's boastfulness is in contrast to St Antony's humble admiration for the feats of his fellow-anchorites. See *Life*, p. 21.

The Nicene Fathers. See note to p. 63 above on *Arius*. St Antony was of course not present at the Council, but was profoundly respectful of the clergy. See *Life*, p. 76. Antony's half-envious scorn of the orthodox party suggests Flaubertian anticlericalism.

Paphnutius. Christian confessor who suffered the standard mutilations of those condemned to work in the mines.

Diocletian. Roman Emperor from 284 to his abdication in 305, famous for his administrative reforms and military discipline. His increasingly savage persecution of the Christian Church, encouraged by the future Emperor Galerius, began in 303.

Theophilus . . . John . . . Spiridion. The presence of two bishops from outlandish countries, the pastoral occupation of a third, and the great age of Alexander (Athanasius's predecessor as bishop of Alexandria) were normally mentioned with admiration, as in Socrates, *Ecclesiastical History*, book I, chapter xii. Flaubert twists these details into grounds for Antony's contempt.

p. 72   *Antony falls onto the mat.* The description of Antony's hallucinatory crisis may be compared to the account which Flaubert made to Taine of his own attacks, in which just such a contrast between a lightning fugue of images and a slowly spreading, engulfing effect is indicated. See *Corr., Supplément* (1864–1871), pp. 93–5.

CHAPTER II

p. 74   *The jackals.* Antony is without the cooperation secured by his prototype, who stemmed the inroads made by wild beasts on his supplies by catching hold of one and admonishing it gently. See *Life*, p. 63.

a table. The following description replaces the pig's dream of the first version, quoted on p. 14 above.

p. 76   *Staters . . . Caesar.* This numismatic cascade includes ancient Persian *cycles* or sigli, darics and Aryandics, Greek staters doubtless bearing the head of Alexander the Great, Macedonian coins perhaps bearing the head of Demetrius I (336–283 BC), Egyptian coins (the Ptolemaic currency being notable for its splendid gold pieces) and imperial Roman coinage.

p. 77   *Hermes.* Greek god of wisdom, also messenger of the gods and guide of dead souls.

Anubis. Egyptian messenger of the gods who guided the souls of the dead to Osiris, god of the underworld, and was therefore identified with Hermes.

p. 78   *to kill the Arians.* St Antony foretold the violence which the Church would suffer at the hands of the Arians. See *Life*, p. 88. But the orgy of killing here described is directed on the contrary against the Arians, and is a case of voyeuristic sadism rather than clairvoyance. Flaubert's account may owe something to the events of 391, when the patriarch of Alexandria, Theophilus, called in bands of monks to destroy the great shrine of Serapis. I also think it possible that he is influenced by St Augustine's account of the book-burning Circumcellions, notorious for cudgels and cruelty. See note to p. 115 below on *Circumcellions*, and *Oeuvres de Saint Augustin* (Desclée de Brouwer, 1936–), especially vol. 30, p. 463, and vol. 32, pp. 185–7, 303. Some details of the description, however, suggest its derivation from the pig's dream of the first version, quoted on p. 14 above.

p. 79   *a new town.* Constantinople, the new Christian capital of the East, completed in May 330 and erected on the site of Byzantium.

p. 80   *Antioch, Ephesus.* Antioch in Syria and Ephesus in Asia Minor, the only two cities of the Eastern Empire to rival Alexandria in importance.

Novatians. Third-century sect who refused to readmit to communion Christians who lapsed in the Decian persecution of 249.

Meletians. Followers of Meletius, excommunicated bishop of Lycopolis; during the Diocletian persecution of 303 he claimed certain rights normally exercised by the absentee bishop of Alexandria, and he later joined the Arians.

Mercury. Roman god of trade.

three bronze serpents. These intertwined serpents decorated the pagan tripod of Delphi, which Constantine purloined for his new hippodrome.

wooden eggs . . . seven dolphins. The dolphins indicate the total number of rounds making up the course; the eggs, one of which is removed at the end of each round, indicate how many are still to run.

Patricians. Constantine conferred the title of *patricius* as a reward for service to the Empire.

the blue faction . . . the green. Spectator support was divided between two factions of chariot-drivers clothed in different colours.

p. 81 *Crispus.* Constantine's eldest son, murdered in 326 in obscure circumstances.

the Fathers of the Council of Nicaea. The degradation of the Nicene Fathers is exaggerated; the normal fate for those in disgrace was exile.

Presently a huge hall. An evocation of the legendary temples and palaces of Babylon, built during Nebuchadnezzar's reign in the sixth and seventh centuries BC.

p. 82 *the tower of Babel.* See Genesis XI, 1–9. The name Babylon is possibly a later form of the Hebrew Babel.

Antony . . . bellows like a bull. Cf. Nebuchadnezzar's temporary metamorphosis into an ox, in Daniel IV, 33.

p. 84 *The Queen of Sheba.* In elaborating this piquant episode, Flaubert drew both on the account in 1 Kings X and on Arab legends; he may also have come across a medieval version of

St Antony's life in which the saint is tempted by a diabolical queen, who proposes marriage, but saves himself by making the sign of the cross. See André Chastel, 'L'Episode de la Reine de Saba dans *La Tentation de Saint Antoine*', in *Romanic Review*, vol. XL (1949), pp. 261-7.

p. 85   *a pebble between their teeth.* This method of encouraging salivation was tried by Flaubert on his travels. See Maxime Du Camp, *Souvenirs littéraires* (Paris, 1882-3), vol. I, p. 491.

p. 85   *Here's balm ... Bactria.* The Queen's tempting offers are
-6   mostly of celebrated provenance. Gennesareth was the principal lake of Palestine; Cape Gardefan or Gardefui was the easternmost headland of Africa, a region so rich in spices as to be known as the *Aromata Promontorium*; south of Cape Gardefan lay the Ethiopian headland of Bazium, notable for its gold mines; Tartessus was a district equivalent to the modern Andalusia in southern Spain, rich in iron, lead, silver, and tin, for which Flaubert uses the Greek word *kassiteros*; Pandion was a region at the southern end of the peninsula of Hindustan, and Palaesimundum is an ancient name for Sri Lanka; even more remote were Bactria, a large province in Central Asia, and Issidonia, a town or region also in Central Asia; Chalybon, Emath or Emesa, and Palmyra were Syrian cities, and Assur was the original capital of Assyria. Ladanum is a resin exuded by the leaves of the Cistus or rock-rose genus, and silphium a plant which the Greeks imported from Cyrenaica for culinary and medicinal purposes. The tacha or tachas is a biblical animal whose hide was used to cover the ark (see Numbers IV, 6); it has been variously identified as goat, ferret, badger, dolphin, sea-cow and (in the New English Bible) porpoise. But the most interesting reference is, implicitly, to the famous Phoenician city which is described as covered with 'blue and purple from the isles of Elishah' in Ezekiel XXVII, 7. The Queen of Sheba's eloquence owes much to the whole of this chapter of the Bible in which the prophet laments the end of the beauty and the affluence of Tyre.

p. 86   *Dgian-ben-Dgian.* Oriental jinn or spirit whose magical shield supposedly belonged to three Solomons in turn.

p. 88   *Simorg-Anka.* Fabulous bird of Persian legends. In the Koran the Queen of Sheba is associated with the Hoopoe, who flies around the world, discovers the marvellous country she rules over and tells Solomon of her existence. See André Chastel, 'La Légende de la Reine de Saba', in *Revue de l'Histoire des Religions*, vol. 120 (1939), pp. 27–44. Cf. also Jorge Luis Borges and Margarita Guerrero, *The Book of Imaginary Beings*, revised, enlarged and translated by Norman Thomas di Giovanni (Jonathan Cape, London, 1970), pp. 204–5.

p. 89   *hopping on one foot.* For references to Oriental versions of the legend in which the Queen of Sheba betrays a hairy leg or a cloven foot as a sign of diabolical origins, see the articles by Chastel cited in notes to pp. 84 and 88 above on the *Queen of Sheba* and *Simorg-Anka.* But Flaubert is obviously not prepared to shatter his erotic *pièce de résistance* too sharply.

CHAPTER III

p. 90   *a Cabirus.* The Cabiri were ancient gods very popular in Hellenistic times, whose mysteries were celebrated on the island of Samothrace. In art they were depicted as squat, dwarf-like figures.

p. 91   *Paul the hermit.* Paul the Simple, who was determined, aged sixty, to qualify as an anchorite and was put through some gruelling ascetic paces by St Antony.

       Schebar. Or Schebat. The eleventh month of the Jewish religious year.

p. 92   *Athanasius.* See note to p. 64 above. The accusations cited by Hilarion were part of the virulent campaign mounted by his enemies to secure his exile in 335.

p. 94   *Moloch.* Israelite god whose cult was notorious for the live incineration of children. Cf. 2 Kings XXIII, 10, and Flaubert's account of Carthaginian sacrifices to the god in chapter XIII of *Salammbô*.

p. 95 *Montanists.* Apocalyptic sect of the latter half of the second century, followers of the Phrygian Montanus, who claimed that the Holy Spirit had inspired him to announce the third revelation, superceding that of the Law and the Gospel. Their rigid discipline and millenarian fervour made them seek out persecution.

Denys, Cyprian and Gregory ... Peter of Alexandria ... the Council of Elvira. The Decian persecution of 249–51 threw into relief the moral choices connected with martyrdom. Denys, bishop of Alexandria, fled from the city and subsequently recommended that lapsed Christians, i.e. those who had sacrificed to pagan idols and so were guilty of apostasy, should be treated leniently. Cyprian, bishop of Carthage, also hid to avoid persecution, but was beheaded in 258 during the Valerian persecution. Gregory, bishop of Neocaesarea in Pontus, not only fled from the Decian persecution but also used his thaumaturgic powers to transform himself and his deacon into two trees when found out by his enemies. Half a century later Peter of Alexandria drew up a series of 'canons' advocating leniency to the lapsed, and himself fled during the Diocletian persecution. The Council of Elvira, held in Spain at about this time, condemned the seeking of martyrdom through deliberate acts of provocation.

p. 96 *Balaam.* Seer who foretold the coming of the Star of Jacob. See Numbers XXV, 17.

Aeschylus. It is as the author of the *Prometheus* trilogy that Aeschylus qualifies as a pre-Christian seer. Edgar Quinet saw him in this light and also drew attention to Tertullian's claim that Christ was 'the true Prometheus', adding that Prometheus was 'the true prophet of Christ'. See his characteristic discussion in *Prométhée* (Paris, 1838), pp. xii-xxi.

the Sibyl of Cumae. Seer who predicts the birth of a wonderful child in Vergil's Fourth Eclogue. Constantine identified this child with Christ.

Denys the Alexandrian. See note to p. 95 above.

Saint Clement. Clement of Alexandria, sometimes called the first Christian scholar, head of the catechetical school c. 190–203. He taught that pre-Christian philosophy contained partial truths which were perfected in Christianity.

Hermas. Supposed author of a book of visions much admired in the latter half of the second century. A woman called Rhoda plays an important part in these dreams, as does a sybilline figure identified as the Church.

p. 97   *calamus.* Ancient reed pen.

Origen. Born c. 185, one of the greatest scholars and theologians of Christian antiquity, head of the catechetical school of Alexandria from c. 202, exponent of the allegorical interpretation of the Scriptures, believer in the divine unity of all creation, but often remembered for his early self-castration. He was tortured in the Decian persecution and died soon after.

p. 98   *And yet the angel.* Hilarion's objections in this and in his following speech may all be traced back to the arguments of David Strauss. See *The Life of Jesus Critically Examined* (SCM Press, London, 1973), pp. 119, 343, 402, 459–60, 679, 706 and 728ff.

the haemorrhoidal woman. The French is '*hémorroïdesse*', i.e. a woman suffering from haemorrhoids, instead of the more normal '*hémorroïsse*' which is closer to the Greek *haimorrous* or 'flowing with blood' (see Matthew IX, 20). David Strauss (see note above) attributed the woman's condition to menstrual disorder, as do many other commentators; but I note that in F. Vigoureux's *Dictionnaire de la Bible* (Paris, 1903), vol. III, articles *Hémorroïdes* and *Hémorroïsse*, the alternative interpretation is suggested, backed by reference to the Mosaic law regarding women with abnormal discharge of blood in Leviticus XV, 25–30 – a passage which is, however, also open to varying interpretations. Flaubert has at least one eminent precursor in Sir Thomas Browne, who refers to 'the statue of Christ, erected by his haemorrhoidal patient' (see *Pseudodoxia Epidemica*, vol. VII, pp. xviii, 13, and note to p. 121 below on *Eusebius of Caesarea*).

CHAPTER IV

p. 101 *agapae.* Early Christian love-feasts, which the poor were invited to join. They sometimes included a eucharistic celebration, but were of variable solemnity and could degenerate into abandoned good cheer.

sayons. Peasants' jackets.

Procula ... Poppaea. Dubious models of feminine piety. Apocryphal literature relates that both Pilate and his wife Procula ultimately became Christian converts. Poppaea, who was everything except good, flirted with various beliefs including Judaism, but I have not identified the source of Flaubert's allusion to her Christian inclinations. He was very much fascinated by the violent and extravagant character of Nero (37–68).

p. 102 *'I have ... unto you.'* See John XVI, 12.

Mani. Born c. 216 near Ctesiphon in northern Babylonia, Mani started a powerful religious movement which survived into the Middle Ages. He was tortured and killed c. 276–7, and those who adhered to his rigorously dualist religion were fiercely persecuted in the following centuries.

p. 103 *Origen.* See note to p. 97 above.

a leper. Flaubert uses the rare Greek word *célèphe*; see Seznec, pp. 18–19.

p. 104 *Saturninus.* Native of Antioch in Syria whose ascetic sect appeared about the reign of Hadrian (117–138).

p. 105 *Cerdo.* Gnostic teacher of the second century who came from Syria to Rome, where he was influenced by Saturninus.

Marcion. Gnostic from Sinope on the Black Sea who reached Rome c. 139. Influenced by Cerdo, he tried to de-Judaise Christianity and was soon excommunicated.

Saint Clement of Alexandria. See note to p. 96 above.

Bardesanes. Syrian Gnostic (155–223) who composed religious hymns and was influenced by the astrological art of the Chaldeans.

Herbians. I cannot trace a sect of this name; but the belief that angels created men's souls was attributed to Hermias, a Galatian heretic possibly identical with Hermogenes (see note to p. 118 below).

Priscillianists. Followers of Priscillian, Spanish heretic of uncompromising asceticism; despite his appeal to the emperor he was burnt alive in 385 and his death is a landmark of religious intolerance.

p. 106   *Theodas.* The only reference to this alleged disciple of St Paul is that made by the Valentinians and recorded by Clement of Alexandria.

Valentine. One of the most illustrious and popular of the Gnostics, who taught his complicated system at Rome c. 138, and was like Marcion excommunicated. R. M. Grant points out that 'neither stood for the cardinal Christian doctrine of the unity of God and the goodness of his creation'; see his *Gnosticism and Early Christianity* (New York, 1966), p. 137.

Eons. See note to p. 63 above on *Gnosticism.*

Sophia. In the Old Testament, *Sophia* or 'Wisdom' has a separate existence which precedes the creation of the world (see Proverbs VIII, 22ff.). The Gnostics elaborated the concept to solve their problem of relating higher to lower, and Valentine's double Sophia acts both as fallen divinity and as redemptive force.

Pleroma. The word means 'fulness' and indicates the Gnostic heaven. Cf. note to p. 63 on *Gnosticism.*

p. 107   *Acharamoth.* Or Achamoth. Possibly a transcription of the

Hebrew word for 'wisdom'. See Werner Foerster, *Gnosis* (Oxford, 1972), vol. I, p. 24.

Basilides. Gnostic active in Alexandria during Hadrian's reign (117–138). The scorn of personal suffering and moral behaviour is more characteristic of his followers.

Abraxas. Many talismanic gems exist inscribed with this word, which in Greek characters represents the number 365.

Kaulakau. A name for the Saviour seemingly based on the Hebrew characters of Isaiah XXVIII, 10 ('precept upon precept, line upon line'), whose import for the Gnostics is obscure.

p. 108 *Elkhasaites*. Followers of Elkhasai, Syrian prophet active during Trajan's reign (97–117). They introduce into Flaubert's text a series of permissive heretics whose antinomianism was directed against the Mosaic Law.

Carpocratians. Followers of Carpocrates of Alexandria, who taught in the first half of the second century that transmigration must be avoided by experiencing everything in one lifetime.

p. 109 *Nicolaitans*. A sect charged with eating food sacrificed to idols and committing fornication. See Revelation II, 13–14.

Prounikos. The word connotes voluptuousness, and was sometimes given to the Valentinian Sophia. See note to p. 137 below.

Marcosians. Second-century Gnostic sect named after Marcus, perhaps a disciple of Valentine; they were accused of practising magical rites.

Sabaoth. i.e. the Lord of Hosts, god of the Jews. The ass-headed Egyptian god Seth was associated with him, so the Gnostics had a precedent for this offensive image of the Demiurge. See Jean Doresse, *The Secret Books of the Egyptian Gnostics* (London, 1960), p. 42.

Helvidians. Late fourth-century sect who opposed celibacy.

Adamites. Obscure second-century sect, who claimed their nudity helped them to practise self-control.

Messalians. Fourth-century Mesopotamian sect who justified their negative life-style on the grounds that assiduous prayer alone chased out the devil.

p. 110 *Paternians.* Fourth-century sect remembered only for their licentiousness.

Aetius. Extreme and formidably eloquent Arian referred to as 'the ungodly'.

A Man. Tertullian, born in Carthage c. 160, passionately hostile to intellectual subtleties. His scandalous charges against the heretics highlight his rhetorical skills, and his glee at the martyrdom of Mani shows his harsh intolerance. In disgust at the laxity of the Roman clergy he joined the rigorist Montanist party (see note to p. 95 above).

p. 111 *Priscilla.* Disciple of Montanus. See note to p. 95 above.

Esculapius. Greek god of healing.

p. 112 *Maximilla.* Disciple of Montanus. See note to p. 95 above.

Tarsus. Chief city of Cilicia, a commercial and scholarly centre.

p. 113 *Magdalene, Joanna, Martha and Susan.* i.e. Mary Magdalene and other disciples of Jesus who figure in the Gospels.

Leontius. Bishop of Antioch (348–357); he had earlier mutilated himself for the sake of the virgin Eustolium. In 325 the Council of Nicaea condemned self-castration.

Sotas couldn't cure me. Both Priscilla and Maximilla fell into ecstasies and delivered prophecies which Christians attributed to demons. The Thracian Bishop Sotas tried to exorcise

Priscilla. Schism was inevitable between the Montanists and the Church disciplinarians who rejected their claims to divine inspiration.

p. 114 *Pepuza*. Phrygian village, headquarters of the sect.

Ah! How wildly you scream ... Legend clearly states that Priscilla and Maximilla left their husbands in order to follow Montanus, but this masochistic eroticism has a Flaubertian ring. Contemporary detractors accused them of more straightforwardly heathen orgies.

p. 115 *Archontics*. Fourth-century sect who believed in seven archons or rulers of the heavens.

Tatianians. Followers of Tatian, a second-century Syrian Gnostic noted for his rigid sexual abstinence.

Valesians. Obscure Arabian sect said to castrate both themselves and their guests.

Cainites. A branch of the Ophites (see note to p. 121 below on *A Voice*), hostile to the Jewish Creator; they reversed the moral judgments of the Scriptures, praising the fratricide Cain and the Sodomites (see Genesis, IV and XIX), and regarding Judas as the agent of a higher god who would free mankind from the evil Demiurge.

Circumcellions. Literally, 'hut-haunters': North African fanatics who roamed about in bands committing atrocities. They allied themselves with the persecuted Donatists, who formed a schismatic sect at the beginning of the fourth century in protest against the secularisation of the Church.

p. 116 *Audians*. Fourth-century Syrian sect, also known as the Anthropomorphites because they believed God had a human form.

Collyridians. Fourth-century female sect whose rites honoured the Virgin Mary and included the offering of cakes (Gr. *collyris*).

Ascites. An offshoot of the Montanist sect nicknamed after their habit of dancing on skin bottles.

Apelles. Disciple of Marcion; his companion Philumene's miracles included the insertion of a large loaf into a narrow-necked glass vase.

Sampsenes. Fourth-century branch of the Elkhasaite sect (see note to p. 108 above) who revered two women-descendants of Elkhasai.

false prophetess of Cappadocia. Third-century prophetess who impressed the people of Eastern Anatolia with the Invocation she used to consecrate the Eucharist.

Arius. See note to p. 63 above. Arius appropriately introduces a chorus of christological heresies.

p. 117 *Sabellius.* Third-century priest whose heresy was at the opposite pole to that of Arius, since he denied the distinct personalities of Father, Son and Holy Ghost.

Council of Antioch. Council of 269 which rejected the term 'consubstantial' later judged orthodox by the Council of Nicaea.

Sethians. Post-Valentinian sect who claimed descent from Seth, third son of Adam, and believed that the Messiah went through successive incarnations.

Theodotians. Followers of Theodotius the Tanner, who left Byzantium for Rome c. 192. They regarded Melchisedek as a celestial counterpart of the human Saviour, and based their belief in the priest's divinity on the text of Hebrews VII, 3, which describes him as 'without father, without mother, without descent, having neither beginning of days, nor end of life; but made like unto the Son of God'.

Merinthians. Or Cerinthians; followers of Cerinthus, a contemporary of the first apostles, whose belief in the resurrection of the human body of Jesus distinguishes him from later Gnostics.

p. 118   *Apollinarists.* Followers of Apollinaris the Younger, bishop of Laodicea, who seceded from the Church in 375 after denying Christ's genuine humanity.

Marcellus of Ancyra. Fourth-century bishop of Ancyra in Galatia, condemned by the Arian Council of Constantinople in 336 for his advanced Sabellian heresy.

Calixtus. Originally a slave, Pope from c. 218 to c. 223, accused of 'modalism', i.e. a version of Sabellianism.

Methodius. Fourth-century Lycian bishop of Olympus in Asia Minor, who suggested that the Word was incarnated in Adam until he sinned.

Paul of Samosata. Patriarch of Antioch from 260, deposed and excommunicated for his antitrinitarian views by the Council of Antioch in 269.

Hermogenes. Heretic of the second and third centuries, who taught that Jesus Christ left his body in the sun before ascending to the Father, quoting Psalm XIX, 4.

A Jew. This Jew is not a historical individual but a spokesman for various snippets of anti-Christian propaganda discovered by Flaubert in his reading. See Seznec, p. 19, and Beausobre, vol. II, p. 492.

p. 119   *Esau.* Son of Isaac and Rebecca. See Genesis XXVI.

the Bellerophontian disease. Intense melancholia, named after the sufferer Bellerophon, a legendary Greek hero who slew the Chimera.

all brandish ... strips of cloth. Many apocryphal gospels circulated in early Christian times; it is argued that they were formed by interpolating versions of the canonical gospels.

Marcosians. See note to p. 109 above.

Encratites. The word points to self-control, and was applied to various ascetic sects of the second century.

p. 120 *Barcouf*. The writings of this prophet are as often associated with the Basilidians as with Mani.

Ebionites. Judaising Christians contemporary with the first apostles; they denied Jesus's divinity.

the locust-eater. John the Baptist, who baptised Jesus in the River Jordan not far from Jericho. See Matthew III and Mark I.

p. 121 *Eusebius of Caesarea*. Born c. 260, a learned and prolific writer, for a time in sympathy with the Arians, bishop of Caesarea in Palestine from c. 313 to his death c. 339. His writings refer to the legend that a monument in the northern Palestinian city of Paneas (a stone column supporting the bronze figures of Jesus extending his hand and a woman kneeling in supplication) was erected by the woman whose miraculous cure is related in Matthew IX, 20–22, Mark V, 25–34, and Luke VIII, 43–8. See also note to p. 98 above on *the haemorrhoidal woman*.

Marcellina. Flaubert has noted the few details about this woman mentioned by Augustine and Epiphanius; see Seznec, p. 18. The order of deaconesses was known in the ancient Roman Church but ceased to exist in the tenth or eleventh century.

A Voice. This introduces the Ophites, an early Gnostic sect who worshipped the serpent (Gr. *Ophis*), finding proof of its identity with the Saviour in John III, 14: 'And as Moses lifted up the serpent in the wilderness, even so must the Son of man be lifted up.'

p. 122 *Knouphis*. Egyptian god pictured on Ophite gems as a serpent with human head.

Kyrie eleison. 'Lord, have mercy', words used in the opening of the Mass. Cf. Psalm CXXII, 3, and Matthew XV, 22.

p. 123 *Astophaios, Oraios, Sabaoth, Adonai, Eloi, Lao.* These six auxiliaries of the evil Demiurge Ialdabaoth were associated with the seven planets and with certain animals. R. M. Grant suggests that the titles are all names or attributes of God in the Old Testament; see his *Gnosticism and Early Christianity* (New York, 1966), p. 47.

Sophia. See note to p. 106 above.

p. 124 *Epidaurus.* Greek town famous for its sanctuary of Esculapius; there was a statue of the god holding his hand over a serpent.

King Ptolemy . . . Moses . . . Glaucus son of Minos. In ancient Egypt as elsewhere the serpent was revered for its healing powers; for the account of how Moses made a serpent of brass to heal the snake-bitten, see Numbers XXI, 6–9; the legendary Glaucus choked when he fell into a vat of honey, and was saved with the same herb as had been used by one serpent to reanimate another.

p. 125 *broken by Hezekiah.* King Hezekiah broke the brazen serpent made by Moses because of the idolatrous practice of burning incense to it; see 2 Kings XVIII, 4.

p. 126 *Peter of Alexandria.* See note to p. 95 above.

p. 127 *Cyprian.* See note to p. 95 above.

Pionius. Priest of Smyrna martyred in 251 in the Decian persecution.

Polycarp. Bishop of Smyrna martyred under Marcus Aurelius, c. 156. Flaubert was given to referring to himself as Polycarp in his letters.

p. 128 *Montanus.* See note to p. 95 above.

p. 130 *Lucius.* A Lucius was martyred at Rome c. 161. The road to the neighbouring town of Tibur started from the Esquilean door on the north-east side of the city.

Domitilla. A Domitilla was exiled c. 96 and later beheaded. As in the case of Lucius, Flaubert elaborates the circumstances of martyrdom.

p. 131 *pultis.* A kind of porridge made from water and flour, to which could be added eggs, honey, and cheese.

p. 132 *The Gymnosophist.* This Brahman or Hindu priest, addressing Antony as his fellow, figures unexpectedly among the heretics and has in fact been shifted from the place among the Hindu gods which he occupied in earlier versions of the work. The new niche can be justified both by Flaubert's discovery of allusions to the Indian travels of certain heresiarchs (see Seznec, p. 221), and by the account of a community of Ethiopian gymnosophists, supposedly preserving Indian traditions, which occurs in Philostratus. Cf. *Apollonius de Tyane,* trans. A. Chassang (Paris, 1862), pp. 237 ff.

p. 134 *Kalanos . . . Augustus.* Kalanos was an Indian ascetic whose self-immolation was a protest against the invasion of India by Alexander the Great in the fourth century BC; later a member of an Indian embassy burnt himself at Athens in front of Augustus (63 BC–AD 14).

p. 135 *Simon.* Samaritan sorcerer from a village called Gitta, active in Rome in the first century, identified by early heresiologists with the Simon Magus whom the Apostle Peter condemned (see Acts VIII, 9–24). He believed that he was an incarnation of God, and that a woman called Helen was his first Thought, 'Ennoia'. She was supposed to have undergone many transmigrations, notably one as Helen of Troy, before being rescued by Simon from a brothel in Tyre. Simon's miracle-working life was further elaborated in the writings attributed to Pope Clement I, from which Flaubert takes some allusions to his magicianship.

p. 136 *On each . . . with my face.* For the idea that this evocative description is based on the elegantly spare diagram representing the *Valentinian* Pleroma, with the eons grouped in pairs, in Matter's *Histoire du Gnosticisme,* see Seznec, p. 27.

p. 137 *Sigeh, Ennoia, Barbelo, Prounikos.* Sigeh is 'Silence', one of
the highest eons; Ennoia is 'Thought'; Barbelo is of un-
certain meaning, also one of the highest eons; Prounikos
means 'lustful' or 'lechery', and refers to the fallen eon
separated from divine life; see Werner Foerster, *Gnosis*
(Oxford, 1972), vol. I, pp. 24–5.

Stesichorus. Lyric poet (c. 632–c. 553 BC). According to legend
he was blinded as a result of his defamatory account of the
story of Helen, and recovered only after having recanted in a
second version.

Lucretia. Roman wife of the sixth century BC who stabbed
herself to death after her rape by Sextus, son of Tarquinius
Superbus.

Delilah. See Judges XVI.

pp. *Caius Caesar Caligula . . . Pope Clement.* The assiduous court-
137–8 ship of the moon by the Roman Emperor Caligula (12–41)
is recorded by Suetonius, and Flaubert makes a bizarre
rapprochement between this source and Clementine litera-
ture. See Seznec, p. 25.

p. 138 *. . . Ephraim . . . Damascus.* Ephraim and Issachar were
districts of Palestine named after two of the tribes of Israel.
Simon's topographical rhetoric shifts from within the con-
fines of Palestine (Bizor, Houleh, Mageddo) to the cities of
Bostra and Damascus lying beyond in Syria.

I am Jupiter. There is some method in Simon's messianism.
He was convinced that the Holy Ghost had communicated
itself to other peoples, including the Greeks (see Matter, vol.
I, p. 207); Sophia, as the first Thought, is obviously comp-
arable to Minerva, identified with the goddess of wisdom,
Athena, who was born from the head of Zeus or Jupiter.

p. 139 *Dositheus.* Leader of a Jewish or Samaritan sect, possibly
pre-Christian. Simon's discipleship is likely to be mythical.

Saint Paul . . . Saint Peter. Tradition has it that both Peter and Paul visited Rome in the reign of Nero. The encounter between Simon Magus and Peter recorded in Acts VIII gave rise to fictitious dialogues between the magician and the apostles.

I flew. This legend of levitation may have originated from the spectacle of an unfortunate Icarus staged for Nero. See Beausobre, vol. I, p. 203.

I came to life. Flaubert turns to ironic account the legend, recorded in the third century by Hippolytus, that Simon asked his disciples to bury him alive but failed to rise again on the third day as promised.

p. *140*   *two men.* Apollonius and Damis. Apollonius of Tyana, a Greek city in Cappadocia, was born at the beginning of the first century. His biography was written c. 200 by Philostratus, encouraged by Julia, wife of the Emperor Septimius Severus. Philostratus professed to base his account on that of Damis, the disciple who accompanies Apollonius on his peripatetic career and acts as a foil to him. That Apollonius was regarded as more than a great sage is suggested by the fact that the following emperor, Alexander. Severus, placed Jesus and Apollonius alongside each other as household gods. The engagingly imaginative biography came to be used for anti-Christian purposes, and Eusebius found it necessary to refute the claim that Apollonius was superior to Jesus; in the eighteenth century, deists took the parallels between the miracles performed by the two leaders as grounds for general scepticism. The threat to Antony's faith which this appearance represents is well discussed in Seznec, pp. 47–58. In a manuscript note Flaubert wrote: 'Apollonius is the most intelligent of all the heretics. He is the equal, the antagonist of Christ. He has done things quite as astonishing, is as pure, and he knows rather more.' See *OC* (1971–5), vol. IV, pp. 303–4.

p. *143*   *Asbadean fountain.* Or Asbamean; the spring was sacred to Jupiter and salutary to the sincere; see *Apollonius de Tyane*, p. 7.

cnyʒa. Or conyza; odorous plant used in antiquity for treating bites, probably a species of fleabane.

p. 144   *a hierodule.* Slave of either sex, sometimes a sacred prostitute, living in a temple and dedicated to a god.

the governor of Cilicia. His threats were provoked by the rejection of his homosexual advances; see *Apollonius de Tyane*, p. 13.

Pythagoreans. Apollonius was a great exponent of the precepts of Pythagoras, the philosopher-scientist of the sixth century BC who founded a religious brotherhood imposing a strict discipline of silence and self-examination.

p. 145   *Samaneans.* Early Indian Buddhist sect whose name has been interpreted to mean 'those who have conquered their passions'; see Creuzer, vol. I, p. 303.

astrologers of Chaldea ... mages of Babylon. According to Herodotus, the Chaldeans were the priests of Belus at Babylon, expert in astrology and oneiromancy. The Magi, famous for similar skills, were originally a priestly caste of Medians, whose influence spread westwards to Babylon. There is thus some overlap between the terms 'Magian' and 'Chaldean'.

mounts of Olympus. The massif of Olympus covers a large area in the north-east of the Greek peninsula; the highest peak was regarded as the home of the gods.

Hyrcanian sea. The Caspian Sea, largest inland sea of Asia.

Bucephalus. Alexander the Great's favourite horse, buried during the Indian expedition after the battle of Hydaspes (326 BC).

Niniveh. Capital of the Assyrian empire.

Ctesiphon. Chief city of Babylonia, north of Babylon on the River Tigris.

Babylon. Like Philostratus, Flaubert allows Apollonius anachronistic experience of the splendour of the city.

p. 247 *Belus*. The name 'bel' or 'baal' was originally applied to many gods in the sense of 'lord', but came to be used to refer to the chief god of Babylonia.

empusa. A one-footed bogy-woman who could assume different shapes.

Taxilla. Town in the Upper Punjab between the Indus and the Hydaspes visited by Alexander the Great.

Phraortes. Indian king described by Philostratus.

Porus. Indian king, one of whose elephants showed such courage in battle that Alexander the Great dedicated it to the sun; Philostratus reports that 350 years had elapsed since this battle; see *Apollonius de Tyane*, pp. 61–2.

p. 248 *Iarchas*. Hindu sage who figures importantly in Philostratus's narrative.

Sesostris. Legendary king of Egypt credited with great conquests, possibly through a confusion of the exploits of Ramses II with those of some predecessors.

p. 249 *Cynocephales*. 'dog-headed' creatures, presumably baboons.

Taprobane. Ceylon or Sri Lanka. On this mythical expedition, see Creuzer, vol. I, pp. 199–203, and vol. IV, plate XI, fig. 58.

Gangarides. People of the delta region of the Ganges.

Comaria. Southernmost cape of Hindustan.

Sachalites . . . Adramites . . . Homerites. Peoples of the south coast of Arabia.

Cassanian mountains. Probably the region of Mount Gazuan,

to the south of Mekka, inhabited by the Cassanite tribe.

Pygmies. Dwarf-like people said to live near the sources of the Nile in Upper Egypt, which would be on the last lap of Apollonius's return journey.

p. 150 *Ephesus.* See note to p. 80 above.

Cnidos. Greek city in the south-west angle of Asia Minor, famous for its statue of Aphrodite by Praxiteles, a copy of which exists at the Vatican.

Tarentum. Southern Italian city on the north shore of the Gulf of Tarentum.

p. 151 *Vespasian.* Emperor 69–79. Here Flaubert begins to counterpoint two stories: while Apollonius describes one of the omens which announced the fortune of Vespasian, as recorded by Suetonius, Damis tells the famous story of Menippus and the vampire, taken from Philostratus. See Seznec, p. 53.

Corinth. Greek city near the isthmus between Peloponnesus and central Greece, reputed to be prosperous and profligate.

Baia. Favourite resort of wealthy Romans on the coast of Campania.

p. 153 *Nero.* See note to p. 101 above on *Poppaea.* The emperor was flatteringly hailed as Apollo despite the heavy-handedness of his verses.

p. 154 *Sporus.* Nero's lover, a eunuch said to resemble the dead Poppaea.

Domitian. Emperor from 81, assassinated in 96 on 18 September (which Flaubert should designate as the 14th day *before* the October calends). He twice banished the philosophers from Italy, in 89 and 95, and his reign culminated in ruthless terror.

p. 155 *Pozzuoli.* The ancient Puteoli, a port and trading city not far from Naples.

p. 156 *Trophonius.* One of two architect-brothers of Boeotia, legendary builders of the temple of Apollo at Delphi. He was swallowed underground in the grove of Lebadeia which became the site of an oracle.

cakes for the Syracusan women. Cakes representing the sexual organs, made of sesame and honey, were offered to their goddesses by the women of Syracuse in ancient Sicily.

Mithra. Persian god of light whose cult spread from the Orient to Rome where its popularity rivalled that of Christianity.

Sabasius. Phrygian or Thracian god often identified with Dionysus. During the celebration of his mysteries a golden snake was passed beneath the clothes and across the chests of initiates.

Cabiri. See note to p. 90 above. A purple scarf featured in the initiation ceremonies of the cult.

Cybele. Fertility goddess of Anatolia whose cult spread to Italy, where her image was ritually bathed in the Almo during festivals.

Samothrace. See note to p. 90 above.

the Good Goddess. Flaubert refers either to Cybele (see note to p. 178 below) or to Ceres, who enjoyed Cabiric status and a mysterious cult; cf. Creuzer, vol. I, pp. 426 and 506.

p. 157 *hippopods.* 'Horse-footed' men mentioned by Pliny; see *Natural History*, book IV, chapter 27.

myrrhodion. Probably the very pungent oil extracted from the Indian tree called *myrodon*.

Junonia. One of the Fortunate Isles, the modern Canaries.

p. 158 *Balis.* Miraculous plant mentioned by Pliny; see *Natural History*, book XXV, chapter 5.

androdamas. Very hard black hematite which earned the title 'man-taming'; see Pliny, *Natural History*, book XXXVI, chapter 20.

p. 159   *divine forms.* The stone fetishism of antiquity is well documented, and particularly famous was the conical figure in the Greek city of Paphos in Cyprus; Aphrodite was said to have risen from the sea nearby.

Pythia. Female medium through whom Apollo's oracles at Delphi were delivered.

CHAPTER V

p. 162   *Elephantine.* Island on the Nile. Its position at the point where the river becomes navigable, at the southern limit of the Roman Empire, meant that its garrison was often at war with the tribes of Nubia.

Diocletian. See note to p. 69 above.

Heliopolis. City of Lower Egypt on the south-east point of the Delta, famous in Pharaonic times for its temple to the sun-god Helios. It was partially deserted by the time Strabo visited it in the first century BC, and was plundered after the fall of paganism. Flaubert is doubtless assimilating the temple with the ancient tombs which St Antony inhabited earlier in his life.

p. 163   *One . . . devours children.* Moloch; see note to p. 94 above.

p. 164   *The valley becomes a lake of milk . . .* Flaubert's notes to the first version of *Saint Antony* indicate that he forbore to name the Indian gods because they were still worshipped and so did not strictly belong in a procession of defunct deities; his descriptions are in fact largely inspired by the plates in Creuzer's work, but the anonymity of the gods perhaps adds to their vividness. Anyone wishing to break the picturesque code may refer to Jean Seznec, 'Flaubert and India', in *Journal of the Warburg and Courtauld Institute* (vol. IV, 3–4,

1943), pp. 142–50, to Seznec, p. 87, and to Creuzer, vol. IV, pp. 1–24 and figs 1–115.

p. 167   *A Naked Man.* The Buddha, born c. 560 BC. See pp. 42–3 above.

      '*And when ... great joy!*' See Matthew II, 9–10.

p. 168   '*A man ... the Christ!*' See Luke II, 25–6.

      '*In the midst ... wisdom*'. See Luke II, 46–7.

p. 169   '*Pharisees ... vipers!*' See Matthew XXIII, 27, 33.

p. 171   *Oannes.* Primitive Babylonian god, bringer of arts and civilisation. Flaubert possibly refers to him as Chaldean because he figures in the *History of Babylonia* by the Chaldean priest Berosus. The distinction between Chaldean and Babylonian has long been confused.

p. 172   *they gaze at the stars.* On the Babylonian star-gazers, see note to p. 145 above.

p. 173   *Pythagoras and Zoroaster.* Tradition has it that Pythagoras (see note to p. 144 above) was taught by the Babylonian mages. Zoroaster, the founder of what was to be the national religion of Persia until the Mohammedan invasions of the seventh century, was also credited with the astrological expertise of Magians and Chaldeans. The time of Zoroaster's life is very uncertain, but the idea that the two men were contemporaries and could have had 'frequent conversations' is to be found in Beausobre, vol. I, pp. 30–31.

      Belus. See note to p. 147 above.

p. 174   *Gangarides.* See note to p. 149 above.

      the goddess. The cult of Mylitta, a Babylonian Venus, is described by Herodotus and discussed in Creuzer, vol. II, pp. 23–5. See p. 42 above.

p. 175   *Ormuz ... Ahriman.* In the dualistic system of Zoroastrianism, Ormuz is the good principle in conflict with the evil principle, Ahriman.

Kaiomortz. Androgynous creature born of the bull in which Ormuz placed the seed of life.

Meschia . . . Meschiana. Ancestors of the human race seduced much like Adam and Eve by tasting first goat's milk and then pieces of fruit.

Mithra. See note to p. 156 above.

p. 176 *Homa.* The creative Word, one of whose incarnations was a sacred tree of life, the stems of which were crushed to give an intoxicating juice drunk during sacrifices.

Amschaspands . . . Izeds . . . Ferouers. Orders of spirits controlled by Ormuz. The Ferouers or Fervers were emanations of his essence and very numerous, because every living being had its own Ferver or ideal prototype. Flaubert's description of Ormuz is based on that of a monarch's Ferver in Creuzer, vol. I, pp. 722–3.

Caosyac. Or Saoshyant. Zoroaster's unborn son, a prophet who would destroy Ahriman and bring about resurrection.

Diana of Ephesus. Fertility goddess whose images were usually made of ebony, to symbolise her affinity with night. She is the first of three great syncretistic goddesses whom Flaubert places between the divinities of the East and those of Greece and Rome.

p. 178 *Good-Goddess, Idean . . . Mother of Syria.* Cybele, the great fertility goddess worshipped at mount Ida in Phrygia. Her cult was similar to that of the Syrian goddess which is described in Lucian of Samosata's *De dea Syria*, and Flaubert is also indebted to Apuleius; see Jean Seznec, *Les Sources de l'épisode des dieux dans la Tentation de saint Antoine* (Paris, 1940), pp. 125ff.

Archigallus. The chief of the Galli, eunuch priests of Cybele.

p. 179 *Atys.* Cybele's partner, whose legendary self-castration was imitated by his devotees.

p. 180 *A large catafalque.* The appearance of this catafalque marks a transition to the widespread cult of Adonis, Aphrodite's lover who was killed by a boar, and was like Atys a god of vegetation and fertility. Flaubert seems to have noted the distinction between the 'gentle, tender, effeminate' character of the Adonia and the 'male, energetic, and frantically savage' character of the Phrygian festivals, pointed out in Creuzer, vol. II, p. 76.

p. 182 *Persephone.* Demeter's daughter, goddess of the underworld.

Isis. Although Isis was referred to as myriad-named and was worshipped in Hellenistic times throughout the Mediterranean world, Flaubert concentrates on her Egyptian setting. See also pp. 43–4 above.

Amenthi. Egyptian underworld.

Nomes. Ancient administrative districts of Egypt, associated with local gods.

Osiris. The legend is that Isis and her twin brother Osiris had intercourse while still in the womb, and that even after his death and dismemberment they managed a union which resulted in the birth of the premature and feeble Harpocrates.

Byblos. Phoenician port.

Anubis ... Cynocephalus. See notes to pp. 77 and 149 above. Anubis was associated with the baboon, which the ancient Egyptians tamed and trained.

Typhon. The Egyptian Seth, evil power identified by the Greeks with their monstrous Typhon.

p. 183 *coucoupha.* This is the Egyptian name for the hoopoe, but in Creuzer's illustrations a canine head appears to be referred to. See Creuzer, vol. IV, fig. 159.

labyrinth. This vast construction was near the city of Arsinoe about fifty miles west of Pispir and comprised a dozen palaces and thousands of apartments, many of them underground.

p. *184* *bearing a ... nacelle*. A nacelle is a small boat. Possibly the French '*qui portaient*' is a persistent error for '*que portaient*', or 'borne by'.

paterae. Round flat ornaments.

Philae. Island in the Nile above the first cataract, the site of a large temple to Isis where libations of milk were offered on the tomb of Osiris.

Apis. Sacred bull worshipped at Memphis; it was mummified when it died and a successor was chosen.

p. *186* *a mountain*. Olympus, the home of the classical gods. Flaubert uses their Latin names although, as Taine objected, the Greek counterparts would have been more fitting.

the gorgon. Petrifying monster whom Minerva (Athena) helped to kill.

peplos. The draped costume of Greek women.

p. *187* *Mimalloneids ... Maenads ... Bacchantes*. Frenzied female followers of Bacchus (Dionysus).

Vulcan ... the Cabiri. The Cabiri (see note to p. 90 above) were sometimes treated as children of Vulcan (Hephaestus), and depicted with hammers in their hands.

caduceus. Winged wand entwined by two serpents.

talaria. Winged sandals, or wings on the ankles.

petasus. Low broad hat.

Venus Anadyomene. Venus 'rising from the sea'; she sprang

from the foam formed around the mutilated genitalia of Uranus, castrated by his son Kronos (Saturn).

p. 188   *Proserpina.* The Latin Persephone, goddess of the underworld.

Aristeas. Flaubert's *Aristée* may be Aristeas of Proconnesus, a legendary poet and worshipper of Apollo who lived in about the sixth century BC; the story is that he dropped dead in a fuller's shop, which was then shut up; but Aristeas was subsequently seen and spoken with on the road, and when the shop was opened it was found to be empty; seven years later he reappeared, wrote another poem, and vanished again. See Herodotus, *History*, book IV, chapter 14. The minor Greek deity Aristaeus, benevolent to cattle and fruit-trees, is a less plausible alternative.

the symbol of Jerusalem. The Jerusalem Symbol or Creed dates from 348 and is an amplification of the Nicene Creed. Antony recites a slightly shortened version of it.

p. 189   *Titans ... Giants ... Hecatonchyres ... Cyclopes.* Sons of the sky god Uranus, punished for their rebellion; the Hecatonchyres were hundred-handed, the cyclopes one-eyed.

phratries. Greek brotherhoods or kinship groups, admission to which meant religious recognition of citizenship.

Agamemnon. Commander-in-chief of the Greek forces in the Trojan War.

Erebus. Underground region through which dead souls had to pass.

Camp of Mars. Area of Rome full of magnificent temples, mausoleums and crematoriums.

p. 190   *what triumphs is the mob's imbecility.* These typical Flaubertian sentiments are expressed at greater length in the first version, where the Muses deplore the artist's prostitution to the appetites and whims of the crowd. See *OC, La Tentation de Saint Antoine*, pp. 477–8.

Hebe. Goddess of youth, cup-bearer to the gods.

Athens. Minerva (Athena) was the patron goddess of the town.

p. 191   *Hecatombeon*. The first month of the Athenian calendar; it began with the first new moon after the summer solstice and was named after the customary sacrifices or hecatombs.

Propylaea. Magnificent roofed gateway on the west side of the Acropolis.

Kerkopes ... Amazons ... Centaurs. The Kerkopes were ape-like creatures whom Hercules slung upside-down from a pole across his shoulder, from which vantage-point they ridiculed his body; his fight against the Amazons had as its object the winning of queen Hippolyte's girdle; and the quarrel with the Centaurs started because Hercules insisted on broaching a jar of their wine.

Achelous. Horned river-god whom Hercules fought to win his wife Deianeira.

Omphale. Lydian queen to whom Hercules was sold as a slave.

p. 192   *Amphytrionades*. i.e. son of Amphytrion, a mocking title: Alcmene (wife of Amphytrion) conceived twins, the first of which was Hercules, son of Zeus who visited her disguised as her husband early in the night.

down into my empire. One of Hercules's twelve labours was to carry off the guard-dog Cerberus from Hades.

Tityos. Giant who raped Zeus's mistress, Leto.

Tantalus. Lydian king condemned to stand chin-deep in water which vanished when he tried to drink.

Ixion. Would-be rapist of Zeus's wife, bound to a flaming wheel.

Keres. Death-bringing spirits, depicted as birds of prey.

Amphitrite. Wife of Poseidon (Neptune) and one of the Nereids, daughters of the sea-god Nereus often depicted riding on the fish-tailed Tritons.

p. *193*   *three hundred men withstood the whole of Asia.* In the battle of Thermopylae of 480 BC, the Spartan King Leonidas and his three hundred companions were killed defending the pass against the Persian armies. Flaubert's enthusiasm for this heroic episode was such that he planned to write a work about it; see Marie-Jeanne Durry, *Flaubert et ses projects inédits* (Paris, 1950), pp. 11–12.

Ceres. The corn-goddess Ceres (Demeter) regrets the disappearance of the Elusinian mysteries, whose rites probably included a dramatic presentation of her wanderings after the abduction by Pluto of her daughter Kore-Persephone, also called Daira.

p. *194*   *Archon.* Highest officer of the ancient Greek state, who would supervise the Dionysia at which his wife represented the wife of the god.

Pan. Herdsman god of Arcadia.

Silenus. Spirit of the woods, sometimes seen as the dignified instructor of Dionysus (Bacchus), sometimes as a pot-bellied drunkard.

Delos. Smallest island of the Cyclades in the Aegean, the birthplace of Apollo.

Pythia. See note to p. 159 above.

p. *196*   *Axieros, Axiokeros, Axiokersa.* Divine triad of Cabiri; see note to p. 90 above.

Samos and Telesphorus. Minor gods of healing.

Sosipolis. Literally, 'city-saving'; the legend is that the Eleans were saved from the Arcadians by a miraculous new-born child who turned into a serpent and put the enemy to flight.

Despoina. Arcadian goddess of the underworld, daughter of Poseidon and Demeter.

Britomartis. Cretan nymph who jumped over a cliff when pursued by Minos and was caught in fishermen's nets.

Gelludes ... Striges ... Empusas. The Gello was a child-snatching female demon; the Striges, named after the *strix* or screech-owl, flew by night and strangled children; on the Empusa, see note to p. 147 above.

Eurynome. There is a confusion here between Eurynome, daughter of the Ocean, and Eurynomus, the repulsive demon who devoured corpses.

Orthia, Hymnia ... Laphria, Aphaea ... Bendis ... Stymphalia. All these local goddesses were identified with Diana-Artemis. On the altar of Orthia, worshipped by the Spartans, boys were ritually whipped; marble statues of bird-legged girls were to be seen in the temple of Diana of Stymphalia.

Triopas. Three-eyed god, perhaps an ancient sky-god.

Erichtonius. Attic hero born of the fertilised earth after an amorous struggle between Hephaestus and Athena; as a child he was partly serpent-shaped. But Flaubert may be confusing him with Erysichthon, son of Triopas, who offended Demeter and was condemned to an insatiable hunger which at last forced him to eat his own flesh.

Xerxes. King of Persia 485–65 BC.

p. 197 *Zalmoxis.* Hero and god worshipped by the Thracians; said to be a former slave of Pythagoras, he preached the immortality of the soul.

Artimpasa. Scythian goddess identified with Aphrodite Urania, the celestial Venus.

Orsiloche. Crimean goddess identified with Artemis.

Cimmerians. See note to p. 63 above.

Thule. In ancient times the northernmost limit of the inhabited world, variously identified with Iceland, Norway and the Shetlands.

Aesars. Ancient Etruria was eventually subjugated by the Romans, and the Etruscan gods or Aesars naturally appear before the minor Roman divinities.

Tages. Child-like god of wisdom unearthed by a peasant.

Nortia. Flaubert follows Livy's interpretation of this goddess's nail-driving activity.

Kastur and Pulutuk. The Etruscans adopted many Greek divinities including Castor and Pollux, twin sons of Zeus.

p. *198* *Capitol.* The most sacred hill of Rome, site of many temples.

Janus. God of beginnings, perhaps originally a sky-god, whose symbol was a double-faced head.

Summanus. God of nocturnal thunderstorms; the wheel-shaped cakes baked for him perhaps symbolised his chariot.

Vesta. Goddess of the hearth.

Bellona. Goddess of war, companion to Mars.

goddess of Aricia ... demon Virbius. The wood-goddess Diana was worshipped in a grove on the shores of Lake Nemi, a few miles from the town of Aricia. Her male partner Virbius was an obscure god honoured at the same spot. The presiding priest was traditionally a runaway slave who had to break a bough from a sacred tree within the grove and then kill his predecessor.

Salarian Way. Ancient highroad running north-eastwards from Rome to the Adriatic coast.

Pons Sublicius. Early wooden drawbridge in Rome, considered sacred.

Subura. Dirty and disreputable district of Rome.

Mark Antony's time. i.e. c. 82–30 BC.

Libitina. Ancient goddess of burials, who was confused with Venus Lubentia and treated as a goddess of love and death.

pp. 198–9 *Larvae . . . Lemures*. Ghosts of those buried without proper rites.

p. 199 *Terminus*. God of boundary-marks.

Vertumnus. God of the changing year, or of autumn.

Sartor. God of menders and cultivators.

Sarrator. Cf. the latin *sarritor*, a hoer or weeder.

Vervactor. Cf. the latin *vervagere*, to plough fallow land.

Collina, Vallona. Goddesses of hill and vale.

Hostilinus. God of equal-eared cornfields.

Sabina. Region north-east of Rome.

pp. 199– 200 *Domiduca . . . Naenia*. Flaubert took great pains to document himself on what Creuzer calls the 'domestic Olympus' of Latin paganism, which proliferated as each circumstance of life was personified; see Creuzer, vol. II, pp. 1237–41, and

Seznec, *Les Sources de l'épisode des dieux*, pp. 141–9.

p. 200   *Lares*. Family ghosts of the Romans, also guardians of home, farm land, and crossroads.

Feralia. Roman All Souls' Day, when each household honoured its dead.

p. 201   *Crepitus*. Flaubert could not bring himself to leave out this scatological god although he learnt from his friend Frédéric Baudry, who had consulted Alfred Maury, that 'poor little Deus Crepitus does not exist: it's a modern invention'; see Seznec, *Les Sources de l'épisode des dieux*, p. 142.

Aristophanes. See *The Clouds*, pp. 388–91, where the thunder of the heavens is compared to a flatulent stomach, as evidence for the non-existence of Zeus. The point was not lost on Flaubert, judging by the thunderous entry of the Lord of Hosts who follows in the wake of Crepitus.

Claudius Drusus. Sic. The reference is to the Emperor Claudius Drusii (10 BC–AD 54), who planned an edict permitting farting at table after he heard of the discomfort of one of his guests. See Seznec, *Les Sources de l'épisode des dieux*, p. 179.

p. 202   *my temple is destroyed*. The temple of Jerusalem was destroyed when the city was stormed by Titus in AD 70.

CHAPTER VI

p. 206   *Plato's antichtone, Philolaus's central fire, Aristotle's spheres*. In line with a number theory which concentrated on the decad, the antichton or counter-earth was conceived as a tenth planet, invisible from the inhabited side of the earth. Philolaus, a Pythagorean philosopher of the fifth century BC whose work was known to Plato, taught that the earth and the other planets revolve around a central fire. Aristotle developed the theory which explained the movement of the planets in terms of concentric spheres revolving simultaneously.

p. 209   *Extension.* It should be remembered that the Devil is expounding a broadly Spinozist philosophy (see pp. 11–12, 15 and 17 above). The distinction between Extension or what is physical and Thought or what is mental was emphasised by Descartes. But Spinoza insisted that the mental and the physical could not be regarded as irreducibly separate, so that Thought and Extension were attributes of a single substance, a single reality. The Devil's arguments throughout chapter VI can be usefully compared to Part I of the *Ethics*, entitled 'Concerning God'; there Spinoza argues, among other things, that substance absolutely infinite is indivisible (*Prop.* XIII) and that besides God no substance can be granted or conceived (*Prop.* XIV); that there is no vacuum in nature and that extended substance is in no way unworthy of God (*Prop.* XV. *Note*); that God's will and God's essence are identical (*Prop.* XXXIII. *Note* II); that God does not direct things towards a particular goal, that natural phenomena are not adapted for the benefit of man, and that human notions of what is good or bad bear no relation to the laws of nature and the true perfection of things (*Appendix*). The passionless perfection of God is further emphasised in Part V (*Prop.* XVII).

CHAPTER VII

p. 213   *Didymus.* See note to p. 63 above.

Xenophanes. Monotheist philosopher of the sixth century BC, reputed founder of the Eleatic school which emphasised the pantheistic unity of the universe and argued that the notion of change was due to the false reports of the senses.

Heraclitus. Philosopher who flourished c. 500 BC and conceived the universe as a changing whole of conflicting opposites, whose order could be recognised only through the rational discourse of the philosophic soul.

Melissus. Greek philosopher of the fifth century BC, last member of the Eleatic school; he denied the existence of the void and believed in the spatial infinity of the universe.

Anaxagoras. Greek philosopher (c. 500–c. 428 BC) who taught that matter consists of minute and infinitely divisible particles.

Ammon. See note to p. 64 above.

p. 214   *my mother.* See note to p. 62 above.

Ammonaria. See note to p. 62 above.

p. 215   *An Old Woman.* See p. 45 above.

Saul. First king of Israel, who fell on his sword after being wounded by the arrows of the Philistines. See 1 Samuel XXXI, 3–4.

Razis. Elder of Jerusalem unjustly informed against, who avoided arrest by a gory suicide described in 2 Maccabees XIV, 37ff. Augustine criticised his action.

Saint Pelagia of Antioch. Fifteen-year-old virgin who flung herself from the top of the house c. 306 to avoid being raped and tortured by Diocletian's soldiers.

Domnina of Aleppo. Woman of Antioch who fled from the Diocletian persecution with her two daughters, Berenice and Prodoscia; they drowned themselves when pursued. Augustine supposed that a special revelation might have justified their action.

virgins of Miletus. Flaubert could read in Plutarch of the 'strange reverie and terrible mood' which drove these virgins to suicide; they were dissuaded by the threat of having their naked corpses exposed in public. See *Oeuvres morales de Plutarque*, trans. Amyot (Paris, 1802), vol. XVI, pp. 155–6.

Hegesias. Hegesias of Cyrene, philosopher of the third century BC.

p. 216 *Herostratus*. Arsonist who made a name for himself by burning down the temple of Ephesus, reputedly in 356 BC on the night when Alexander the Great was born.

Racotis. Egyptian quarter of Alexandria.

p. 220 *a gigantic worm*. This image, new to the third version, was partly inspired by a little drawing of a death's head on the end of a worm which was sent to Flaubert by Maurice Sand. See *OC, La Tentation de Saint Antoine*, p. 678, and Seznec, pp. 62–3.

p. 221 *figures ... at Babylon, and ... in the port of Carthage*. The little-travelled St Antony is at this point well eclipsed by the Flaubertian spokesman, rich in learning. For a description of the monstrous images in the temple of Belus, see Creuzer, vol. II, p. 889. Augustine refers to a Carthaginian mosaic representing semi-human monsters in *De Civitate Dei*, book XVI, chapter viii.

the Sphinx ... the Chimera. See pp. 19 and 45–7 above.

p. 223 *Porsenna*. King of Etruria whose tomb was a vast square monument surmounted by pyramids, each topped by a bronze globe and a chaplet of bells. See Pliny, *Natural History*, book XXXVI, chapter xiii.

orichalc. Yellow copper ore, possibly brass, prized by the ancients.

Atlantis. Fabulous island off the Straits of Gibraltar.

p. 225 *At last ... human bodies*. The procession of the monsters and their significance for Flaubert is excellently discussed by Seznec, who provides a thorough survey of Flaubert's documentation (mainly in Pliny, Aelian, Berger de Xivrey and Bochart) and draws attention to other contemporary treatments of the theme, e.g. by Hugo and Huysmans; see Seznec, pp. 59–85. See also p. 48 above. And cf. the creatures described in Borges, *The Book of Imaginary Beings*.

p. 228   *His stupidity attracts me.* See pp. 33–4 above. The name 'Catoblepas' is supposed to mean 'that which looks downwards'.

p. 230   *spiders . . . in their mesh.* The image of the spider, alert at the centre of its mesh of sensitive points, is characteristic of materialist and pantheist philosophy; it occurs in *Le Rêve de d'Alembert*: see Diderot, *Oeuvres philosophiques* (Garnier Frères, 1964), pp. 314–17.

Ahuti . . . Alphalim. Flaubert has changed these creatures from apes into birds; see Seznec, pp. 73–4.

p. 231   *horns of Ammon.* The old name for ammonites, thought to resemble the ram's horns of the Egyptian god Ammon.

Dedaims of Babylon . . . Mandrakes . . . Baaras root. Dedaim is apparently an error for the Hebrew Dudaim, a kind of mandrake; these narcotic plants were credited in ancient times with all sorts of fabulous properties, were supposed to shriek when uprooted, and were sometimes depicted with human faces; the Baaras herb belongs in the same fabulous tradition and was described by Josephus as a flame-coloured root which raced too fast to be uprooted. See Seznec, pp. 74–5.

Vegetable and animal. The notion that there are no clear-cut distinctions between animal, vegetable and mineral was already well established in the eighteenth century. Diderot, acknowledging the authority of Buffon, argues in the *Encyclopédie* that the freshwater polyp is 'the last of animals, & the first of plants' (article *Animal*, vol. I, p. 472), and in *Le Rêve de d'Alembert* that minerals, like all matter, may have sensibility; see *Oeuvres philosophiques*, pp. 258, 263–4 and 311.

remains of may-flies. In *Le Rêve de d'Alembert* Diderot mentions 'the sophism of the may-fly', whose ephemerality might lead it to regard humans as eternal, in support of his

critique of any belief in the immutability of things. See
Oeuvres philosophiques, pp. 303–4.

iron flower. Flos ferri, a kind of Aragonite, coral-like in form,
occurring in association with beds of gypsum and deposits of
iron ore.

p. 232   *a vibration quivers across them.* In one short phrase Flaubert
suggests the vital movement of spontaneous generation. For
a fuller imaginative description of the first erethism or
'orgasm' of tiny gelatinous bodies, see Lamarck, *Histoire
naturelle des animaux sans vertèbres* (Paris, 1815), vol. I, pp.
174–6. Taine indeed objected that Flaubert's finale seemed,
in its Alexandrian context, too exact an anticipation of
Lamarckian zoology; see *OC, La Tentation de Saint Antoine*,
p. 683.

There in the middle ... the face of Jesus Christ. Christian,
pagan and personal connotations all contribute to this much
decoded conclusion. Jean Seznec draws attention to Flau-
bert's reading of Adolphe Didron's *Histoire de Dieu*, and
especially to the passage expounding how 'God is light, the
sun is his image', and the plate illustrating 'the Saviour in an
aureole of clouds which mould themselves to his body', as
well as other illustrations of the nimbus; see Didron, *op. cit.*
(Paris, 1843), pp. 113 and 147, and Seznec, p. 26, n. 4. But
one should also note Flaubert's familiarity with the *Bhagavad
Gita*, where he might read that 'the glory and amazing splen-
dour of this mighty being may be likened to the sun rising
at once into the heavens, with a thousand times more than
usual brightness', a passage which leads up to the apostrophe
'I see thee, difficult to be seen, shining on all sides with light
immeasurable, like the ardent fire or glorious sun ... The
sun and moon thy eyes; thy mouth a flaming fire, and the
world shining with thy reflected glory!'; see *The Bhagvat-
Geeta*, trans. Charles Wilkins (1785), Facsimile Reproduction
by George Hendrick (Gainsville, 1959), pp. 90–91, and *C*, vol. I,
p. 1003. Moreover, Gnostic influence cannot be excluded: 'the
Manicheans, in line with the ideas of Scripture, placed God
the Father in an *invisible & inaccessible Light*; & in line
thereafter with the ideas of the Persian Philosophers, they

believed that the Son, who is the Image of the Father, had chosen for his sojourn the visible Light, or the Body of the Sun'; see Beausobre, vol I, p. 565. However, the descriptive elements of the vision can certainly be traced back to Flaubert's experience in Greece; for the argument that Flaubert, on the basis of this initial experience, developed a setting for the book as a whole, touching in the golden dust of the opening description and emphasising the golden clouds of the close, see Benjamin F. Bart, *Flaubert's Landscape Descriptions*, (Ann Arbor, 1956) pp. 53–7. See also pp. 17–18, 24–5 and 30–1 above.

FIND OUT MORE ABOUT PENGUIN BOOKS

PENGUIN CLASSICS

FLAUBERT

SENTIMENTAL EDUCATION

Translated by Robert Baldick

'I know nothing more noble', wrote Flaubert, 'than the contemplation of the world.' His acceptance of all the realities of life (rather than his remorseless exposure of its illusions) principally recommends what many regard as a more mature work than *Madame Bovary*, if not the greatest French novel of the last century. In Robert Baldick's new translation of this story of a young man's romantic attachment to an older woman, the modern reader can appreciate the accuracy, the artistry, and the insight with which Flaubert (1821–80) reconstructed in one masterpiece the very fibre of his times.

THREE TALES

Translated by Robert Baldick

With *Madame Bovary* Flaubert established the Realistic novel. Twenty years later he wrote the *Three Tales*, each of which reveals a different aspect of his creative genius and fine craftsmanship. In *A Simple Heart*, a story set in his native Normandy, he recounts the life of a pious and devoted servant-girl. A stained-glass window in Rouen cathedral inspired him to write *The Legend of St Julian Hospitator* with its insight into the violence and mysticism of the medieval mind. *Herodias*, the last of the three, is a masterly reconstruction of the events leading up to the martyrdom of St John the Baptist.

and

MADAME BOVARY

BOUVARD AND PÉCUCHET

SALAMMBO

PENGUIN CLASSICS

STENDHAL

SCARLET AND BLACK

Translated by Margaret R. B. Shaw

To Stendhal (1783–1842) the novel was a mirror of life reflecting 'the blue of the skies and the mire of the road below'. *Le Rouge et le Noir*, his greatest novel, reflects without distortion the France of the decades after Waterloo – its haves and have-nots, its Royalists and Liberals, its Jesuits and Jansenists. Against this crowded backcloth moves the figure of Julien Sorel, a clever, ambitious, up-from-nothing hero whose tragic weakness is to lose his head in a crisis. Margaret Shaw's translation keeps intact the plain, colloquial style of a writer who, in an age of Romantics, set the pattern for later Realists such as Flaubert and Zola.

THE CHARTERHOUSE OF PARMA

Translated by Margaret R. B. Shaw

Stendhal's second great novel, *La Chartreuse de Parme*, was published in 1839. He adapted the theme from a sixteenth-century Italian manuscript and set it in the period of Waterloo. Amid the intrigues of the small court of Parma the hero, Fabrizio, with his secret love for Clelia, emerges as an 'outsider' whose destiny is shaped by events in which his character plays relatively little part. Fabrizio's final withdrawal into a monastery emphasizes his lack of contact with real life and his similarity to the ingrown hero of the twentieth century.

and

LOVE

ZOLA

GERMINAL

Translated by L. W. Tancock

Germinal was written by Zola (1840–1902) to draw attention once again to the misery prevailing among the poor in France during the Second Empire. The novel, which has now become a sociological document, depicts the grim struggle between capital and labour in a coalfield in northern France. Yet through the blackness of this picture, humanity is constantly apparent, and the final impression is one of compassion and hope for the future, not only of organized labour, but also of man.

THÉRÈSE RAQUIN

Translated by L. W. Tancock

The immediate success which *Thérèse Raquin* enjoyed on publication in 1868 was partly due to scandal, following the accusation of pornography; in reply Zola defined the new creed of Naturalism in the famous preface which is printed in this volume. The novel is a grim tale of adultery, murder and revenge in a nightmarish setting.

L'ASSOMMOIR

Translated by L. W. Tancock

'I wanted to depict the inevitable downfall of a working-class family in the polluted atmosphere of our urban areas,' wrote Zola of *L'Assommoir* (1877), which some critics rate the greatest of his Rougon-Macquart novels. In the result the book triumphantly surmounts the author's moral and social intentions to become, perhaps, the first 'classical tragedy' of working-class people living in the slums of a city – Paris. Vividly, without romantic illusion, Zola uses the coarse *argot* of the back-streets to plot the descent of the easy-going Gervaise through idleness, drunkenness, promiscuity, filth and starvation to the grave.